THE
Lock3t

BRITTANY BESSONETT

Lauren —
Keep the faith... always!
XOXO

Dedicated to my dearest friend. Your case may remain unsolved, but I'm thankful you finally found your peace.

Chapter 1
PRESENT

I've got you.

Those were the last three words she remembered hearing before being jerked from her sleep. The three words that resonated in her head as her feet repetitiously pounded the pavement. It wasn't uncommon for the intensity of her nightmares to increase this time of year, and each one ended the same way … with those three eerily familiar words …

I've got you.

The sky boasted a kaleidoscope of colors as the sun began to peek over the horizon. The fiery shades of orange and red welcomed a new day, and the meteorologist predicted yet another record-breaking high temperature. Summer refused to let go. Only a mile into her morning run, Katie's tank top clung to her body and sweat rained down her chest. Her ponytail bounced behind her with every stride.

She rounded the corner by the local convenience store and continued up Main Street. Her route took her through highly populated neighborhoods, and although traffic occasionally broke her stride, she was never bothered by the interruption. It was a small price to pay for peace of mind. There was a nature trail nearby, typically flooded with runners and bikers, but it was too similar to the trail she had trained on growing up in Brownsboro, a small town about three hundred miles north of Victoria. A town she would rather forget.

The Victorian homes along her route offered a therapeutic escape for Katie. She often caught herself daydreaming about what life would be like living inside one of the majestic beauties. Her favorite was a white two-story, with a large wraparound porch, over-sized windows, and ornate trim. Framing the front of the property was a black wrought-iron gate that opened to a concrete sidewalk. It purposefully led to a set of stairs, slightly crumbling on the edges, surrounded by flowerbeds full of manicured shrubs and accented with soft touches of seasonal flowers. The dark shutters matched the front door, and she imagined what was on the other side: tall ceilings framed with crown molding, arched entryways, and intricate chandeliers. An antique piano nestled in front of the windows of the great room with a view of the giant oak, whose protective limbs covered the front yard. It was apparent this home had been well taken care of and, although she could not pinpoint why, it exuded a sense of safety.

She had never seen anything like it before moving to Victoria. The only thing remotely close was a bed and breakfast her parents took her to when she was eleven. The name of the town they visited that week escaped her memory, but the details of the time they spent inside that mansion, as she often referred to it, she will never forget. That trip was the last vacation her family took before her mother passed away. Maybe that was the attraction to this particular house: it reminded Katie of her mom.

Katie stopped, flipped the cap on her water bottle, and took a drink. The cool water offered a welcome reprieve from the heat. A sweltering ninety-four degrees at sunrise was not uncommon for an August morning in Texas, and she felt every degree. The hair beneath her ponytail was soaked, and she could taste the saltiness of the sweat that dripped down her face. After a few more gulps, she refastened the cap and kneeled down to tighten the laces on her running shoes.

A black car approached and slowed to a stop only a few feet from where Katie was kneeling. She instinctively cut her eyes in the car's direction, but did not recognize the vehicle nor did she have any idea what the driver was doing. It was an odd place for a car to stop. There were no traffic lights nearby, and the only visible road sign read *No Parking Any Time*. She pulled the double knot tight on her left shoe and glanced up again to take another look at the car. It was Amanda, her face finally visible as she leaned towards the windshield to wave at Katie. She stood up and exhaled, completely unaware that she had been holding her breath.

Amanda rolled down the passenger side window and Katie walked over to the car. When she leaned down and propped herself on the door with her forearms, the sweet smell of Amanda's perfume tickled her nose. Sweat dripped from her cheeks and splashed against the car.

"Are you some kind of crazy?" Amanda joked as she peered over the rim of her sunglasses. "You know it's August in south Texas, right? Most sane people like to stay inside where we have this thing called air conditioning!"

"Yes, I should probably have my sanity questioned," Katie scoffed. "But you know me, never one to play the 'normal' card. Whose car is this, anyway?"

Amanda placed her glasses on the console and fidgeted with the knobs on the stereo as if the car was smarter than she was. "Oh, it's my stepmom's. Dad took mine to the shop today to get that annoying noise checked out. He said it was something like my brakes or my rotors or something minor like that."

Katie grinned and rolled her eyes. *Only Amanda would think something like brakes on a car would be insignificant.* "Well, I hope it turns out to be nothing major," she laughed. "Will you still be able to meet at Joe's later today?"

"Yes, but that is why I stopped when I saw you. Can we move it up to six? My dad is having an impromptu get together at the house tonight around eight with some work buddies to celebrate the completion of their latest project. I'm not really sure why he even wants me there, it will probably just be a bunch of dudes having a few drinks and patting each other on the back. Not particularly my idea of fun, but something about family and support blah, blah, blah," Amanda chuckled. "Of course, you know you are welcome to come?" Her inflection turned the statement into a question.

Katie paused, staring blankly. Amanda knew that look all too well, the *I'm trying to come up with a reason why I can't make it* look. She was accustomed to it, so she didn't press the issue. She simply said, "I know, I know, maybe next time," and flashed Katie a reassuring wink and a smile.

Katie let out a sigh of relief. "Thank you."

"You got it, cupcake! Well, I better be off. Errands to run and nails to polish," Amanda slid her rhinestone-rimmed sunglasses back on her face and put the car in reverse. "And I guess I will let you get back to this running thing you do. Crazy, I tell ya. You are just plain crazy."

"You're so kind," Katie said sarcastically. "Have fun and I will see you at six."

She pushed herself up from the window and stepped back from the car. Amanda rolled up the window and waved as she drove away.

Amanda didn't have a care in the world. She was twenty-five, one year younger than Katie, and was the epitome of a ditsy blonde. It didn't help that she came from money. Her father was the CFO of the contracting company responsible for a large portion of the industrial development around the Port of Victoria. Her skin was a beautiful olive color and her body was oddly fit. Oddly, because Katie had never seen her exercise, not once, and she always poked fun at Katie for running so much, as if she didn't understand why she did it. The health benefit was only a bonus for Katie, it was not her real motivation, but Amanda had no idea. Katie never told her the real reason why.

Even though Amanda's life appeared perfectly effortless and at times Katie felt a twinge of jealousy toward her, she appreciated that Amanda had patience enough to be her friend. A task only one other person had been able to accomplish over the last nine years. She wanted to come clean about her past, especially before something happened like it did in Austin, but she was always afraid that if Amanda knew the truth, she may not look at her the same way. And that was a risk she wasn't willing to take. Not yet, anyway.

Katie was a little behind schedule now, thanks to her unexpected visit with Amanda. She quickened her pace until steps became leaps and she ended up sprinting her last half mile. She had to be at work by nine and didn't want to be late. Most of the end of her route was uphill, so by the time she reached the front door of her apartment she was spent. Unable to remember the details of the nightmare that awakened her in a panic that morning, the run was a success.

When she opened the front door to walk inside, the cool air hit her like a train. The corner of her mouth instantly pulled up in a grin, thinking of her conversation with Amanda. She took a deep breath, holding the air in her lungs for a few seconds before exhaling, and her breathing gradually returned to normal. She closed the door and latched the chain lock, locked both dead bolts, turned the lock on the doorknob, and tossed her keys on the hutch in the entryway.

She did not get permission from management to add the two extra locks, but she really didn't care. If she knew anyone from maintenance would be coming by she left them unlocked, but that didn't happen very often. They had only been to her apartment once in the three years she had lived there, and that was when the heating element went out in her oven. The thought of having a strange man in her apartment was enough for her to make most minor repairs on her own without bothering to call the landlord. Maintenance didn't seem to notice the locks, or at least they never mentioned them.

Running short on time, Katie kicked off her shoes and headed to the bathroom. She took down her hair and peeled off her sweaty clothes, dropping them on the floor near the sink. After starting the shower, she caught a glimpse of herself as she passed the mirror and stopped to gaze at her reflection while waiting on the water to warm up. Her long brown hair was creased from the rubber band of her ponytail, her cheeks still crimson red from her run. She possessed a natural beauty evident to everyone but herself. All she could see was the aching loneliness behind her pale blue eyes and often wondered if anyone could ever love something so damaged. And if they could, would she let them?

The steam rolling from the shower snapped her out of her daze and back to reality. She was in and out in record time, although her showers never really lasted that long. She dried her hair and then checked the clock to see how she was doing on time. *Eight forty. Crap!* she thought. *I will have to drive today.*

Even though she had a car, Katie normally rode her bike to work. It wasn't too far from her apartment, and she usually only drove when the weather was bad or if she had errands to run after work. She knew riding her bike would keep her from having to make deliveries, the only part of her job that bothered her.

She threw on some blue jeans and a light-blue satin blouse that brought out the color of her eyes. One of the nicer items of clothing she owned and much more appropriate than joggers and a baggy sweatshirt, which made up the majority of her wardrobe. The outfit was a little fancier than usual for a day at the flower shop, but she knew she needed something that would transition from work to Joe's. Amanda would be dressed to the nines as usual, and since they were now meeting at six, Katie wouldn't have a chance to come home and change. She walked through a mist of body spray, grabbed her purse and day planner, snatched her keys from the hutch, and headed out the door.

It was a quick trip to work and she arrived just in time. Mrs. Greyson probably wouldn't mind if Katie was late, but she didn't want to find out. She respected her boss dearly and was thankful she had offered her a job since she had no previous experience. It didn't pay much, but after a year of job hopping when she came to Victoria and on the verge of giving up and moving to yet another town, Katie had finally found a place where she was not only comfortable but enjoyed what she was doing. That was worth more to her than a hefty paycheck.

When she pushed open the front door, the bell overhead rang, announcing her entrance. The aroma of apples and cinnamon with a hint of freshly baked cookies filled the air; an inviting scent that Katie loved walking in to each day. She could see Mrs. Greyson working diligently in the back, sorting through the fresh flower deliveries from this morning. She was short in stature, a little plump through the middle, and the most genuine soul Katie had ever met. Her long, full hair was a combination of silver and brown, and she wore it the same way every day: slightly frizzy from her natural curl, with the sides joined together in the back with a clip. Even though she was widowed at the early age of fifty-eight and her two children were grown and gone, she was full of love and worked each day with a smile on her face and a song in her heart. Katie could hear her singing as she closed the front door.

"Good morning, Mrs. Greyson," Katie called out. She flipped around the OPEN sign on the front door, dropped her purse behind the counter, and headed to the back room.

"Good morning, Katherine." Mrs. Greyson was the only person other than her mother who called Katie by her full name. She looked up as Katie walked in to the room and did a bit of a double take. "Well, don't you look beautiful today?"

"Oh, umm, well, thank you." Katie blushed, as if undeserving of the sweet words. She had never been any good at taking a compliment.

"You must have big plans this evening?" Mrs. Greyson inquired with a sly grin across her face.

"No. Not too big. I'm meeting Amanda after work at Joe's for drinks. We still try to get together once a week for girl's night, you know, before she and Kyle get married and I get replaced." Katie feared deep down that what she said as a joke would soon become a harsh reality.

"Well, shoot," Mrs. Greyson said, almost as if disappointed.

"What? You don't like Amanda?"

"Oh, of course I do dear. She's one of my best customers. I just thought this might have something to do with that striking young man who came by asking about you this morning. I've never understood how a sweet little thing like you has remained single for so long. You are quite the catch!"

Katie froze. "Someone came here? To the shop? Looking for me?"

"Well, you are the only young brunette working here. I was in the parking lot helping unload the delivery truck and he pulled up beside me in his car. He asked me if you were working today and I told him yes, that you were usually here by now, but that we didn't officially open until nine. He was very polite and told me thanks for the help, he would stop by later." Mrs. Greyson's tone went from playful to concerned when she saw the bewilderment on Katie's face. "Is everything alright, dear?"

"Oh … yes … sorry." Katie exhaled and tried to loosen up, hoping to avoid any further suspicion. "It, it was probably this guy I met last week at the flea market when Amanda and I were shopping," she stuttered. Instant nausea filled the pit of her stomach. She had never lied to Mrs. Greyson before.

Until now.

"Hmmmm, sounds interesting," Mrs. Greyson perked back up. She was always a sucker for a good love story. "I can't believe you didn't tell me sooner. How exciting, I sure hope things work out!"

When she turned to put the roses in the refrigerator Katie whispered to herself, "Yeah. Me too."

Katie spent the rest of the day in turmoil, but tried to carry on like it was any other normal day. She had two orders for fresh flower arrangements to deliver to Mrs. Hicks down at the Methodist church for her birthday, and a candy bouquet to make that a customer wanted to pick up around four. As much as she was opposed to going to the church, she didn't mind making the deliveries today because she didn't want Mrs. Greyson to leave her at the shop alone. She was thankful she had to drive today. Luckily, she was able to stay busy, but each time she heard the bell ding as someone came through the front door, nerves riddled her body.

As the hours ticked away, Katie found herself obsessing over her conversation with Mrs. Greyson and the possibility that her past had finally come back to haunt her. She knew deep down there was no way possible he could be there looking for her. *He was in prison and besides, how would he know where to look? But who else could it be?* Amanda was the only person Katie associated with, and although she had been introduced to Amanda's fiancé, Kyle, on several occasions, she didn't necessarily consider them to be good enough acquaintances that would require a visit. She didn't want to seem suspicious by probing Mrs. Greyson for details such as asking how tall he was, what color of hair he had, and if he had a small scar on his cheek below his right eye.

Katie wondered if the incessant paranoia was for nothing. Less than an hour until closing and she still had received no visitors, for which she was relieved. She could tell Mrs. Greyson had also been on the lookout, but for entirely different reasons—she thought Katie had a potential beau coming by. She had never spoken of her past with Mrs. Greyson before, but her boss was very intuitive. She could sense Katie's loneliness, and knew there must be a reason why in the two years she had known her, that Katie had never shown the slightest interest in being in a relationship, but Mrs. Greyson never asked why.

Katie decided to try to push the thoughts of her past away and start closing up the store so she could go meet Amanda. She put the unused stems back in the refrigerator to keep them fresh, washed her pruning shears, and put away her hot glue gun. She wiped down the table, then dusted and neatly restacked the vases on the bottom shelf. She hung her red apron on the hook beside the back door and began to sweep. With her head down looking at the floor, she did not notice Mrs. Greyson coming up behind her.

"I'm sorry your fella didn't come back for you today."

Katie jumped and spun around quickly, allowing an expletive to blurt from her mouth.

"Shit!" Katie cringed. "Shoot! I mean shoot! I'm so sorry," she apologized, still standing in attack mode, broom gripped with both hands out in front of her like a weapon. She knew Mrs. Greyson had probably heard worse, but she felt like she had just cursed in front of her mother and was going to get in trouble. She lowered the broom and her shoulders fell. "You startled me. I didn't hear you come in."

"I gather," Mrs. Greyson chuckled. She patted Katie on the shoulder and whispered, "It's okay honey. I've let that word slip once or twice in my day."

Katie sighed and attempted a grin. Mrs. Greyson always had a way of making her feel better. When her head quit spinning, it finally registered with her what Mrs. Greyson had said.

"Oh, and about the guy? It's really not a big deal," Katie blew it off nonchalantly.

"Not a big deal?" Mrs. Greyson protested. "I saw you watching that front door like a hawk and how you got all jittery every time it opened. Ah, young love, I remember how that feels. Butterflies. Nerves. I had that with my sweet Phillip, God rest his soul. What a wonderful feeling," she said, gazing at the ceiling with a dreamy look upon her face. Mrs. Greyson had married Phillip just out of high school, much to her father's dismay, but their love withstood the test of time, outlasting all predictions of her family naysayers.

Katie doubted she would ever know what that felt like and didn't want to rain on her boss's love-parade by telling her the anxiety and nerves she was experiencing had nothing to do with love. She admired Mrs. Greyson's feelings for her husband and was amazed that she harbored no bitter feelings over his untimely death. Katie often felt she had a lot to learn from Mrs. Greyson.

"Well, I've about got everything cleaned up for the day. I'm going to head out, if that's okay." Katie used the dustpan to collect the pile of trash from the floor and dumped it in the wastebasket. "Is there anything else you need me to do?"

Mrs. Greyson looked around the room. "Everything looks good, sweetie. If you could, turn the closed sign around on your way out. I will lock up the store. You and Amanda have a good time tonight, enjoy being young." She pushed her glasses up from the tip of her nose.

"Thank you, Mrs. Greyson. We will. See you tomorrow." Katie placed the broom back in the corner, grabbed her purse, and, by the time she reached the front door, she could already hear Mrs. Greyson singing. *How can someone be so happy all of the time?* She flipped the sign around to CLOSED and, once she was outside, scanned the parking lot before getting in her car. *Better safe than sorry.*

Joe's was a quaint little coffee shop downtown on the square, nestled between a vintage furniture store and a children's clothing boutique. It was one of the few places Katie was comfortable hanging out, and she was glad she had finally let Amanda convince her to go. It was never overly crowded and the atmosphere was relaxed, unlike the pub at the end of the street where the rest of the people her age typically went. That place was a regular drunken frenzy of bombarding hormones and loud music. Katie never cared to experience that again.

As she pulled up to park, Katie looked at the clock and realized her quick exit from work to avoid any further conversation about the mystery man caused her to arrive a little early. She had about fifteen minutes to kill, but decided to go ahead and go in and try to get her favorite table—the one at the far end of the room, where her back faced the corner.

On her way to the door, she stopped. She turned around, expecting to see someone standing behind her, but there was nothing more than the normal flow of people, coming and going from the local businesses. To her left she could see the gazebo and grassy area of De Leon Plaza, and to her right, the white pillar entrance of the museum. She turned back around and continued towards Joe's.

Katie had only been seated a few minutes when Amanda came bouncing in the door, as beautiful and carefree as always. She looked like she had just stepped out of a magazine, and every man in the place stopped to stare as she walked by. Katie loved that Amanda didn't even seem to notice—it was part of her charm.

"Do you think they are trying to tell us something by always putting us in the back corner?" Amanda asked, unaware it was at Katie's request.

"Yes, they said it is because you smell bad."

Amanda sniffed under her arm.

"Geez, I was kidding. And you said I'm not normal," Katie laughed. "I knew you would be crunched for time, so I just ordered the usual. Hope that was okay."

"Now you're ordering for me? Maybe I should be marrying you, not Kyle," Amanda joked, her chair legs screeched against the tile floor when she scooted closer to the table. "Speaking of getting married …"

The waitress interrupted as she placed a glass of decaffeinated peach tea in front of Katie and a tall, frothy latte in front of Amanda, not the type of beverages someone would expect to see if two girls in their twenties said they were going for drinks. Steam rolled out from beneath the blob of whipped cream in the top of Amanda's cup. It looked delicious, but Katie knew that if she drank something like that she wouldn't sleep for days, and she didn't need anything else contributing to her insomnia.

"Can I get you ladies anything else?" The waitress clasped her hands together.

"No, thank you." Katie took the silverware from inside her napkin, set it on the table, and draped the napkin across her lap.

Amanda did the same and then picked right back up where she left off. "About my wedding, I have a huge favor to ask you. What would you say if I asked you to be my maid of honor?" The hesitancy in her voice let Katie know Amanda wasn't sure how she would answer.

"Seriously?" Katie's voice raised about three octaves. "I would love to be in your wedding."

"Oh my goodness, that makes me so happy," Amanda squealed and clapped her hands together in excitement. "This is going to be so much fun."

She took a drink of her coffee and it must have given her a jolt of energy because she barely took a breath for the next ten minutes. Amanda rambled on about wedding plans, dress shopping, and how her stepmom felt Amanda should have asked her cousin to be the maid of honor, not her best friend. Katie fiddled with the napkin in her lap and tried to focus on what Amanda was saying, but couldn't shake the strange feeling that she was being watched. She lifted her tea glass to take a drink and peered over the rim, scanning the room for anything suspicious, but nothing appeared out of sorts. There was an elderly couple at the table by the front window, sharing an oversized helping of peach cobbler, and a group of teenage girls in line at the register, waiting to check out. Amanda's voice was still droning in the background. The only car visible from her chair was empty and the people on the sidewalk were engaged in conversation with their backs to the window. Katie sighed and shook her head. *I think I'm losing my mind.*

"Helloooo?" Amanda banged her spoon against the side of her glass three times. "Earth to Katie?"

"Sorry, what did you say?" She tried to refocus, curious if Amanda had asked a question she didn't respond to, and wondering exactly how much of the conversation she missed.

"You seem a little preoccupied. Is everything okay?"

"Actually ... no, not really." Katie had debated for a long time whether to tell Amanda about her past and assumed one day she would. With her unknown visitor at the flower shop, she really needed that day to be today. She needed someone to talk to, someone she could trust. She took a deep breath and with all the nerve she could muster finally said, "Listen, I need to tell you something. Something I've actually wanted to tell you for quite some time now."

"Anything, girlie. What is it?" She sensed Katie's angst. "Hey, if this is about the wedding ..."

"No, no, that's not it at all." Katie looked past Amanda at two guys approaching the table.

Amanda spun around to see what she was looking at. "What are you doing here?" She asked, genuinely surprised to see Kyle standing there.

"Nice to see you too," he protested.

"Oh, stop it, you know what I mean. I thought you were going to have dinner with Ty before dad's party?" She leaned over, surprised again that the guy with him wasn't her brother.

"I tried calling him several times and he never answered. He must be working late or something. So when Brad called and asked if I wanted to hang out, I said sure."

Amanda looked at Kyle sternly, her eyes widened, nodding slightly toward Brad.

"Oh, pardon my manners. Brad, this is my fiancée, Amanda, and this is her friend, Katie," motioning respectively. "Girls, this is Brad Sanderson."

Brad stood over six feet tall with dirty blonde hair that was long on top and shaved on the sides. He had hooded brown eyes and a square chin. His pink polo shirt and khaki shorts made him look like he was ready for eighteen holes of golf.

"Hey, Brad." The bracelets on Amanda's wrist clanged together as she reached out to shake his hand. "Nice to meet you."

"Nice to meet you, too." He shook her hand and turned towards Katie, offering to do the same. "Good evening."

"Hi," Katie replied awkwardly with a wave, denying his request to shake hands and refusing to make eye contact. He pulled back his arm, not sure to make of what just happened.

Kyle chimed in, "We were thinking about going down to the pub to shoot some pool, and since Joe's was on the way I thought we would stop in and see if you two wanted to join us."

"I would love to kick your butt at a game of pool," Katie's heart sank at the sound of Amanda's response, "but I don't really want to show up at the party smelling like cigarette smoke. You shouldn't want to either," she looked down at her watch. "As a matter of fact, we should probably head that way pretty soon."

"You go ahead. Brad and I are in the same car. I know how your dad's parties are. We have plenty of time to shoot a game or two and still be there before things really get going. I will just meet you at your dad's house. If I smell like an ashtray, I will stop and change clothes beforehand, I promise," Kyle said. "Katie, do you like to play pool? You could go with us if you would like."

"I can't. I have to be up early for work tomorrow. Thank you for the invite, though." Katie was quick to respond. She wouldn't have gone even if Amanda had said yes. Not only was the pub the last place she wanted to be, there was something about the way Brad kept looking at her that made her uncomfortable, like this entire meeting wasn't just a coincidence.

"Maybe next time then. Did Amanda tell you the good news?"

"Yes, she just did, and I would be honored to stand up for her at your wedding. I'm looking forward to it." This time she was being honest. She didn't care much for being around a group of people she didn't know, but she would do anything for Amanda and was happy she had asked her to be a part of their special day.

"See, I told you she would say yes." Kyle nudged Amanda on the shoulder. "You were worried for nothing."

Amanda looked horrified that Kyle brought that up. Sometimes he didn't know when to keep his big mouth shut. "You can leave anytime, you know."

Kyle and Amanda constantly gave each other fits, but Katie had never known two people more suited for each other. Kyle absolutely adored Amanda. It was obvious by the way he looked at her. She watched them playfully teasing each other and smiled when he leaned down and kissed her on the tip of the nose. Katie took a drink of her tea, trying to ignore the heat coming from Brad's stare.

"I guess we should get going. Katie, it was nice to see you again," Kyle nodded and then turned to Amanda. "I will see you shortly, beautiful."

Amanda stood and gave Kyle a hug. She stepped back and looked from him to Brad. "You boys stay out of trouble. Brad, it was nice to meet you. Don't let Kyle be late."

"Likewise," Brad was responding to Amanda, but his eyes never left Katie, "Maybe we can all get together another time."

Katie faked a smile, trying to keep her tea from coming back up into her throat. "Bye, guys."

They finally left.

"I'm so sorry about that, I had no idea he was going to stop by." Amanda sat back down.

"No biggie." Katie finished off her tea and the ice rattled in the glass as she set it back on the table. "Call me crazy, but for a minute there I thought it was an ambush attempt to set me up on a blind date."

"With Brad? Girl, Kyle knows better than to pull a stunt like that, that is, without asking me first. And I surely wouldn't let him do that to you with someone I didn't know."

"You've never met him before?" Katie asked.

"No, honest. I've just recently heard Kyle mention his name. I think he said he works in the service department at Kyle's dealership. Well, not Kyle's dealership, but the dealership where Kyle works. You know what I mean. Anyway, I've never seen the guy before tonight." She took a drink of her coffee and then used her tongue to clean the whipped cream it left behind on her lip. "He was kind of checking you out though, wasn't he? Not a bad looking guy, either. Kind of has that mysterious yet preppy thing working for him," her eyes widened. "If you're interested, I can have Kyle …"

"No, I'm good," Katie interjected, squashing that thought before it ever fully left Amanda's mouth. She didn't need any mysterious men in her life. That had not worked out too well for her last time.

Amanda looked at her watch again and sighed. "Dad will be pissed if I'm late. He wants me to help set everything up. I had better go. Are you sure you don't want to come with me?"

"I'm sure, thanks anyway. It's been a long day and I'm exhausted. Plus, I have to work tomorrow and need my rest. You know Mrs. Greyson, she's quite the slave driver."

Amanda pulled some money out of her wallet and put it on the table to cover the tab plus a hefty tip. "Yes, she's just wretched. I'm not sure how you put up with her every day, with her constant singing and incessant happiness, and such. But I forgive her, after all, she's the reason we are friends." She smiled.

"No, the fact that you order and send so many flowers is the reason we are friends," Katie exclaimed.

"Good point."

They both stood up and gathered their things. As they were walking out the door, Amanda suddenly remembered, "Shit, girl, I'm so sorry. With all of the excitement about asking you to be in my wedding and then Kyle stopping by, I completely forgot you wanted to talk to me about something. What is it?"

"Don't worry about it," Katie assured her. She knew she didn't have the time or the nerve at this point to attack that conversation, and definitely not while walking out of the coffee shop. "We can talk about it some other time."

"Promise?"

"Yes, I promise."

"Okay, I'm holding you to that." She pressed the button on her key fob and unlocked her step mom's car. "I will call you tomorrow."

"Sounds good." Katie knew Amanda's attention span rivaled that of a squirrel. If she wanted to finish the conversation, she would have to bring it back up. "Have fun at your dad's party."

"Oh, you know it!" Amanda responded.

Katie took a quick shower and threw on her favorite University of Texas sweatshirt and a pair of black yoga pants. She plopped down on the couch, grabbed the remote, and started flipping through the channels when the rumble in her stomach reminded her she hadn't eaten all day. She went to the kitchen and opened the refrigerator. *I really need to go to the market.* Her options were bleak: old milk, lunchmeat, ketchup, mustard, leftover Chinese food, and a bottle of Moscato Amanda had given her for Christmas last year that she never opened. Drinking wasn't really her thing. Fortunately, the bread hadn't gone stale and she scrounged together enough stuff to make a turkey sandwich. She devoured it as if she hadn't eaten in days.

It was still early, but Katie was ready to call it a night. She cleaned up her mess in the kitchen and turned off the light. On her way to the bedroom, she checked all the locks on the front door, the same as she did every night. She lay down on her bed, a nightlight keeping the darkness at bay, and the events from the day scrolled through her head. The nightmare, an unknown visitor, her past, Amanda's wedding, Brad. She was completely exhausted, staring at the ceiling, yet afraid to close her eyes.

Chapter 2
NINE YEARS EARLIER

"I said stop calling me!" Katie shouted, then slammed down the receiver. Damon had not left her alone since she ended things with him a few weeks ago. She was through trying to be nice about it because that obviously wasn't working.

"Honey, is everything okay?" Carl asked.

"Yes, dad. It's fine," Katie lied. "I'm going for a run." She leaned down and kissed him on the head as she passed by his desk. It's where he spent most of his time while at home, working on his books for the hardware store. It was something her mom used to take care of. "I will be home in time to cook dinner."

Katie made her way through the living room toward the front door and glanced at the picture of her mom on the mantle above the fireplace. She missed her so much it hurt, and she resented God for taking her away. It was a feeling that plagued her with guilt, but all the time she had spent in church on her knees, the relentless praying for her mom to get well, and He obviously didn't listen. The cancer ate away at her mom's body until there was nothing left but a lifeless shell that no longer resembled the woman Katie knew. Didn't He understand how much girls needed their mothers? To help shop for bras and to give advice on boys? Maybe her mom could tell her how to handle Damon, something she wasn't comfortable talking about with her dad. How could she tell him about his propositions? That the reason she broke up with Damon was because he kept pushing her to have sex, and at seventeen, she just wasn't ready? Her dad struggled enough getting through her first menstrual cycle, she was certain he couldn't handle a conversation about sex. Neither could she.

Katie felt her throat tighten and the tears start to build in her eyes. She knew she needed to go. She pushed open the screen door and turned toward her father before walking out. "Be home soon, dad," she offered with a fake smile.

"Okay, sweetheart. I love you, be safe."

Katie stepped off the porch and took a moment to collect her thoughts. Her head overflowed with images of her mom, coupled with the resonating sound of Damon's voice and the profanity he had spewed on the phone moments ago. She knew she would see him Saturday, she was sure of it, and the thought of it made her queasy. Damon had not missed a single cross-country meet since he came to town, not one, and she believed this weekend would be no different.

Their relationship had ended after only six months, and she hadn't known him much longer than that. He moved to town just before the end of their junior year to live with his grandparents and he took the school by storm. A new student in a small town always generated a buzz of interest and it didn't help that he had bad-boy charm and rugged good looks. He was tall with dark, wispy hair and full lips. The rigid edges of his jawline were covered in stubble, and he had a tribal tattoo with bold black loops and hooks that rested high on his right shoulder. The boys automatically hated him and the girls all wanted to date him, but he paid them no attention. He quickly had eyes for a quiet, blue-eyed brunette who sat next to him in Mrs. Berkeley's government class. It didn't take long for him to build the reputation of someone who got what he wanted—and he wanted Katie.

She shook her arms out simultaneously and rocked her head side to side, stretching her ears toward her shoulders. A good run would help her escape the mental demons lurking in her head as it had done so many times in the past. She breathed in the sweet smell of East Texas pines, zipped up her jacket, and took off, disappearing into the trees.

It was a short hike from her house through the woods to get to Black Bear Trail; a trip she had made often over the last four years. Katie took up running when she was thirteen as a suggestion from her grievance counselor, Ms. Riley. Teenage angst combined with the loss of her mother had her spiraling into a state of depression, and she needed an outlet for her emotions. Katie thought the entire idea of running therapy was absurd; after all, what did Ms. Riley know? She had no children and her mother was still alive, but much to Katie's surprise, it actually worked. Not only did running help, it turned out she had a knack for it. Her sophomore year, Coach Fletcher recruited Katie to be on the varsity cross-country team for the Brownsboro Bears.

The sun was low in the western sky and Katie knew she needed to pick up the pace if she was going to make it home before dark. Fall had already begun to rob the trees of their leaves, and with every step, she heard the earth crunch beneath her feet. She darted between trees, careful to dodge fallen limbs hidden in the shadows, and with one long stride she cleared the creek without even a trace of mud on her shoes. She knew this path like the back of her hand and could probably do it blindfolded if the need arose.

A few moments later, she emerged from the woods into the clearing that surrounded Black Bear Trail. Katie used this as her starting point, even though the official entrance to the trail was about a half mile around the path near the parking lot. The trail appeared vacant, just as she had expected. It was Wednesday evening, and the normal running crowd was more than likely at church, a place she hadn't been since her mother's funeral and she had no interest in going back.

Katie replaced her MP3 player in her pocket with her necklace, took off her jacket, and draped it across the wooden park bench beside the trail. She scrolled through her playlists until she found the one titled Black Bear Three Mile. She ran the trail so many times that she used the songs in her playlist to help measure her pace. By the time Linkin Park came on, she should be at the park entrance. The sound of Finger Eleven had her crossing the wooden bridge over the creek, and when Maroon 5 started singing, she would be passing the restroom area on the backside of the trail. When she got back to her starting point, 3 Doors Down would signal the end of lap one for a total of one and a half miles. She paced the second lap using the same method.

Long-distance running was about endurance, and she learned from all of her cross-country meets that the key to success was finding a stride that would allow her to maintain a consistent speed. Too fast, and she would run out of gas before the race was over. Too slow, and she would find herself so far behind the other competitors that even with a sprint to the finish, she would not be able to catch up. Coach Fletcher had Katie on a strict running schedule. She was his star athlete, and having her on the team was his best chance for making it to state. Three days a week she ran for distance, anywhere from five to seven miles at the track or along neighboring country roads. The other two days he had her working on stability by running through dirt and gravel or up large hills. Outside of athletics, Katie put in hours of work on her own, even on the weekends, determined to beat her personal record at the district meet on Saturday.

Nickelback blared through her ear buds as she placed them in her ears. She bent over at the waist, reaching for her ankles, and felt the muscles pull in her calves and hamstrings. She lunged to the right and then to the left to widen her hips and to stretch her inner thighs. After a few tuck jumps to get her heart rate going, she hit the trail. She hadn't stretched as much as usual before a run, but she was racing against the sun that was quickly setting and needed to get moving.

Half a mile down and Katie knew she was right on pace. With Linkin Park drowning out the sound of her footsteps, she passed the parking lot at the trail entrance. There were two people loading up their bicycles on the back of a red Jeep Wrangler, but otherwise the parking lot was empty. She had the trail all to herself.

Her breathing settled to a steady rhythm and as she ran, she took in the beauty around her; the golden tones of fall evident in every direction. Leaves strewn about blanketed the ground. The nearly barren trees boasted their unique network of branches, some of which encroached upon the narrower parts of the trail. Their trunks were so wide she often wondered how old they might be. She crossed the wooden bridge over the creek and then breezed by the restroom area right on schedule, and before she knew it, she was starting the last leg of her run.

Katie was uncertain of the physics behind the therapeutic nature of running and, at seventeen, she really didn't care. Whether it was pure adrenaline or the release of endorphins that numbed her pain, it worked. The thoughts of Damon had vanished and the sad memories of her mother's passing were replaced with visions of the beautiful woman who used to read her bedtime stories at night and kiss her forehead each morning before school.

Almost completely out of daylight after she finished her three miles, Katie darted directly into the woods toward her house. She knew her dad would be worried if she wasn't home before dark, especially since she had left right after Damon's phone call. Halfway home she realized she left her jacket on the park bench. The jacket itself wasn't all that important, but she couldn't stand to lose what was inside the pocket so she turned around. On her way back to the trail, a side stitch stabbed beneath her ribs. She slowed her pace to a walk and raised her arms above her head to help ease the pain. This was something she'd become accustomed to with all of her running and knew it would pass quickly, once her breathing returned to a normal pace. Focused on the pink glisten of her jacket in the distance, she was caught off guard when her arms dropped from the after-shock of a crushing blow to her gut.

Someone was there, behind her. In an instant, she was immobilized, her arms pinned to her sides. *What is this? Is this some kind of joke?* A hand covered with a black glove clenched over her mouth and another arm squeezed tightly around her chest. Her ear buds, ripped from her ears during the commotion, now dangled over the arm of a stranger. She tried to yell, but the glove muffled her voice. This person's strength was undeniable and she was physically exhausted. Her lungs screamed. Not able to breathe through her mouth, she fought to get them air. Sweat caused the glove to shift slightly, and the scent of leather overpowered the little bit of oxygen she was able to take in as it moved. Her feet came off the ground as she kicked and thrashed, but her muscles were fatigued from running. Her attempts to break free failed. The burning in her lungs intensified and the trees around her appeared to be melting. Dizziness took over and Katie's body succumbed to the pressure. The world around her went black, but not before hearing a faint whisper and feeling the breath of her assailant against her face.

Chapter 3
PRESENT

Katie shot straight up in her bed, gasping for air, covered in sweat, her heart pounding. She blinked rapidly, begging her eyes to come in to focus as she turned on the lamp. Waking up like that had not gotten any easier over the last nine years. Counseling, pharmacotherapy, imagery rehearsal therapy sessions, she had tried it all, until she finally accepted one day that this would be a normal part of her life from now on. The nightmares weren't an everyday occurrence, but they occurred more frequently than she cared for this time of year and almost always happened after a stressful day … like yesterday.

She glanced at the clock and decided to get up. Thirty more minutes of lying in bed staring at the ceiling waiting for the alarm to go off hardly seemed worth it. She made her way to the kitchen to start a pot of coffee, decaf, using the last scoop of grounds from the bottom of the can. Yet another reminder she needed to go to the market. Out the window, dense fog hovered in the air. The rising sun had yet to burn through its looming blanket, so instead of a run she opted for the next best thing when it came to needing a distraction.

"Hello?" Carl's voice resonated through the telephone receiver.

"Hey, Daddy."

"Good morning, sweetheart. How are you?" he knew the reason behind early-morning phone calls, but would never directly broach the subject.

"I'm okay. I haven't talked to you in a while, so I thought I would call and check on you. How's your knee?" she asked, avoiding the obvious reason for her call.

"I'm feeling much better than the last time we talked. My incision is healing nicely and it's getting easier to maneuver around the house. They finally upgraded me from a big, clunky walker to a cane. Your dad is getting old."

"You've been old for a long time, Daddy," Katie joked, thinking of his bushy, grey hair. "Do you think you will still be able to make it down for Thanksgiving?" Carl always tried to travel to Victoria for holidays or if there were an emergency, but the drive was too taxing on him to make more than a few times a year.

"That's the plan. I have one more month of physical therapy and then a follow-up consultation with Dr. Kerstal the first week of October to see if he will release me to make the drive. There is still plenty of time, so I'm sure it won't be a problem."

"What a relief. I was worried that with everything that's been going on you wouldn't be able to, and I feel like it has been forever since I've seen you."

Eight months, to be exact. He had come down for Christmas last year, but missed her birthday in March due to his knee replacement.

Katie and her dad talked for almost an hour. He listened intently as she rambled on about how busy they had been at the flower shop and how Amanda asked her to be in her wedding. He told her all about his experience with home health and the recovery process since his surgery. The conversation flowed so naturally she was surprised when she noticed the time.

"Well, Daddy, I guess I better go. I have to get ready for work."

"Okay. I'm so glad you called. It was good to hear your voice. I will talk to you soon."

Just as Carl was about to hang up the phone he heard Katie's voice shout, "Daddy, wait!"

"Katie?" he asked, bringing the receiver back to his ear.

"I … I need to ask you something." He could hear the hesitancy in her voice. "Is there anything you may have forgotten to tell me?"

"Not that I can think of. Why? Is everything okay?"

"Well, I think so," Katie replied, honestly not sure of the answer to that question. "Mrs. Greyson said that someone stopped by the flower shop to see me yesterday before I got to work. A man."

He knew by the sound of her voice what she was thinking.

"Honey, Detective Burns told me that we would be notified before his release or any change in his incarceration status. I know he doesn't know where to reach you, but he hasn't tried calling me. You would definitely be the first to know." Carl feared for the day that actually happened.

So did Katie.

"I know. You're right. It's just that nobody here really knows me, so when Mrs. Greyson told me I had a visitor I couldn't think of anyone else it could be."

"I really don't think you have anything to worry about," Carl said, "but I will call Detective Burns to make sure so you can have some peace of mind. I will let you know as soon as I get in touch with him."

"Thank you so much, Daddy. I appreciate it."

Katie loved talking to her dad, yet the end of each conversation left her with the same guilty feeling inside. Carl understood why she never came to see him, even while he was in the hospital, but he didn't blame her. After Katie moved and the house was empty, it was his choice to stay in Brownsboro, a town cursed by the memory of a past she longed to forget. He worried about her constantly, but couldn't bear to say goodbye to the home he had made with his beautiful wife, Mary. Although she had been gone for quite some time, Carl felt as if her spirit were still with him, and he didn't want to move and risk the possibility of losing her again.

Carl and Mary were married for thirty-four years when she passed away. He loved her from the moment he laid eyes on her. He was working behind the counter at Upton Hardware, his father's business, when she walked through the door one sunny afternoon. It was as if the world around him melted into a hazy blur and all that remained in his line of sight was the most exquisite creature he had ever seen. Locks of golden, blonde hair curled up at the end above her shoulders. Big, soulful brown eyes full of mystery, yet warm like the sun. A small, button nose and full, pale lips, all atop a petite frame clothed in a sleeveless turquoise A-line dress that hit just above her knees. When she approached him to pay for her soda and peered up at him from beneath her long, black eyelashes, he knew his heart would belong to her and only her for the rest of his life.

After a short year of courting, Carl proposed to Mary. She was only seventeen at the time, but without hesitation, she said yes. They were head over heels in love with each other and everyone in town knew. Carl spent every second he could with Mary, and on days when he had to work, she hung around the hardware store. Carl's father often joked about putting her on the payroll with as much time as she spent there.

Carl emptied his savings account to put a down payment on a quaint little farmhouse a few miles outside of town. It was a single-story with two bedrooms, and although it was in desperate need of repair, Carl and Mary were both able to see the potential in what would become their forever home. It was a place where they could be together and eventually grow their family.

They spent months working around the house, breathing life into their dream. Carl repaired the damaged hardwood floors, replaced the missing pickets in the porch railing, and exhausted himself night after night repairing the leaky roof. Mary was able to utilize the limited furnishings they had to create a cozy, functional living space amid the construction mess and each night, atop a mattress that lay directly on the wooden floor, they made love.

In the winter of that same year, Mary became pregnant. Even though it felt like they were about to place the last piece into their life puzzle, her body was unable to support the pregnancy, and at only twelve weeks gestation she had a miscarriage. Devastation shook her to the core and for the first time since they'd met, Carl saw her weep.

The following weeks were the hardest they faced as a couple. Not only did they lose their child but in one of her follow-up appointments the gynecologist revealed that Mary had endometriosis and told her the chances of conceiving again, let alone carrying a pregnancy full term, were minimal at best. Mary ignored what the doctor said regarding the possible complications of another pregnancy, refusing to give up on having a child. She knew in her heart that she was supposed to be a mother, and it pained Carl each month when Mary's natural reminder came, letting her know once again that she was not pregnant.

Carl brought up adoption a few times, but the topic was never open for discussion in her opinion. They both knew it would put a strain on them financially, and deep down, that was the reason behind Mary disregarding the idea. No matter the cost, Carl was willing to do anything to keep her from having to experience that pain again and was concerned for what another pregnancy would mean for Mary's health.

Weeks, months, and years ticked away. Life settled into a normal routine. Carl inherited the hardware store from his father and Mary kept busy with the accounting end of the business. She found that the monotony of crunching numbers and paying bills kept her mind occupied and less focused on her inability to conceive. The repairs on the house were complete, but the emptiness of the room Mary insisted on turning into a nursery was daunting for Carl. He cherished his life with Mary, but that room represented the one thing he hadn't been able to give her—a child.

Owning their own business proved very demanding of their time, so they vowed to do something together each Sunday after church. When the weather was nice, they liked to drive out to the lake and spend the day fishing or hiking the nature trails. Mary would pack a picnic basket with fried chicken, fruit salad, and sweet tea, and they would spread a blanket beneath the large willow tree next to the water and have lunch. More than once, on that same blanket beside the lake, as the sun danced across the water, Carl and Mary would get lost in one another. The two of them never let making love solely become about having a child, they loved one another hard, but deep down Mary held on to the hope each time they were together that life would grow inside of her. None of their attempts at creating life resulted in another pregnancy.

The trips to the lake were eventually replaced with Sunday afternoons spent at home. They took up gardening and celebrated in dance when the first signs of life poked out from beneath the dirt. They had given birth to a field of fresh vegetables that suddenly grew faster than Mary could prepare. She loved to cook, and Carl was thankful, because he loved to eat. She canned what she could and packaged up the rest in brown paper sacks to deliver to members of their church. On days when it rained and they couldn't work in the garden, they would rock in the wooden porch swing where Mary would read to Carl. Those days were his favorite. The soothing sound of her voice mixed with the tapping of the rain on the roof made the rest of the world, and all of its troubles, disappear. There were no worries about the hardware store or failed pregnancies or an empty locket. Just the sound of an angel, his reason for being and the woman he would sacrifice his life for, and there was no place he'd rather be than in that very moment—on that front porch he'd built for his Mary.

It was a Thursday evening when Carl received the phone call that would change their lives forever. Pastor Ray asked if he and Mary would meet him down at the church. When they arrived, across from Pastor Ray sat a disheveled young woman wearing what appeared to be a man's shirt, stained pants that were two sizes too big, and the skin of her feet showed through the holes in her shoes. She was holding a baby, one she knew she was incapable of caring for. She had come to the church looking for help.

Pastor Ray knew of Carl and Mary's situation, as they had gone to him for guidance in prayer. He asked if they would be interested in fostering the child with the possibility to adopt. Without a second thought, they simultaneously said yes. Pastor Ray took the baby from her mother and placed the child in Mary's arms. For the second time in her life, Mary fell in love. This chubby faced, brown-headed bundle of joy was everything she had ever hoped for and with one glance into her big blue eyes, Mary knew …

It's you. You're the one I've been waiting for all this time. I knew in my heart you would come to me and I've finally found you. My little Easter egg. My Katherine.

The flower shop buzzed with orders. Mrs. Greyson handled all of the fresh flower arrangements, and left Katie in charge of starting the homecoming mums for the big football game next week. Her workstation was chaotic, sprinkled with glitter and spilling over with blue and gold ribbons. It wasn't her favorite project, but it gave her a sense of satisfaction, knowing Mrs. Greyson trusted her creativity enough to get the job done.

"Katherine, are you in your car today?" Mrs. Greyson called out.

"Yes, ma'am. If I don't make it to the market after work, there is a large possibility I may starve to death. You wouldn't believe how empty my fridge is."

"We can't have that, at least not until after you are through making all of those homecoming mums."

"I'm touched to know you care so much," Katie laughed. "Did you need me to make a delivery?"

"Yes, please. Two, actually. The rose bouquet in the front cooler goes to the Baymont Inn, and the arrangement I am finishing now needs to go to the hospital, room 3212. I have a couple of sprays for the funeral home I need to finish before six."

"I bet I can handle that." Katie welcomed the break from the sadistic hot glue gun. She felt she could rob a bank undetected due to her lack of fingerprints.

Abandoning her workstation in a giant mess, she loaded an oversized box with the two arrangements and put it in the back seat of her car. She fastened the seatbelt snugly around the box to help keep it from moving, having learned the hard way that a quick and unexpected stop resulted in a watery mess in the floorboards. The Baymont Inn was on the other side of town, so she decided to deliver the rose bouquet first. It was a stunning combination of canary yellow and deep fuchsia roses in a bulbous glass vase. Katie secretly tried to avoid deliveries as much as possible, but she had to admit that the expression on the recipient's face when she handed them one of Mrs. Greyson's creations was priceless. A powerful message came with an unexpected delivery of fresh flowers, a magic she had witnessed herself many years ago as the unexpected recipient of a bouquet of yellow tulips.

She got in her car, pulled her cell phone from her purse, and plugged the address for the hotel into her GPS. Seeing her phone reminded her she had promised Amanda she would call her. *Am I ready to have that conversation? Why did I even bring it up?* Katie knew she didn't have time to dive into that nightmare right now, but she didn't want Amanda to think she was avoiding her. She was honestly surprised Amanda hadn't blown her phone up with text messages the night before, giving Katie play-by-play details on her dad's party, about how boring it was or how someone from her dad's crew was hitting on her, which seemed to happen quite frequently. Amanda didn't like to attend those parties, and had a tendency to use Katie as an outlet to pass the time during situations like those.

She opened a text message to Amanda:

> Sorry I haven't called. Crazy busy at work. Out on deliveries
> today. Can't wait to hear how last night went. TTYL.

She pressed send and put her phone in her cup holder.

Between the traffic and catching what seemed like every red light on the way, it took Katie longer than expected to get to the Baymont Inn. She parked her car and grabbed her phone to end her trip in GPS. It wasn't that she didn't know how to get to the hotel; she used the GPS as more of a verbal reminder to turn if she let her mind wander while driving. With her phone in her hand, she checked her messages. No response from Amanda.

Katie delivered the roses to Lisa, the day shift manager at the hotel, and when she handed her the bouquet, Lisa squealed so loudly her voice echoed off the walls of the lobby. She explained to Katie that the arrangement was from her husband in celebration of their fourteenth anniversary and proceeded to tell her the story of how they met. Katie often got an earful from strangers. Each time Katie would try to break free from the conversation, Lisa would suck her back in with another story about her husband.

Katie smiled as she walked back to her car, thankful for the needy hotel guest that allowed for her getaway. Katie buckled up and grabbed her phone. Still no response from Amanda. No acknowledgement she'd received her text, no sarcastic remark about having to wait, nothing.

That's odd.

Katie pulled into the delivery lane in front of the hospital, hoping to make a quick trip in and out. She'd already been gone from the shop longer than anticipated, and she didn't want Mrs. Greyson to have to handle everything on her own. The oversized revolving door at the hospital entrance carried her inside the lobby. Katie glanced at the card sticking out of the flowers nestled in the bed of a blue ceramic replica of a '48 Ford pickup:

TYLER DUNCAN

ROOM 3212

She took the elevator to the third floor. The nurse at the front desk had a phone up to her ear and waved Katie on to deliver the flowers directly to the room. Katie knocked on the door to announce her delivery and waited for a response from the other side that it was okay for her to come in. She pushed open the door.

There was a man lying in the bed, his face scabbed with dried blood and his neck cuffed with a grey, plastic brace. The extent of his other injuries hidden beneath stark white linens. Wires and monitors surrounded the bed, an atmosphere all too familiar for Katie, and she could think of nothing more than getting out of the room, and quick. She quietly set the flower arrangement down on the counter near the sink and the woman sitting next to the bed lifted her head and turned toward Katie.

"Amanda?"

Chapter 4
NINE YEARS EARLIER

The light above her head pierced through her swollen eyelids as they fluttered, trying to open. She couldn't move. Her head was pounding and every inch of her body ached. *Where am I? What happened? How did I get here?* Thoughts raced through her head, amplifying the pain. Katie searched the room with her eyes for something familiar. Anything. The walls were foreign, the ceiling hidden in the bright light. The rhythmic sounds coming from beside the bed made no sense to her. BEEP … BEEP … BEEP … They weren't in sync with the tick of the clock, which seemed to drag with every passing second. *Oh, my head.*

The room smelled sterile. The aroma of disinfectants and the metallic taste in her mouth made her want to gag, but the thought of expending that much energy was exhausting. Her upset stomach was no match for the pulsating pain radiating from her head, and the plastic brace around her neck kept her from repositioning. She desperately wanted some relief … and some answers.

Katie had no luck deciphering her surroundings with her limited movement, so she closed her eyes and tried to think of the last thing she could remember. A series of events scrolled through her mind: *Damon, fighting on the telephone, running at Black Bear Trail, getting dark, looking for my jacket.* Her eyes popped back open when a rustling noise came from the corner of the room. *I'm not alone.*

"Hello? Is … someone there?" her voice squeaked. The vibration of her vocal cords made her throat feel like she had swallowed glass shards doused in gasoline.

A shrill squeal from metal chair legs scooting across the floor confirmed her suspicion. She was not alone. Her anxiety level hit code red with the sound of shuffling footsteps growing closer. Before she knew it, someone was standing next to her.

"There are those beautiful blue eyes I've been waiting to see," Carl spoke softly. He reached toward Katie and gently brushed the hair back from her forehead, thankful to see she was finally awake

"Daddy?" Although relieved by his presence, the calming sound of his voice and his comforting touch broke the dam and tears began to flow down her cheeks. "Where am I?"

"Honey, you are in the hospital. You are going to be okay, just try to stay calm. The doctors and nurses are taking very good care of you."

Hospital? Confused and trying to make sense of everything going on, Carl's appearance told Katie things were not good. His tear-stained face was red and puffy, as if he'd been crying for days, and although he tried to fake a smile, the sadness in his eyes told a different story. The wrinkles in his shirt were evidence of hours spent sleeping in a chair. His coarse hair was a tousled mess. Katie had only seen him look this disheveled once before, and two days later, they buried her mother.

"Daddy, what happened? The last thing I remember was going back to the trail to get my jacket and then I woke up here."

That was still the million-dollar question of the day. *What happened?* Almost everything to this point was speculation, and what little the doctors and police did know was based on the statement of a passerby who found Katie beaten, lying crumpled on the ground at Black Bear Trail, and then called 9-1-1. Carl had a strong suspicion of who was responsible for this and hoped that once Katie woke up she could fill in the blanks, but that didn't appear to be the case.

Before Carl had a chance to translate his thoughts into words, Dr. Sheffield walked into the room. He was a tall, fit man in his early forties, with light brown hair and hazel eyes. He moved in a fluid manner and his shoes slightly drug the floor with each step. The swooshing noise was almost hypnotic.

"Katherine, I'm Dr. Sheffield. I'm going to be taking care of you today. Can you tell me where you are?" He asked as he approached the bed.

"Yes. I'm in the hospital."

"That's right. Do you know how you got here?"

"No, sir." She felt deflated.

Dr. Sheffield glanced over at Carl, concerned, and then back to Katie.

"Can you tell me what you do remember?"

Having just recited the events in her head, they were fresh on her mind.

"I went for a run, just like I always do. On the way home, I realized I left my jacket on the bench beside the trail, so I turned around to go back after it. That's the last thing I remember."

"That's a good start," he said, trying to encourage her. "I'm going to take a quick look at you, listen to your heart and your lungs, and then we will go over a few things, okay?"

"Okay," Katie replied.

Dr Sheffield took the stethoscope from around his neck and placed it on Katie's chest. She flinched.

"It's okay, Katherine. Take a few deep breaths for me and I will try to hurry."

Hearing her full name made her think of her mother. *I need you so bad, Mom. I wish you were here.* The feeling of this strange man hovering over her, examining her battered body, made her uneasy. Those few moments felt like an eternity. A lump began to swell in her throat as she choked back the tears.

Dr. Sheffield finished his exam and hung his stethoscope back around his neck. He picked up a wooden clipboard from the bedside table and began to write in the chart. Katie hoped that hidden somewhere in those pages was the explanation to this mystery.

"Katherine ..."

"Call me Katie," she interjected.

Dr. Sheffield made a note in her chart of her preferred name, and before he proceeded, he pushed the button on the bed rail to raise Katie to an upright position.

"Katie, some of this may be tough to hear. Since you can't remember exactly what happened, I will tell you a little of what we know so far. You were brought to the hospital by an ambulance late yesterday evening."

Yesterday? I've lost an entire day?

"A young man found you on the ground outside of the park area at Black Bear Trail. He called 9-1-1 and requested an ambulance. He was questioned by the police, but so far they have been unable to locate any witnesses to give an account of your attack."

With those words, Katie could no longer control the urge and she threw up.

Dr. Sheffield pushed the button to call for the nurse. She entered quickly and immediately tended to Katie.

"That is probably enough for right now. I will have the nurse get you something to calm your nerves and something to help with your pain. I will come back this afternoon during rounds and check on you to see how you are doing. Try to get some rest. If you need anything, tell the nurse and she can reach me by phone." Dr. Sheffield turned to look at Carl. "Mr. Upton, may I speak with you outside for a moment?"

Carl assured Katie he would return quickly, and then followed Dr. Sheffield into the hallway. As the door closed behind them, Dr. Sheffield began to speak.

"I have the results back from Katherine's, pardon me, Katie's tests," he corrected her name. "The extent of her injuries is worse than we originally anticipated. The x-rays confirmed a hairline fracture to the base of the skull, more than likely due to some type of blunt force trauma. Her neck appears to be okay, so I will put in an order to remove her neck brace. Katie's inability to remember what happened may be the result of some minor swelling around the temporal lobe of her brain. The MRI ruled out an intracranial hemorrhage, which is good, but we will need to keep her here for a few days for observation and follow up testing to monitor the swelling."

Carl's head reeled with all of the medical jargon, but he knew from the tone in Dr. Sheffield's voice that there was more to come.

"Mr. Upton, do you know if your daughter is sexually active?"

"No," Carl answered immediately.

"No, you don't know? Or no, she isn't?"

Carl didn't want to think about Katie having sex. She was seventeen, but she was still his little girl. *Are dads supposed to know that anyway?* Katie had been dating a boy and he came to the house on occasion. *But sex? Surely not.* He would like to think that wasn't the case, but he didn't know how to honestly answer that question. So he didn't. "Why are you asking me this?"

"Because there is also evidence of a sexual assault."

"Oh my God," Carl fell back into the wall.

"She has visible bruising and bleeding around her vaginal area and the lab tests revealed a spermicide commonly used in condoms. There was no semen detected so it isn't necessary to proceed with an STD prophylactic treatment, but Katie experienced significant trauma. It is too early to determine if there will be any residual long-term effects on her reproductive health."

And there it was. The news he feared the most. The blood drained from his face and his knees began to shake.

"Mr. Upton, do you need to sit down? I know this is a lot to take in, but we will do our best to ensure that Katie is taken care of. The detectives are working diligently at the scene, searching for any evidence that may lead to an arrest. Detective Burns will be by soon to get a statement from Katie now that she is awake. When you go back in to see her, she will undoubtedly look to you for answers. Try to avoid giving her any details of what we found regarding the sexual assault. We don't want to sway her recollection of what happened. It is best if she is able to remember the order of things on her own."

Dr. Sheffield's phone rang and he excused himself from the conversation. Carl stood paralyzed in the hallway, the life sucked from his body by the doctor's words. To everyone else around him, it was business as usual. A nurse scurried by with two bags of IV medicine and a handful of plastic tubing. Housekeeping reloaded the linen cart from the storage closet across the way. A woman in the waiting room rattled on to her friend about every place she had registered for her upcoming baby shower. All the while, his daughter was lying in a bed on the other side of the door. Her innocence had been brutally stolen from her, and possibly her ability to have children as well. A nightmare he'd lived through once before with his wife now potentially stared his daughter in the face.

Chapter 5

PRESENT

Headlights whizzed by with every passing car. Traffic was heavier than usual for a Tuesday evening as he headed south of town toward the party. He didn't bother putting the top down because he was already running late. It was too hot for that, anyway, and the thought of sweating in a pair of starched jeans didn't appeal to him.

Nothing in him wanted to go. He only succumbed to the invitation after a plea from his sister. She always had the ability to talk him into anything, even going places he didn't want to go. After a long day at work, and ending it with a flat tire, all he wanted to do was ride.

His parent's house was as far out of town as his, but in the opposite direction. Both houses had a Victoria address, but the drive between the two was so long it felt like they were in separate counties. He took his exit and merged on to the farm market highway, ten miles per hour above the speed limit. The road felt abandoned compared to his previous travels. The pathway was narrow and lined with trees, surrounded by darkness.

A pair of headlights in the distance pierced the night, resembling a glowing set of animal eyes. As the road passed beneath him, the eyes increased in size. It was a truck—a big one—and it was barreling his direction. The headlights veered toward his side of the road and he laid on the horn. No response. He jerked the wheel but it was too late, and the oncoming truck clipped the driver's side corner of his vehicle, sending him into a tailspin. Tossed from the road, he finally came to a stop when his car slammed into a tree. The sound of crumpling metal echoed in his ears, followed by an eerie silence.

Water hissed from his busted radiator, sending clouds of steam into the night. He opened his eyes and blinked. *I'm still breathing. I'm alive,* he mentally assessed the situation. The taste of blood strong in his mouth, he ran his tongue across his lip, revealing a huge gash. A cut higher on his head produced a warm trickle of blood, snaking its way down the side of his face.

The impact with the tree had him pinned under the dash, wedged tightly into a space that looked more like a wadded-up metal ball than a vehicle. He tried to remain calm, but his inability to move allowed panic to slide in. "Help!" he yelled out. The words forced from his mouth sent a piercing pain through his chest.

Things started to get a little woozy. His heart raced and a tingling sensation pulsated through his body. *Am I losing too much blood?* His head fell forward, landing on the mangled steering wheel. The deflated airbag hung limp in front of his face. He closed his eyes in an attempt to stave off the dizziness, even though he knew that during a situation like this he should never go to sleep. But he was getting tired. Very tired. "Help!" This cry was weaker than the last. "Somebody please help me. Anybody …"

A faint light flickered in the window, followed by the sound of a voice. A woman's voice.

"Hang in there, help is on the way," she spoke in a calming manner.

Ty tried to speak. "What about the other guy?" he asked, but his words came out choppy and inaudible.

"Don't try to talk, save your energy," the woman replied. "Focus on your breathing."

She reached through the broken glass and placed her hand on the back of his head. Her touch was calming, as was the news that help was on the way.

"Can you open your eyes for me?" She gently stroked his hair. "You will get through this. Don't give up. I need you not to give up."

The night sky was full of flashing beams of red and blue lights. There were two highway patrol cars on the scene with another on the way, plus an ambulance and a fire truck. Two men passing by in a pickup pulling a cattle trailer also stopped to offer assistance, and one of them worked for the Texas Department of Transportation. He immediately went to the far edge of the scene to help slow oncoming traffic, not that this road was heavily traveled. Especially at night.

Paramedics gently pulled Ty's head back toward the seat and secured his neck with a brace. They covered his body to shield him from any debris and, using the Jaws of Life, the firefighters freed him from his vehicle. They slid him from the wreckage and placed his crumpled body on a nearby stretcher, paramedics attending to him on either side. As they loaded him into the back of the ambulance, he caught a glimpse of the woman that had waited with him until help arrived.

"You're such a fighter. I'm so proud of you," she said.

Amanda spent the night in the hospital at Ty's bedside. Although he was her stepbrother, they were very close. Amanda's parents had divorced when she was only four and her mother moved away, leaving her to live with her dad. At times, Katie felt this common bond drew them closer together, both knowing what it was like to be without their mother at an early age. The only difference was that Amanda's father eventually remarried, and when he did, she inherited an older brother.

Katie dropped her keys and cell phone on the bedside table next to a Styrofoam cup and looked around the room for something to sit on. The sterile smell of antiseptic spray made her want to gag. A glance at the sofa bed near the window, buried under wadded white sheets and two wrinkled pillows, flashed her back nine years. She could see her dad sitting there with frazzled hair and sunken eyes, staring blindly out the window. Chills danced up her spine. She detested hospitals; nothing good ever came from being in one.

Not for her anyway.

Amanda sat in the only chair in the room, a tan vinyl recliner perched on casters and accented with dark brown urethane arm caps. She wore a pair of denim skinny jeans cuffed just above the ankle, leopard print wedges, and a black blouse that hung loosely off one shoulder, exposing a thin white line left behind by the strap of her bathing suit. Smeared mascara streaked her cheeks and chunks of blonde hair had escaped her once-tight ponytail and fell against her face.

Katie fetched one of the pillows from the sofa bed, dropped it on the floor, and kneeled down next to Amanda's chair. She took a quick glance at Ty. "I still can't believe I didn't know this was your brother."

"What do you mean? I know you've never met him, but I talk about him all the time."

"Yeah, but you call him Ty. And it's not like you two have the same last name. It never dawned on me that Tyler Duncan was *the* Ty."

"Please never refer to him as the Ty to his face. I'll never hear the end of that."

"Noted." Katie smiled.

"I take it your car was still there?"

"Yeah. Luckily, it hadn't been towed. I should have known better than to leave it parked outside the front door like that."

"In your defense, it's not like you intended on being here this long. Did you call Mrs. Greyson? Is she okay with you staying for a while?"

"Of course," Katie assured her. "She told me to stay as long as you needed me. Is there anything I can do? Or anything I can get you?"

"No, I'm fine," Amanda yawned. "Just tired. Thank you for staying with me, though, and keeping me company."

"You don't have to thank me. I would have been here last night had I known. I was wondering why I hadn't heard from you."

"You wouldn't have wanted to be here last night." She swept a piece of hair from in front of her eye. "It was total chaos."

"Tell me everything," Katie fell back on her heels. "What happened?"

"Ugh, where do I start?" she sighed. "After I left Joe's, I tried to call Ty to see if he was still coming to the party, but he didn't pick up. I remembered Kyle saying he didn't answer his calls either, so I started to get worried. It's not like him to not answer his phone. But when I got to the house, Dad told me I was overreacting and worrying over nothing. He told me Ty was a grown man, and if he didn't want to answer his phone, then he didn't have to," she rolled her eyes. Even at twenty-five, that same philosophy didn't apply to her, but she still lived under his roof and Ty didn't, so she kept her mouth shut. "Dad's buddies started showing up soon after I got home and I lost track of time. Regardless, I should have suspected something was wrong with Ty when Kyle got there before he did. Ty is rarely ever late to anything. Kyle, on the other hand, is always late. It drives my dad crazy. Dad says he'll probably be late to our wedding."

"I highly doubt that."

"I know, me too. But dad doesn't cut him any slack. He always says he's not good enough for me. Which is ridiculous. Anyway, at least he didn't smell like an ashtray when he got there. That would have really pissed Dad off. He stopped and changed clothes on his way over from the pub after he dropped his friend off. He asked about you."

"Who asked about me? Kyle?" Maybe Kyle *was* the one who stopped by to see her at the flower shop.

"No, Brad. He wanted to know if you were dating anyone. What your story was."

"My story?" Katie scoffed. "That's a book nobody wants to read." She was not fond of the two of them talking about her, but it wasn't like Kyle knew any details about her life or even enough information to keep that conversation going for very long. "What happened next?"

"We were all standing around the pool and Brayden, this guy who runs heavy equipment on one of dad's crews, dropped his beer. The glass bottle shattered everywhere. When I went inside to get the broom to clean up the mess, the phone was ringing. I answered it and they asked to speak to my stepmom. I had no idea who it was. I yelled out the door for her to come inside instead of taking the phone to her. The music was loud and so were the guys. There's no way she would have been able to hear someone on the phone. I walked into the laundry room to get the broom and heard her cry out for my dad. She was hysterical. We both made it into the kitchen at the same time and she told us Ty had been in an accident and was in the hospital. They didn't give her any details, just said he was in serious condition. I absolutely lost it."

"Girl, why didn't you call me?" Katie asked.

"I would have, but we bolted out of the house so fast I left my purse and cell phone sitting on the kitchen table. I rode with Dad and Linda because my car is still in the shop. Kyle stayed behind to make sure all of the guests left and to take care of the house, and to be there in case anyone else called before we made it to the hospital. I kept in contact with him on my dad's phone. I would have called you from it, but I don't have your cell phone number memorized. I barely know my own number. When I called information to try and get your landline, they told me it was unlisted."

"What time did all of this happen?" Katie slid right past the topic of her unlisted phone number.

"I don't remember." Amanda squinted her eyes trying to recall. "I think we made it here around ten? I don't know; it's been a long night."

When they arrived at the hospital, Ty was still in the emergency room. Only two visitors were allowed at a time, so Amanda had alternated going back and forth with her dad. Linda never gave up her seat. The space was cramped and uncomfortably warm without a lick of privacy. The curtain exterior did little to shield conversations from neighboring patients. In the bed directly across from Ty's, nurses held down a screaming boy to sew up his lacerated lip caused from crashing face first into the concrete. His screams were matched in volume by the mother throwing blame at the father for letting the boy ride his bike in the dark. An older woman to the left, brought in by an ambulance for chest pain and shortness of breath, was convinced she was having a heart attack. It was her fourth visit of the year, and according to the whispers among nurses it was again nothing more than anxiety. And to the right, a very embarrassed gentleman fumbled through explaining that he had taken more Viagra than prescribed. It was something he clearly wished the entire room hadn't been privy to, but the bulge in his pants did nothing to hide his secret.

Even though it felt as if she were stuck in a bad episode of *Grey's Anatomy*, Amanda's time spent with Ty behind the curtain was far better than that in the waiting room. The automatic sliding doors never got a break. The plastic chairs offered no comfort and were lined with people waiting to be seen. Some with obvious injuries—broken limbs, cuts, and scrapes—and others with no visible signs of trauma, yet they wore white admittance bracelets around their wrists. Among the crowd, a stocky middle-aged man with a thick black beard and a bald head clutched a small trash can to catch his vomit. A Hispanic woman wearing a red apron over a white button-down shirt and black pants rocked to console her crying baby. Her other child sat in the seat next to Amanda, eating Cheetos and laughing at cartoons that blared from his iPad. He left cheesy, orange fingerprints on everything he touched. The room was littered with paper cups from the water dispenser and smelled of hand sanitizer and vomit. Relief washed over Amanda when her father came out to tell her Ty was being admitted and transferred to a room on the third floor.

"Did you at least get some sleep?" Katie nodded toward the disheveled sofa bed.

"No. That's Linda's mess. She tried to get some sleep once we moved up here, but I don't think she ever really did. Doctors and nurses kept coming in, throwing on the light, and checking on Ty. I sent her and dad home this morning to get some sleep and told them I would stay. I didn't want him to be alone. Kyle is going to come by and sit with me after work, and I'm sure my parents will be back at some point after dinner." Amanda's chest inflated as she drew in another big yawn. "It's impossible to rest in this place."

"Trust me, I know."

"You do?" Amanda raised a brow.

Katie saw the opportunity to finish the conversation she started the day before, but Amanda stopped her.

"I guess from when your mom was sick?" Amanda continued. "Did you spend a lot of time in the hospital then?"

"Yeah," Katie sighed. "From then."

"Oh."

The room fell silent. Katie picked at the peeling edge of a safety sticker stuck to the side of the bed rail and remembered what it was like to be in Ty's place. She wondered what it must have been like for her dad to get that late-night phone call. To have a random person call and say *Someone found your daughter in the woods. We don't have any details other than she's badly beaten, unconscious and in the hospital.* How scary that must have been for him. And to have to face that alone. She heard a buzzing sound and looked around to see if she had accidentally triggered something on the bed.

"Katie, your phone is ringing."

The ringer was off, and the vibrations of the incoming call caused it to dance across the table. Katie stood from the floor and looked at the screen, but didn't answer. She pushed the button on the side to stop the vibrating.

"Is that Mrs. Greyson?" Amanda asked.

"No, it's my dad." She knew he was probably calling to say he talked to Burns, and she didn't want to take that call in front of Amanda. "I will call him back when I leave." She fell back down on the pillow, this time landing on her butt rather than her knees, and crossed her legs in front of her. A single buzz jerked from her phone, alerting her of a new voicemail.

"I hate not having my phone," Amanda sighed. "I probably have a hundred missed calls and texts from people wanting an update on Ty."

"Make that a hundred and one. My text wasn't about Ty, but I did send you a message earlier."

"I can't believe I left it at home. I never go anywhere without that thing. Kyle even joked that my phone would need to be part of our wedding somehow. Maybe the ring bearer."

Katie belted out a laugh, and then immediately slapped her hand over her mouth. "Sorry!" she said quietly from beneath her fingers. "But that was funny."

Amanda didn't see the humor.

"If you need your phone, why don't you run and get it? It will probably feel good to get out of this place for a few minutes and to change your clothes."

Amanda looked down at the same outfit Katie had seen her in at Joe's the day before. "But what if Ty wakes up?"

"If our talking and your death grip on his hand haven't made him wake up, he's probably going to be out for a while."

Amanda hadn't let go of his hand since Katie walked in the door. She looked at the time, then at Ty sleeping in the bed, then back down to Katie sitting on the floor, considering her offer sternly. "I don't know. Every time I think about him being alone on the side of the road, waiting to be rescued, my heart aches. I don't want to leave him alone again. I want someone here when he wakes up. You probably think I'm crazy, huh?"

"No, not at all." Katie thought back to her dad, wearing the same clothes for days and never leaving her side. "I can stay here while you run home."

Wait … what?! Did you hear what you just said?

Amanda's eyebrows pinched. "You would seriously stay here with Ty while I went to get my phone? Are you sure you don't mind?"

Yes! Tell her you mind!

"Yes … I mean, no … I mean, yes and no." The thought of sitting in a hospital room alone with a man she didn't know tripped her up. "Let me try that again. Yes, I will stay. No, I don't mind." The familiar fingers of anxiety slithered around her neck and started to pinch, constricting her airway. It felt like she was breathing through a straw. She forced out her breath and counted to five.

"Oh … crap." Amanda's shoulders fell. "My car. It's not here. I rode with Dad, remember?"

"It's okay, you can take mine."

What?! Quit talking! Every time you open your mouth, things get worse.

"Seriously? I can take your car, too?"

Anxiety's grip tightened and choked the last breath from her lungs.

"Yes," she squeaked. "It's on level two of the parking garage. Near the elevators."

"Thank you so much, Katie. It really means a lot that you would do this for me. I owe you big time." She grabbed Katie's key ring from the table, not realizing exactly what she held in her hand. "I will be right back. I promise I'll hurry."

"Ummmm … Amanda?"

"Yes?" Amanda stopped in the doorway and turned back to Katie.

"What happens if he wakes up before you get back? He isn't going to have a clue who I am. Don't you think that will freak him out a little?"

Amanda grinned. "Just tell him your name. Trust me; he will know exactly who you are."

Chapter 6
NINE YEARS EARLIER

Detective Burns barely looked old enough to carry a gun; however, his youthful appearance was deceiving. He held a bachelor's degree in criminal justice from Midwestern State University and had worked for the Tarrant County Sheriff's Department for five years before transferring to Henderson County. He and his wife had moved to the area after she took a teaching position at the local elementary school. The stressful existence of being a detective in the big city had left him and his family searching for a simpler way of life, and Brownsboro seemed to be the answer.

Brownsboro was only a blink of a town dotted on a highway in the middle of east Texas: a quick stretch of road across flat terrain with only a single flashing light to slow the flow of traffic. Large corporate-owned shopping centers had yet to penetrate the city-limit signs and probably never would due to its size, but that only added to the charisma of the tiny town. With a population just above one thousand, it housed a tightly knit community that prided itself on the strong foundation of its Christian faith. Any given morning, a gathering of older men could be found having coffee at the donut shop, reading the newspaper or playing dominos. Saturday evening was always the best time for grocery shopping at the locally owned market and for catching up on gossip. The local rumor mill was the busiest business in town.

Burns thought he'd seen the last of his days interviewing victims like Katie. Crimes of this nature were unfortunately a common occurrence in the Dallas–Fort Worth area, but this sort of thing didn't happen out in the middle of nowhere, in small town America, where it was not uncommon for doors to be left unlocked at night. Where everyone knows everyone and everyone knows everything—sometimes before it even happens. His extensive work with belligerent drunks, domestic disputes, and even homicides had hardened him, but cases involving sexual assault, especially with a minor involved, were something he never got used to.

And this was the hardest part.

There was no way to prepare for the initial encounter with the victim. Asking questions to make them relive their attack, in detail, was an emotional roller coaster that was tough to watch. Rage, sadness, anger, guilt, embarrassment—the wheel of emotions was an unpredictable beast—with no clue as to how it may manifest itself. The complexity of this particular case added an entirely new dimension to the game, even for Burns. He knew the physician's report confirmed a sexual assault, but from what he had been told … the victim didn't. Katie sat in a bed with her dad by her side, and Burns knew that his very line of questioning might ignite the fire that brought this trauma to light. Something he didn't want to be responsible for.

He brought in a small, wooden chair and placed it next to the wall. It sat low to the ground and was quite uncomfortable, but it helped ensure he seated himself in a submissive position. His size had a tendency to be somewhat threatening, which was helpful when interrogating a suspect, but under these circumstances, he wanted to keep from coming across as authoritative or intimidating. With both feet planted on the floor and his knees pointed toward his chin, he managed to leave a reasonable amount of space between his chair and Katie's hospital bed in an otherwise cramped room. He was willing to do anything he knew of to make her as calm and relaxed as possible, preserving her emotional well-being during this process.

"Katie, I'm Detective Burns," he introduced himself. "I work for the Henderson County Sheriff's Department. I've been assigned to your case. Did your dad tell you I would be coming by to see you today?"

Katie nodded in acknowledgement.

"Good. Before we get started, I want to make sure you are comfortable with me being here and asking you a few questions. I know you've been through a great deal and certain things may not be very easy to talk about, so if you would prefer to speak with a female officer, I would be glad to call one in for you."

Katie looked up towards her dad with a question in her eyes.

"It's up to you, sweetheart. Whatever is easier for you," Carl spoke softly, answering her question before she even asked. "I will be right here with you either way."

"It's fine," Katie answered Burns. She took two fists full of her blanket and pulled it up close to her chest. "You can go ahead. I haven't been much help anyway."

Burns took a deep breath and proceeded. "I'm going to ask you some questions and I want you to answer them the best that you can." He had a notepad in his left hand, a pen in the right. "Can you tell me what happened yesterday?"

For the hundredth time ... no. She sighed. "Like I told everyone else, I went for a run at the trail near my house. I go there all of the time. On my way home, I remembered I left my jacket on the park bench, so I went back after it. That's the last thing I remember."

"Did you notice anyone else at or around the trail? Any cars? Maybe other walkers or runners?"

"There were a couple of people loading bikes on the back of a Jeep while I was running, but from what I could tell they left when they were done. Other than that, it was empty out there. I ran alone."

"Could you tell if the people loading the bicycles were male or female? And what color the Jeep was?"

"Two guys. And I think it was black," she answered. "No, wait, it was red."

"Were they young? Old?"

"They were really too far away to tell. They were in the parking lot, I was on the trail. I barely caught a glimpse of them."

"Okay. Do you remember what time it was when you were running?"

"I remember when I got done thinking it was getting pretty dark. So I finished probably around 7:30? 7:45 maybe?" she shrugged.

"You're doing great, Katie. This is all very helpful information." Burns shifted in his chair and jotted a few things in his notepad. "Now, you said the last thing you remember was going back after your jacket. Do you know about where you were?"

"There's a path through the woods that runs from my house to the trail. I was between the creek and the park when I turned around to go back for my jacket. Somewhere near the big oak tree that looks like it has three legs."

"Did anything seem different to you on your way back? Did you notice any changes in your surroundings, see any other people? Maybe hear any strange noises?"

"I was listening to music on my mp3 player; I couldn't hear anything … oh my God …," her words tapered off.

Carl saw the tension building as Katie sat up in the bed. She drew her knees in toward her chest and wrapped her arms around her shins. He reached out and placed his hand on her shoulder. Burns noticed the gesture. "We can take a break at any time; all you have to do is say the word."

Katie started to tremble.

"What is it, Katie?" Burns asked. "What's wrong?"

"There was someone there. Behind me."

"Behind you in the woods?"

"Yes. When I headed back to get my jacket, my side started hurting so I put my arms up over my head to try to catch my breath. That happens sometimes when I run. I remember what song was playing, too. *Yellow* by Coldplay. I remember because I was using the beat to try and slow my breath. And then it felt like someone punched me in the stomach, but from behind." Tears welled in her eyes.

"Did you see this person?"

"No."

"Could you tell if it was a male or a female?"

"Strong, like a man. Taller than me."

"How did you know he was strong? What was he doing?"

"He wrapped his arms around me. I couldn't breathe. I couldn't move." Katie began to cry, and her dad moved in closer.

Burns knew she probably needed to take a break, but he felt he was on the verge of a breakthrough.

"Just a few more questions and we will stop, okay?"

"Okay," she uttered through her tears.

"You said he was taller. How do you know he was taller if he was behind you?"

"I could feel his chin on the top of my head."

"Did you say anything to this person? Or scream out?"

"No, he had a hand over my mouth."

"Did you try to bite or scratch at his hand? Notice what color he was or see any tattoos or scars?"

"No, he was wearing a glove. A black leather glove. I smelled leather. I could feel him breathing on my face."

"Did he say anything to you?"

"Yes," she looked toward Burns with her bloodshot eyes. "I've got you."

Katie's head dropped on to the top of her knees and her sobbing intensified. Carl motioned towards Burns, signaling that she'd had enough. Burns concurred and put away his notebook and pen.

He gathered his things, forced himself up from the chair, and walked around to the side of the bed where Carl was standing. Burns spoke around Carl, toward Katie, not wanting to invade her space. "Katie, we are going to catch this guy. I will do everything I can to make sure of that. I promise."

She stretched back out in the bed and rolled over on her side to face the opposite wall, staring blankly into the distance. She was done talking. To him. To anyone. He could make all the promises in the world he wanted to, she just wanted this nightmare to end.

Before Burns left the room, he had one final question. "Mr. Upton, is there anyone you can think of, for any reason, who may want to harm Katie?"

"Yes," Carl replied without hesitation. "Damon McGregor."

Gravel popped beneath the tires of his squad car as he pulled up the drive. Burns had made a few calls and learned that Damon was the grandson to old man Johnson and his wife Betty, and they lived in the white farmhouse at the edge of town. There was something about the way Mr. Upton uttered his name—with sheer conviction—convinced that this boy was responsible for the attack on his daughter. Burns knew he needed to pay him a visit, the part of his job Burns got off on.

Betty pushed open the screen door when she saw him coming and stepped out on the front porch, letting the door close behind her. Her hair was short and gray, teased into a hive. The housecoat she wore was stained with coffee and her eyes were weathered and tired. "Good afternoon, officer. What can I do for you today?"

"Good afternoon, ma'am. I'm Detective Burns. I was wondering if I might have a word with your grandson. Is he around?"

"Damon? Oh … no, he's out with some friends."

He sensed uneasiness, as if she were covering for him.

"Do you know when he will be back?"

"I'm not sure. Can I ask what this is all about, officer? Is he in some kind of trouble or something?" She feared she knew the answer. After all, being in trouble with the law was the reason he had moved to Brownsboro to live with them.

"Well, I'm not sure. I just needed to ask him a few questions. Maybe find out where he was yesterday."

"He was here," she readily replied.

"And what time was that?"

"For the time you asked about. Yesterday."

"Can you be a little more specific?"

"All day, I suppose."

"Didn't he have school yesterday?"

Tripped up by his line of questioning, she nervously slid her hands into the front pockets of her housecoat. "Yes. I meant he was here all day after school."

This was getting him nowhere. It was obvious she was lying. He took a quick moment to glance around the yard, searching for anything that appeared out of sorts. Stacks from a John Deere tractor peered over firewood piled high between two oversized elm trees. Evidence of a recent fire smoldered from deep within the burn barrel near the back corner of the house, and parked over by the barn was a pickup, a black, jacked-up Chevrolet pickup. Exactly like something a teenage boy would drive, not a retired farmer or his wife. Certain that it was Damon's truck he politely ended the conversation.

"Well, I better be getting back to the station. Thank you for your time. You have a nice day now." He tipped his head in her direction and turned to walk toward his car.

Once he heard the screen door slap shut, he peered over his shoulder to make sure she was gone and then made his way to the truck parked near the barn. The back was full of empty beer cans, but when he looked inside the window, the cab of the truck was rather clean. Not what he had expected. An air freshener shaped like a Christmas tree dangled from the rearview mirror and a Dallas Cowboys baseball cap lay on the dash. He walked the perimeter of the vehicle and, on the ground next to the passenger door, he found a grey loose-knit toboggan. Nothing of interest. *Damn it.* He bent over and grabbed the toboggan, tucked it beneath his arm, and headed back to his car.

The entire trip back to the station, Burns couldn't quit thinking about Katie. How young she was. How fragile. How if something like this ever happened to his daughter, he would kill the son of a bitch responsible. Hell, he might even do that this time. At least rough him up a little. It's not like it hadn't happened before. Nobody would know. Give the creep a taste of his own medicine. Any man that forced himself on a woman, no matter the age, no matter the circumstance, did not deserve to breathe. He gripped the steering wheel tightly as the thoughts continued to barrel through his head.

He tossed his stuff on his desk and flipped on the computer. After his visit with Katie, he knew he had enough information to start chasing a couple of leads. Well, one lead in particular. He didn't feel the need to exhaust too much time and energy on the guys with the red Jeep. It was a public park. People ride their bikes there all the time. Health-conscious folks didn't typically fit the profile of sexual predators anyway. No … his interest was in one thing. Damon. Especially after his conversation with the boy's grandmother.

The monitor lit up, signaling that his computer was ready. He clicked past his screensaver—a black and white photo of a Glock Single-Stack nine millimeter—and entered his password. Perusing social media usually proved to be the most lucrative when digging for dirt on scumbags, so he decided to start there. It was the best way to get a good grasp of what this Damon character was all about. Without any DNA evidence, getting a conviction on the rape charge would be tough, especially since the victim had not seen her attacker, and so far, no witnesses had come forward. Fortunately for law enforcement officers, some criminals were dumb enough to brag about their shenanigans online, down to the most specific details. Social-media sites had become an indispensable resource for collecting evidence. Many times it was a one-stop shop for everything needed to incriminate a suspect.

Burns spent about half an hour scrolling through pictures and reading every post made over the last year or so, but none of it produced any useful information. If Damon had anything to hide, he was doing a great job at it. There were no implicating posts or ambiguous passive-aggressive hints of bad behavior, just an unsettling feeling Burns couldn't quite put his finger on. Maybe it had something to do with the hollowness of Damon's eyes; a characteristic he'd come across numerous times dealing with perpetrators. Each picture on his account was a different version of the same haughty stance, topped with wavy black hair poking out from beneath a grey toboggan—one similar to the one he found on the ground near the black Chevy—and austere green eyes that pierced through the monitor. Damon exuded cockiness in his photos. Not in a pompous or pretentious manner, but in a way that sent a message he wasn't to be messed with. *Man, I'm going to enjoy taking this guy down*, Burns thought to himself. All of this time searching and with nothing incriminating other than underage drinking, unless he could charge him with emanating characteristics of a sociopath, this venture was a dead end

Not ready to give up, he logged in to the National Crime Information Center (NCIC) database to see if by chance Damon had a record. "Jackpot!" Damon's rap sheet read like the *Wall Street Journal*, lengthy and sprinkled with Class-C misdemeanors. Possession, disorderly conduct, criminal trespassing—all charges racked up in Gregg County—he had a rather impressive history for a nineteen-year-old. Although his colorful background would make it easy to build a case against Damon if needed, it was the last entry of his record that sounded the alarms … harassment.

Chapter 7

PRESENT

Katie sat next to the bed, looking in every direction but Ty's, and toyed with the notion that if she didn't physically look at him, he would somehow magically disappear. The beginning of a headache sprouted behind her eyes as she watched the second hand take laps around the clock. It ticked in tune with her pulse, and the sound of both echoed in harmony in her ears. The beat was occasionally accompanied by the thump of a slow drip leaking from the faucet, landing in the sink across the room. With each falling droplet, she replayed how quickly and unexpectedly she had ended up in this situation. How a simple flower delivery—one that she wouldn't have made that day had she ridden her bike to work as she normally did—landed her in a hospital room. It was a place she loathed, and she was strapped to a bed by the hand of a man she knew of, but didn't actually know. A man who, if he woke up, would wonder who in the hell this strange woman was sitting next to him. On top of all of that, she was stuck with no car to escape—no way to leave—even if she wanted to. Panic seethed beneath her skin, waiting for the perfect opportunity to make its ugly escape. She took a deep breath and held the air in her lungs, her chest tight and full, and reminded herself that she was doing this for her best friend, for her only friend, and that it was a temporary situation. Amanda would return soon and she could leave. Hopefully before anyone else even knew she was here.

When Katie started working at the flower shop, she took care of all of the deliveries, the only part of her job she didn't care for. Even though she enjoyed the look of surprise that came with an unexpected delivery, it occasionally forced her into uncomfortable situations, the visits to the churches being some of the most awkward. Between funerals and weddings, churches were a common stop, and no matter which sanctuary she walked into, the pastor always asked her where she attended service on Sundays. She knew they were just being nice and recruiting people into their congregations was what they were supposed to do, but that was never an easy question for her to answer and, honestly, they didn't want to hear the truth. She knew that responding, *Oh yeah, I'm pissed at God, so nowhere*, wouldn't go over too well. After numerous times fumbling through an answer and being asked to try their particular church, she learned to politely respond with something benign like, *I attend the church up the road with my friend*. In Victoria, that could be any number of places, and it was a blanket response she could use anywhere. It was a lie, but it worked.

One morning she decided to ride her bike to work instead of driving. It was only a few miles from her apartment to the flower shop, a trip that barely fazed her conditioned thighs, and it gave her an opportunity to soak up more of the cool spring air she'd enjoyed that morning during her run. When it came time to make deliveries that afternoon, since she lacked transportation, Mrs. Greyson took care of them instead. She soon found herself riding her bike to work more often than not, and whether she had made that decision consciously or subconsciously, she couldn't remember. Mrs. Greyson never said a word, and neither did she.

Katie quickly grew bored with the monotony of the ticking clock in Ty's hospital room. The muted flat-screen mounted on the wall didn't hold her attention long, either, as it was tuned to the local news, something she did her best to avoid on a regular basis. She counted the freckles on the back of her arm, but in doing so she caught a glimpse of Ty's fingers laced in hers and she instantly looked up. *He's not really here. He's not really touching you. He's a figment of your imagination,* she chanted to herself.

Everything in the room became a series of numbers. There were twelve silver rings holding the privacy curtain to a metal track on the ceiling, twenty-four ceiling tiles she could see from her chair, and roughly sixty wooden planks on the floor between her and the door. She knew because she counted each of them. More than once. Over the years, she found that counting helped untangle the web of uneasiness in her mind brought on by anxiety. That, and running. But running wasn't currently an option.

During all of her counting, she kept getting hung up on the number one. The one man in the bed next to her. How, if just one time she had accepted Amanda's invitation to spend time with her family, she would already know him and wouldn't feel the need to put down his hand and jump out the window. Why couldn't she be normal? Just one time.

The door cracked. She knew Amanda hadn't been gone long enough to make it out to her house and back. The headache behind her eyes sprouted another leaf and she bit down on the inside of her cheeks. *Please just be housekeeping.* In walked a tall brunette with milky white skin wearing navy blue scrubs and white sneakers. Her short hair, tucked behind her ears, barely reached her collar. A hint of blush highlighted her cheekbones and her lips were covered in a shimmery, rose-colored gloss. She looked nothing like the picture on her photo ID badge.

"Hi. My name is Raye, and I will be your nurse for the evening." Her shoes squeaked against the floor as she walked into the room. She stopped at the dry erase board hanging on the wall near the door and replaced the name of the day shift nurse with hers. "How's our patient doing today?"

"He's been asleep since I got here, so I'm not really sure." Katie shrugged her shoulders.

Come to think of it, Amanda never mentioned anything about his condition. Katie had no clue what injuries he had suffered, only that he had been in a wreck. That was it.

"I'm glad he's able to rest. That's the best thing for him right now." Raye pulled a pair of disposable gloves from the container mounted on the wall behind the bed and put them on. The plastic snapped against her skin as she straightened them on her fingers. She pushed a button on his vitals monitor that caused his blood pressure cuff to inflate and walked around to the foot of the bed. When she raised the blanket, Katie could see a brace on his right leg. Raye pulled down Ty's sock and gently pressed her thumb over the top of his foot.

"His leg ... is it broken?"

"No, I'm just checking for swelling. Everything looks good, though." Raye rolled his sock back up. "Are you Mrs. Duncan?"

"What? No!" Katie blurted, louder than she had intended. Her face pinched.

"His girlfriend?" Raye continued to fish for answers.

"No, I'm neither of those. I've never met him before." Katie closed her eyes and blew out her cheeks, regretting her words as soon as they came out of her mouth.

Why did you just say that? You moron!

Raye glanced down at their intertwined hands, confused. "Oh, my apologies. I should know better than to assume. So you are …" not exactly sure how to finish that sentence, she left it open for Katie to reply.

"An idiot, that's what I am. I'm so sorry. Your question just caught me off guard. My name is Katie. I'm actually a friend of his sister, Amanda. She went home to get her phone. I told her I would sit here with Ty until she got back." She crossed her ankles and leaned forward in the chair. "You see, it's not that I don't who he is, I just haven't physically met him before today." Katie tried to justify the complexity of the situation and was aware of how bizarre it all must sound. She was also acutely aware of how fast everything was flying out of her mouth, her anxiety graduating from a hum to a bubble. She was socially awkward under normal circumstances, and this was anything but normal. After a brief pause, she continued. "You probably think I'm crazy, don't you?"

"Well, I'm not going to lie. You did have me wondering why you were sitting in a hospital room holding the hand of a man you've never met before."

You aren't the only one.

"This wasn't exactly planned, so trust me; I'm just as surprised as you are. I was actually delivering those flowers over there and before I knew it, my best friend was gone in my car and I was left sitting in this chair, holding his hand." The warmth from his hand served as a nagging reminder that he hadn't actually disappeared.

Raye eyed the arrangement sitting on the counter and then looked back toward Katie. "Wow, that's really pretty. You made that?"

"No. I work at a flower shop downtown. My boss made the arrangement. I just made the delivery."

"Oh, I see." Raye systematically pushed a series of buttons on his IV pump and checked the tubing for kinks. "Not many things surprise me anymore," her words never stopped as she followed the plastic tubing under the blanket to where the IV entered his hand, "but I will say you got me a little with this one. I would have never guessed."

"Guessed what? That I worked at a flower shop?" Katie was confused.

"No," she giggled. "That you two had never met."

"Why's that?"

"Let's just say I see a lot of people each day sitting next to these hospital beds. Sitting next to a friend or family member suffering from some type of illness or injury, and I'm typically a pretty good read on people. I can usually tell who's a friend, who is family, who's just hanging around waiting to cash in on a will. That actually happens, ya know," Raye arched a brow as if to prove her point. "Anyway, when I walked in and saw you two holding hands and you with that concerned look on your face, I thought to myself 'now there's a good-looking couple.' I don't know, some people just fit, and you two look like you go together. Guess I was wrong this time, huh?"

"Guess so," Katie responded with embarrassment, shocked by Raye's bluntness. She couldn't think of anything else to say, so she did the next best thing … changed the subject. "Is there anything I need to tell his sister when she gets back?"

"Technically, I can't give you any details now since I know you aren't family, but I can say the doctor will be making his rounds in a couple of hours and will be able to answer any questions his sister may have." When Raye walked over to the laptop to update Ty's chart, she saw Katie's shoulders fall in disappointment and felt a twinge of guilt for her earlier comments. "Hey, I'm sorry if I upset you with what I said about you two being a couple. I've been told before my mouth doesn't know when to stop. I didn't mean anything by it."

"No, it's not that. It's just the main reason Amanda wanted me to stay was to be here in case anyone came in. To ask questions and get updates, but I honestly don't know what to ask and now I can't get any updates. I don't want her to be disappointed."

"How long have you been sitting in that chair, holding her brother's hand? That you say you've never met? Honey, she's not going to be disappointed at all. She's lucky to have you as a friend," she winked and returned to typing. "Okay, all done." One final tap of the keyboard and Raye folded the top down on the laptop. She carried on loudly, as if there wasn't a patient in the room trying to sleep. "Listen, if it will make you feel better having something to tell his sister, tell her I said his vitals look good. I saw in his chart that the doctor ordered another chest x-ray, and that right now, the best thing for him is rest. Can I get you anything before I go?"

"No, I'm good. Thank you. And thank you for telling me that."

"Well, you two do look like you were meant to be together."

"Not that part," Katie blushed. "The information you gave me to tell his sister."

Raye knew what she meant, but she couldn't help herself. It was just who she was. "Hey, if you need anything at all, push the nurse's call button on the bedrail. There is a convenience station at the end of the hall on the left. Help yourself to anything inside." She took off her gloves and tossed them in the trashcan by the door. She glanced back at Katie. "Do you want the light on or off?"

"On, please."

Raye left and took all of the noise with her. The room fell back into a quiet hum of electronics and fluorescent lights, and for the first time since she sat down, Katie looked at Ty. Not with an accidental passing glance as her eyes wandered the room, but really looked at him. She knew that if that whirlwind of activity hadn't woken him, nothing would.

Ty looked different than she thought he would. Even though he was Amanda's stepbrother, she had it in her mind they would look similar, but that wasn't the case. A lock of his brown hair hung over a gauze bandage on his forehead, and patches of scabbed blood peppered his face. He had fine lines beside his eyes and the texture of his skin indicated he spent more time in the sun than he probably should. His bottom lip was swollen and sutured and his head lay flat on the pillow because of the brace around his neck. Katie remembered that brace all too well. It seemed like just yesterday she was in his place, propped up in a hospital bed with her father by her side, holding her hand. The only difference was that when Ty woke up, he would probably know why he was there.

Ty's hand flinched and she looked down to see his fingers still clasped in hers.

Some people just fit.

Even though that statement was corny and cliché, she knew it was true. Some people truly did fit, like her parents. Two souls bound together by an intangible thread; weaving their way through life together no matter the circumstance. As much as she wanted to experience that type of connection, to find the other half that made her whole, she knew deep down it wasn't in the stars for her. An aching reality that at times was hard to accept.

After many dark years of pain and harbored secrets, her soul bitter and broken, she was not capable of love. Not that kind of love. In her twenty-six years, the only man she ever truly trusted was her father. It would be impossible for someone to assemble her shattered pieces and expecting anyone to do so would be unfair. She saw herself as damaged goods, and was completely convinced that she had nothing to offer anyone in a relationship.

Ty's hand flinched again, except this time it was more like a tug. She looked up at Ty to see him looking back at her.

"Oh … hi," Katie offered shyly, wondering how long he had been awake. The look on his face was a combination of confusion and pain. "Do I need to call the nurse?"

He slightly shook his head no, as best he could confined by the neck brace, and continued to stare.

"Amanda should be back any time," Katie continued, her bubbling anxiety now a roaring boil. "She needed to run shome and hower—I mean run home and shower."

His facial expression didn't change, even with her slip of words.

"Oh, shit!" A light bulb finally went off. "I'm Katie, by the way." She threw up her palm, offering half a wave. "I know you're probably wondering why I'm here, but Amanda said you would know who I was."

He squeezed his hand and she immediately pulled away, not realizing she had yet to let go. "Yeahhhh … about that. Amanda was adamant I hold your hand."

"She can be a little bossy sometimes." His voice was deep and unexpected.

"Wow, you can talk?"

"Am I not supposed to be able to talk?"

"Well … no. I mean yes. It's just … I didn't know what to expect, honestly," Katie stuttered, her heart rate now twice the speed of the second hand on the clock.

"It's nice to finally put a face to the name. Amanda talks about you all the time." Ty cleared his throat and winced. He made his best attempt to get comfortable and ignore the pain.

Katie was horrified at the thought of what Amanda might have told him. Things like 'social weirdness' and 'random panic attacks' flashed in her brain like neon signs. Regardless of what Amanda had said, Ty probably already noticed the social weirdness, and he would likely get to witness the other at any moment. He let out a faint moan.

"Are you sure you don't want me to call the nurse for some pain meds? She said all I had to do was push the button and she would bring you some."

"Maybe in a few minutes. I'm going to try to tough it out a little while longer."

He tried once again to find a position that would keep his ribs from rubbing together. No luck. He reached out his hand and placed it on Katie's arm. Electricity shot through her body like a lightning bolt, exiting her cheeks in a hot flash.

"Actually, there is one thing you can do."

"What's that?" she swallowed hard, wondering if her face was as red as it felt.

"Could you put my hand on the right button to move this bed up a little? So I can try to get more comfortable? I can't look down with this thing around my neck."

"I know. It's impossible. I mean, it looks like it would be impossible, not that I would know or anything. Here," she stood from her chair and placed his hand back on the bed, "let me help." She pushed the button and slowly raised the head of the bed, waiting for him to tell her when to stop. "Is that better?"

"As good as it's going to get I'm afraid." He let out a frustrated sigh. The forced breath panged his chest even more. "I guess I am going to have to call the nurse after all. I thought I could handle this, but I can't. Every time I make the slightest movement, I can feel the two ends of my broken rib grinding together. It's killing me." He spoke calmly, in spite of the pain.

Without hesitation, she pushed the call-button for the nurse. "I had no idea your ribs were broken. I can't imagine how bad that hurts." She sat back down. Suddenly her nerves seemed unwarranted and silly. He was absolutely no threat to her, he couldn't even move.

"Yeah, I've had some broken bones before, but this is by far the worst."

When Raye's voice came over the intercom, Katie didn't even give Ty a chance to speak. She told Raye he was awake and needed something for pain. And fast.

"Hopefully it won't take her long."

They waited in silence. Katie picked at the seam of her pant leg with her fingernails and, out of habit, went back to counting the wooden planks on the floor. Ty lay perfectly still. His broad chest spanned nearly the entire width of the bed, yet there was no visible movement when he breathed. He took the shallowest breaths possible, inhaling just enough oxygen to survive. Katie grew impatient, knowing he was laying there suffering. She'd been in his shoes before, and there was nothing worse than waiting on someone to bring you relief when it was convenient for them. Just as she reached for the button to call the nurse's station again, Raye walked in the door carrying a syringe and a vial of medication. And of course a loudness that swallowed the room.

"I come bearing the good stuff. Do you feel better now that he finally woke up?" she asked Katie.

"You two know each other?" Ty inquired.

"We met earlier." Raye scanned the white medical bracelet on Ty's wrist, followed by the barcode on the vial of medicine she held in her hand. "Funny story, actually. I thought she was …"

"Your sister," Katie interrupted. "She thought I was your sister." *Jesus, lady. Please stop talking!*

Raye took the hint and didn't say another word, but that didn't keep her from smiling while she injected the painkiller into his IV. After only a few moments, his pain began to fade. Raye was gone as quick as she arrived, and Ty's eyelids grew heavy, moving slower with every blink.

"You can leave if you want to. Don't feel like you need to stay on my behalf. I will be asleep shortly." His words were slightly slurred where they hadn't been before.

"I appreciate the offer, but I told Amanda I would stay until she got back. So if it's okay with you, I would like to stay." *Did I really just say that?*

"Of course." His voice was breathy and quiet. "Oh, and she was right."

"Who was right?"

"Amand-err."

"Right about what?" Katie asked.

"You are beautiful." His three final words spoken in a whisper.

He closed his eyes, and just like that, he was out.

Beautiful. That wasn't a word she was used to hearing, not in reference to herself anyway. It was probably the medication talking, so she didn't put much thought into it. She nestled back in her chair and ran her fingers through her hair, thankful to have the use of both hands while she waited. There was no longer an urgency to leave, and the anxiety that had boiled beneath her skin was but a vapor. She grabbed the remote hanging from the bedrail and searched for something more interesting to watch on the television. A cookie-baking competition on the Food Network sufficed, and time passed effortlessly.

"Katie. Wake up." Amanda shook her slightly.

Katie opened her eyes, briefly confused by her surroundings. She glanced over to see Ty still sleeping. "What time is it?"

"It's almost seven. Sorry I took so long. I got held up trying to recover Ty's things from the impound yard," she spoke softly. Amanda had on a fresh set of clothes and her hair looked like she'd been to the salon.

"It's okay. I can't believe I randomly fell asleep. That never happens." Katie sat up straight to stretch her back and a couple of pops escaped her spine. "Were you able to get them at least?"

"Yes, finally. How did things go here?"

"Good. The night shift nurse came by. Her name is Raye, and let me tell you, she is a piece of work."

"Did she give you any updates? Maybe say how long they thought he would be here? When his MRI would be?"

I wish I had known to ask those questions …

"No, none of that. She couldn't tell me much because I'm not family."

"Why didn't you tell her you were a relative? You could have lied, told her that you were my sister or something."

"Well, she did think we were related. Kind of. She thought I was your sister-in-law. She asked if I was Mrs. Duncan."

"Yeah, that's not going to happen," Amanda huffed. "How strange of her to assume you two were married. You don't even know each other."

"Trust me, I know. It was very uncomfortable, and she wouldn't let it go. Anyway, she did say his vitals looked good. She didn't say anything about an MRI, but did say the doctor wanted to do a chest x-ray. Oh, and when Ty woke up, she gave him some more pain medicine."

"Ty woke up? How was he feeling? What did he say?" Amanda fired off questions faster than Katie could respond.

"He was in quite a bit of pain and had a really hard time getting comfortable. You didn't tell me he had broken ribs."

"Yes, and unfortunately there's nothing they can do for that either. And that's not all that's broken. I guess I didn't fill you in very well before I ran off and deserted you; it was a long night and I wasn't thinking. He has a small fracture in his neck, his C3 vertebrae I think they said? I'm not good with that stuff, but I do know that's why he's wearing the neck brace. He doesn't have to have surgery or anything, thank goodness, but he'll have to wear that thing for a while. There are seven staples in his forehead, and of course you can see the stitches in his lip."

"What about his leg? When the nurse was in here I noticed a brace on his leg."

"He was complaining about a lot of pain in his knee. They did an x-ray, but it didn't show any broken bones. They put the brace on to keep it immobilized until they do an MRI. It's the same knee he hurt in high school playing football. His legs were pinned by the dash, and they had to cut him out." Amanda shuddered at the thought. "He's pretty banged up, but it could have been so much worse. After seeing his vehicle … it's a miracle he's alive."

"It sounds like someone was watching out for him for sure." Katie didn't believe in that stuff, but figured it was the right thing to say at the time. She knew some people were just luckier than others and that's all there was to it. The theory of guardian angels, destiny, and fate didn't sit well with her. Nobody was watching out for her the day she was attacked in the woods. Nobody listened to her cries for help when her mom was slowly dying from cancer. Guardian angels were as mythical as the tooth fairy or the Easter bunny in her eyes. They simply didn't exist.

Katie left when the doctor arrived. She found her car parked just a few spots down from where she left it, and when she climbed inside it smelled of J'adore, Amanda's favorite perfume. Attached to the steering wheel was a note. She opened it to find Amanda's writing on a piece of pale green stationary:

> *Dear Katie,*
>
> *I will never be able to thank you enough for staying with Ty and letting me borrow your car so I could run some errands. I don't have many friends who would have done the same. When things calm down a little, I want to treat you to a girl's day. If it wasn't so late, I would have gotten you flowers. You're the best!*
>
> *XOXO,*
>
> *Amanda*
>
> *P.S. In case I forget, remind me to ask you why you have pepper spray on your key ring.*

Katie folded the piece of paper and tucked it away in her purse, pleased that Amanda was unaware of how much she'd struggled to get through the last few hours. There was just enough daylight to stop at the grocery store and make it home before dark, so she decided to swing by H-E-B on her way. She was starving, and there was nothing left in her apartment to eat. Traffic was sparse and, when she turned in at the store, so was the parking lot.

Katie walked up and down the aisles of the supermarket, loading her basket with items to fill her empty cabinets and fridge. It was tough to cook for one person without creating a lot of waste, so she always chose things that made good leftovers or items that came prepackaged in single-serve portions. Working at the flower shop didn't yield a hefty salary, but Katie was good about watching her money. After paying her rent and her utilities, she put a small amount into savings and budgeted the remainder across gas, groceries, and entertainment, making sure to leave a little for those special days out with Amanda.

That was one thing the girls didn't have in common. Amanda had money and wasn't afraid to spend it. She wouldn't bat an eye at dropping several hundred dollars on the latest Louis Vuitton bag or shelling out a wad of cash for a pair of Valentino heels. Katie, on the other hand, wasn't into excessive spending and always shopped for a bargain. Most of her wardrobe came from the thrift shop, mainly because she thought spending an exorbitant amount of money on an article of clothing or pair of shoes was silly when the last thing she wanted to do was draw attention to herself.

She stopped in the dairy section and grabbed a half-gallon of whole milk and a pint of heavy cream. Leftover pasta wasn't her favorite, but she splurged and picked up everything she needed to make chicken alfredo, one of her favorite meals. Maybe she could invite Amanda over for dinner so they could talk. It would give Katie the opportunity to finish the conversation that never really got started at Joe's.

Maybe.

She headed toward the register and began unloading her items onto the conveyor belt.

"Would you like a hand with that?" A man's voice came from behind her.

Katie turned towards the voice. "I can probably manage. It's Brad, isn't it? I'm sorry, I'm horrible with names." She lied. She knew exactly who he was.

"You must not be too horrible, you remembered. Or maybe I just made a good first impression," he winked.

Nope. That's definitely not it.

"Do you live around here? I don't remember ever seeing you in here before." Katie made a mental note that it may be time to change grocery stores. She also noticed he wasn't pushing a buggy.

"Not too far up the road." He thumbed to the right and the edge of a tattoo on his forearm peeked out from beneath his rolled-up sleeve. "What about you? Whereabouts do you live?"

"I live over on the east side of town, going out toward the airport."

Lie number two. Her apartment wasn't anywhere near the airport.

"That's quite a ways from here. What brings you to this side of town? Were you at the hospital with Amanda's brother?" he asked.

"How did you …"

"Kyle told me what happened. That's a raw deal. From what I hear he is lucky to be alive." His voice conveyed anything but concern. He moved a step closer to Katie. "Hey, I know this may seem forward seeing as we just met, but would you like to go out some time? I could take you to dinner," he glanced down at her buggy, "or come by your place and you could cook me some of that pasta?"

Not a snowball's chance in hell would I let you in my apartment!

"That's nice of you to offer, but I'm going to have to pass." Katie nervously strummed her debit card with her fingernails, secretly urging the lady checking her groceries to pick up the pace. "I've recently started seeing someone."

Lie number three.

"Oh," he took a step back. "I'm sorry. Kyle said you weren't dating anyone. I hope it's okay I asked. After we met at Joe's the other night, I couldn't quit thinking about you."

"Kyle probably didn't know. Like I said, it all happened recently and he and Amanda have been busy planning a wedding. I doubt they spend much time focusing on my personal life."

"That will be $76.32," the cashier chimed in.

Katie swiped her debit card, entered her pin number, and took her receipt. She placed it and her card in her wallet and turned back toward Brad. "Looks like I'm all finished here. I better move along so I don't hold up the line." She hurried toward the door. "It was nice running in to you again."

Lie number four.

"Yes it was," he replied. "I'm sure we will be seeing each other again soon," he called out.

The wheels on Katie's buggy screeched to a halt. She turned back toward him, leaving one hand on the handle.

"The wedding?" he responded to her puzzled look. "I heard Amanda tell Kyle you agreed to be in it, right?"

"Oh, yeah. That." They did talk about that in front of him at Joe's. Once again, her paranoia seemed invalid. "Are you in the wedding, too?"

"No. I'm not in it, but I'm sure I will be around for stuff. Kyle and I are pretty good friends."

"I see." Katie forced a smile. "Well, until then."

On the drive home, she spent more time looking in the rearview mirror than watching the road. She even took a different route than normal, just in case, but there was no sign she was being followed. As much as she hated to admit it, Brad was right. With the wedding coming up, she would be forced to be around people she wasn't comfortable with, including him, even if he was harmless. She better learn how to deal with that ... and soon.

Chapter 8
NINE YEARS EARLIER

Detective Burns watched from his squad car as a steady stream of vehicles waited patiently for their turn at the window. The line for the drive thru wrapped around the building and spilled over onto the shoulder of the highway, which was typical for this time of day. Friday mornings at the donut shop were always the busiest in Brownsboro. He took a sip of his coffee and dusted the crumbs from his apple fritter off his chest, thankful that he made it to the popular breakfast stop before the crowd arrived.

Everything in him wanted to stop back by old man Johnson's place last night, but he knew that with Damon's grandmother running interference a repeat visit to the house would be pointless. Burns didn't let that deter him. He knew he needed to come up with another plan, one that Damon would not see coming, one that eliminated a potential cover-up story by a friend or family member. Carl was convinced this prick was the one who attacked his daughter, and Burns had promised Katie he would do everything possible to catch the guy responsible. A promise he would keep. And he knew he wouldn't sleep until he did, either, because cases of this nature all had one common denominator for him: insomnia.

Burns spent the whole night lying in his bed staring at the ceiling. He manifested an entire scenario of exactly what he would do and say when he was finally alone with Damon. This was his favorite part of any case, and he was no amateur when it came to grilling a suspect. While working in Tarrant County, he had learned how to manipulate words and twist stories into the smoothest of confessions, and even if he occasionally crossed the line doing so, he justified his actions by reminding himself he was putting scumbags behind bars where they belonged.

As he continued to watch the flow of cars weave in and out of the parking lot, he replayed every detail of that scenario in his head. He planned to pay Damon a visit at school and have him pulled from class. He couldn't hide behind his grandmother there and it wasn't uncommon to see Burns on campus, as he would often stop to visit his wife or have an occasional lunch with his daughter. His sweet, innocent daughter, Sarah. The thought of her now being only a few buildings away from a sex offender made his blood boil.

Traffic was beginning to thin out as the hour approached eight. It was almost show time, and Burns could feel the excitement begin to course through his veins. He lived for this shit, and couldn't wait to see the expression on Damon's face as he blasted him with questions. Questions structured to have him stammering like a blithering idiot before he knew what hit him. What Burns wouldn't give to be able to walk into Katie's hospital room and tell her and Carl that he had gotten a confession and the person responsible had been apprehended. And for that to take place before her memory recalled any details from the sexual aspect of her attack. Forcing her to relive those tragic moments just for clues that may or may not link to her perpetrator would be unnecessary if Damon 'fessed up to the crime.

Burns downed the last bit of lukewarm coffee from his cup and tossed it into the backseat floorboard where it landed next to the grey toboggan he had snagged from Damon's house. He decided to make a few loops through town to allow enough time for the students and teachers to get situated in their classrooms. The less hallway traffic when he entered the school, the better. This was not a normal environment for questioning a suspect, and Burns didn't want to expose the students to any of this mess if it could be avoided.

When he arrived at the school, he had the secretary summon five different students to the office over the intercom in an attempt to reduce any suspicion of what was about to happen. He needed this encounter to go down just as he had planned, and although the counselor's office wasn't as intimidating as the detainee room at the precinct, it would do. Especially with a kid dumb enough to stick to his normal routine two days after allegedly sexually assaulting his ex-girlfriend.

He may have managed to dodge being questioned at home, but Burns had spotted his black Chevy pickup in the parking lot when he pulled in and knew he was here.

"Well, well, if it isn't Barney Fife. What brings you to school this fine Friday morning, off-i-cerrrr?" Damon did his best to mask his surprise with mockery as he entered the room. He took a seat in the wooden chair directly across the desk from Burns.

"Ahh, we have a comedian on our hands. I knew you were a little old to still be in school, but I didn't realize you were old enough to know who Barney Fife was. That's impressive," Burns chided. He wasn't fooled by Damon's phony over-confidence, and figured he would take a quick stab to knock him down a notch or two. Damon was older than the average senior due to being held back a couple of years, and based on his expression, that was not something he was proud of. Burns had a few other insults he would love to toss Damon's way, but knew he needed to stick to the script.

"Detective Burns," he introduced himself as he extended his hand.

"I know who you are," Damon nodded. "You're the same guy that came by my house the other day."

"You are correct. Did your grandmother tell you I stopped by?" Burns probed, wondering if she told him or if Damon had actually been watching from the window the entire time.

"Yeah, she told me. Not that you really had any business being there. I haven't done anything."

"Who said you did anything?"

"You did," Damon responded in an accusatory tone.

"I don't believe I did. I simply told your grandmother I needed to ask you a few questions."

"The only reason you would need to ask me a few questions is if you thought I had done something. Am I wrong?" Damon asked rhetorically. "I've been around the block a time or two. I know how this works."

"Oh, you do? Well, if you're so smart then why don't you tell me why I'm here?"

"I don't think so." Damon raised an eyebrow and leaned forward in his chair. "I'm not that stupid."

"I never said you were stupid." Burns let out a laugh. He was playing this kid like a fiddle and he knew this was the perfect opportunity to flip the script and begin to stroke his ego a bit.

"What are you laughing at?" Damon's agitation was evident, but the stare from his hollow green eyes never wavered.

"Oh, nothing," he smirked. "It's just that you remind me so much of me at your age."

"That is something to laugh at. We are nothing alike," Damon sternly refuted.

"I beg to differ. Your cocky attitude and smart-ass remarks to everything I say, hell that could have been me sitting in that chair."

"Even if you claim to be like me at this age, which I highly doubt, it would end there. Because if for one second you think I'd ever be dumb enough to become a sorry cop, you're wrong."

"I used to think the same way, man. I had zero respect for authority, especially the cops." He did his best to be relatable to Damon. "I think I did it for the power, honestly. I wanted to be the one telling people what to do, not the other way around. And I'm going to let you in on a little secret ... chicks go crazy for a man in uniform."

"Unlike you, I don't have any problems in that area." Damon wasn't impressed. "I don't need to hide behind a uniform to get lucky."

"I can see that about you. A guy like you has probably had sex with a ton of girls, huh?"

"I have a few notches on my bedpost," he responded arrogantly.

"Heck, you've probably nailed every chick you've ever dated." Burns smiled, as if in approval of such behavior.

"It's not my fault the ladies can't say no." Damon slouched back in his chair, a smug grin on his face.

Burns wanted to knock the flat-rimmed cap off Damon's head and throw him against the wall. Maybe shove a couple of knee thrusts into his groin until he fell to the ground. But Burns knew he had to keep his cool for a little while longer and let his line of questioning do the dirty work.

"I had that feeling about you."

"What can I say? Girls always want the bad boys."

"They sure do." The urge to bash his face in was getting harder and harder for Burns to control.

"And the ones who say they don't, they just need to be convinced otherwise," Damon winked.

BOOM! And there it was. That was quick.

"Like Katie Upton?" Burns asked with a solemn face.

Damon shifted in his chair and a tiny glimmer of light bounced off the round diamond stud attached to his right earlobe. "Somebody said she got roughed up the other day. She probably deserved it. Let me guess …" his words dripped with sarcasm, "… you think I had something to do with that?"

"What I think is maybe she turned you down and that giant ego of yours couldn't handle the rejection so you tried to convince her otherwise," he used his words against him.

"Is that the best you've got? Man, I'm actually a little disappointed in you, Barney. That's circumstantial at best," he snickered.

"Where were you Wednesday evening?"

"Oh, you know, here and there, just riding around," Damon's response was vague, refusing to give Burns any solid information.

"Was anyone with you?"

"No, man, haven't you heard? I travel alone." Damon stopped bouncing his knee and propped his hands on his thighs. "Listen, am I under arrest here?"

"Should you be?" Burns was realizing that he had underestimated this kid.

"I already told you: I haven't done anything. And if you had any proof otherwise," Damon smiled, "this bullshit conversation would have never taken place. I'm going back to class." He pushed himself up, turned, and sauntered out the door.

Damon was right. As much as it pained Burns to admit it, he was right. Although he made a comment that alluded to being forceful with females, that confession was circumstantial at best.

Unless Katie could identify him as her attacker, there was no physical evidence to link him to the crime.

He now knew why Carl was convinced Damon was responsible, and Burns believed he owed it to Katie to figure out how to prove it. The news of her attack had yet to be released to the public, so the sheer fact he mentioned her being *roughed up the other day* could be the sliver of rope he used to hang himself. Maybe he wasn't as smart as he thought he was.

Back at the precinct, Burns cleaned out the trash from the backseat of his squad car. He signed the paperwork waiting on his desk for his return and replied to two emails. One was a personal email from a realtor regarding a lake-house property he had inquired about online, and another from his captain pertaining to a civilian that was contesting her speeding ticket. The speed limit sign at the edge of town, partially obscured by a low-lying limb, was her defense as to why she was going seventy in a fifty. She was from out of town, like most travelers on the main highway in Brownsboro, only passing through.

The top of his desk was relatively tidy. A black mesh desk organizer stood to the left of his computer monitor and to the right, next to his telephone, was a wooden frame that held a photo of his wife and daughter sitting in a pile of crisp, golden leaves, taken last Thanksgiving at his in-laws. He stared intently at the photo, focusing on the innocent smile of his daughter, and flashed back to Katie—badly beaten and confined to a hospital bed. A young girl with her whole life ahead of her now had a childhood tarnished by a merciless attack that she would spend the rest of that life trying to forget.

The need for justice seethed inside him and he yearned to be the executioner. Burns pushed back his chair, grabbed his keys, and radioed for the other officer on duty to meet him at Black Bear Trail.

"Boss, I'm not sure what you're looking for," Officer Wakeland said inquisitively. "We've been over every inch of these woods and haven't found a thing other than the girl's jacket."

"Well, we are going to look again. There's bound to be something we've missed. Sometimes we get so focused that we can't see something staring us right in the face."

"Okay," Wakeland sounded reluctant. "Whatever you say."

They started at the trail and worked their way through the woods back toward Katie's house, each wandering off in a different direction. The heat from the afternoon sun radiated off of their black uniforms as they methodically scanned the ground and surrounding area for anything suspicious. They tossed up leaves, lifted branches, and even inspected trees for potential clothing fragments snagged by jagged bark. As Burns examined a nearby oak tree, he couldn't help but notice the peculiar arc of its trunk with what appeared to be the remnants of a sapling whose growth was stunted by the center of that semi-circle. *A three-legged tree.* He recalled Katie's testimony; this is where the attack took place. He reached into his shirt, bent down, and rifled through the leaves.

"Hey, Wakeland! Over here! I think I found something!" he shouted, his voice bouncing off the trees nearby.

The officer made his way to Burns, who was pointing at an object half buried in the leaves. "What do you reckon it is, Boss?" Wakeland asked.

"It looks like a rag or a sock or something." But it wasn't a rag. Or a sock. Burns knew exactly what it was. "You got an evidence bag?"

"Not on me. Let me go grab one out of the car."

Wakeland retrieved a plastic bag and returned to find Burns still kneeling on the ground. The quick trip up the hill to the car and back left him winded. "Here ya go," Wakeland panted, trying to catch his breath.

Burns grabbed a nearby stick and poked the object. He rose to his feet, and when he hoisted the stick in the air, dangling from the end was a grey toboggan. While Wakeland's head had been down searching for evidence, Burns had been busy planting a little of his own.

Saturday was typically his day off, but Burns knew there was work to be done. He showered and shaved, his harrowed reflection in the mirror barely recognizable. The dark circles under his bloodshot eyes proof of three nights with minimal sleep. He put on his ballistic vest and zipped his uniform shirt before wrapping his utility belt around his waist. It wasn't typical to wear full uniform with what he had scheduled for the day, but something told him to expect the unexpected. On his way down the hall, he stopped and quietly pushed open the door to his daughter's room where she was asleep in her bed. He pulled her pink princess blanket up to her chest and gently kissed her on the forehead. "I will be home soon, Baby. I promise Daddy will play hide and seek with you today," he whispered.

He was running on pure adrenaline at this point. And coffee. An abundance of coffee. Already to the bottom of his third cup, his heart was beating faster than his body wanted to move. He spent the morning typing the reports he'd neglected over the past several days, and although a sense of accomplishment came with catching up on those humdrum duties, that wasn't his goal. It was merely busy work to kill time while he waited for an appropriate hour to visit Katie at the hospital.

It was around a ten-minute drive from Brownsboro to the nearest doctor's office and more than double that time to the nearest hospital, one of the downsides to living in a rural area. The conveniences of urgent care were limited, and any major medical emergency required ambulance transport into the city. It was probably best that Katie was that far from town. Just as Burns was about to walk out the door to head her way with the two bags he'd checked out of evidence, the sound of his desk phone ringing turned him around.

"Burns," he answered.

"Honey, it's me." The sound of his wife's voice came through the phone. "I hate to bother you at work …"

"Is everything okay?" he interjected. It wasn't common for her to call him at the office.

"I think so. Well … I'm not sure. I went outside to feed Atlas and get the Barbie Sarah left in the car, and I noticed a truck stopped in the road at the edge of the tree line. When I started walking down the driveway to get a better look, it drove off."

"What kind of truck?"

"You know I'm not good with brands, but it was dark, either dark blue or black. And it was big. Not one I've seen on our road before."

"You and Sarah stay in the house and lock the doors. I'm on my way."

Burns flipped on his flashing lights and sped out of the parking lot. His house and ten acres of land were on a county road south of town. He grabbed his radio and keyed the mic. "This is 401, all units be on the lookout for a black Chevrolet four-wheel drive pickup, possibly driven by a Damon McGregor, bearing license plate Charlie-Charlie-Alpha-4-5-0-6. The vehicle is being driven by a suspect in an aggravated assault and rape case. Please notify me if the vehicle is found, over."

When he got to the house, he searched the perimeter and found nothing out of sorts. Atlas, their black and tan German shepherd, calmly settled in a patch of dirt beneath the shade tree and there was no sign of the black truck. Once again, he had no proof it was Damon, but every fiber in his body believed it was. And this had gotten personal.

Burns didn't feel comfortable leaving his family at home while he went into the city to visit Katie at the hospital. He didn't want to leave them at all. But he knew the faster he could put this case to rest, the faster he could get that troublemaker off the streets. In order to make that happen, he needed to have another conversation with Katie.

He packed up his wife and daughter and asked if they could go visit her parents for the day. Almost two hundred miles away, it was enough distance from home to ensure their safety while Burns worked the case. He placed the duffle bag his wife threw together in the back of her white SUV and helped Sarah into her booster seat.

"I thought we were going to pway today, Daddy," she pouted. Sarah's Ls always came out sounding like Ws.

"I know, Baby, I'm sorry. Daddy has to work today." He stretched the seatbelt across her lap and fastened it tightly. "Just think about how much fun you'll have with Mimi and Pops, though. You can go swimming and I bet they will take you to the pond to feed the ducks." His in-laws had a heated swimming pool.

"I wuv to feed the ducks!" the excitement in her young voice exploded. "I wish you could feed them with me, Daddy."

"Me too, Baby." He kissed her on the cheek. "Be good for Mommy today, and I promise we will play as soon as you get home."

He shut the door and walked around to his wife. "Please be careful," he pulled her in for a hug and then kissed her on the lips. "I know this isn't what you had planned and there were things you wanted to get done around the house today, but I will feel better if you aren't here while I'm gone."

"Don't you think you're overreacting? It may have been nothing. Whoever was driving could have dropped their phone. Or needed to stop and use the bathroom. You know people often use these back roads for that."

"I know, and you're right. It could be nothing. But it could be everything. The truck you described matches one that belongs to a suspect in a case I'm working. A bad one."

They didn't talk about his work anymore, but she knew what it meant when he wasn't sleeping well. It had happened all time when he worked in Tarrant County. She climbed into the SUV, shut the door, and rolled down the window.

He leaned in for one more kiss and she touched his cheek. "I thought days like these were over," she whispered.

"Me, too," he answered. "Me, too."

Burns parked his squad car near the entrance of the hospital. He took the elevator to the third floor and checked in at the nurse's station before making his way to room 343. When he entered, Katie was watching television and Carl was asleep on the sofa by the window, still wearing the same wrinkled clothes.

"Hey, Katie, do you remember me?" He removed his hat and held it behind his back with the evidence bags, staying close to the door. "I'm Detective Burns; I was here the other day."

"Yes, I remember." Her voice was less raspy than before, but the bruising on her face possessed deeper hues of green and purple.

"That's good. You're sounding better," he encouraged. "Do you feel up to talking with me a little today?" he asked gingerly.

His voice brought Carl from his sleep and he joined Katie at her bedside. "Hello, Detective. I hope you come with good news." Carl coughed to clear his throat.

"Well, maybe. But before we get started," he turned toward Katie, "I wanted to see if you were able to remember any other details about what happened—anything that you haven't already told me."

"No, not really. I've told you pretty much everything I know."

"It's okay. That's perfectly fine." Actually, it was better than fine, but he wasn't going to tell her that. "I want to show you something." He placed his hat and one of the evidence bags on the counter and kept the other in his hand. "May I walk over?"

"Yes," Katie answered.

"We found this yesterday in the woods between your house and the trail. In the general area you described as the last place you remember being. Does this look familiar?" He handed her the plastic bag containing the grey toboggan.

She studied the bag. "May I open it?"

"Absolutely."

Katie peeled open the zippered bag, and as quick as she pulled the toboggan out she shoved it back in and tossed the bag toward the end of the bed. Every hair on her body at attention.

"What is it, Sweetheart?" Carl asked.

"I recognize that hat. It belongs to my ex-boyfriend, Damon McGregor. He wore it all the time. I can tell it's his because of the cigarette burn." Tears pooled above her lower lash line. "It was him, wasn't it? He did this to me, didn't he?"

"That's what we are trying to figure out," Burns spoke calmly. "You said ex-boyfriend. Did he ever go to the trail with you? Have you ever known him to be in those woods?" he asked.

"No. He always came to my cross-country meets and he knew where I lived, but he never went with me to the trail," she stammered. "He didn't know about my path through the woods, at least I didn't think he did."

"You sound pretty convinced it was him. Why do you think he would do something like this to you?"

"He kept trying to get me to have sex with him. He was mad at me because I said I wasn't ready. He said girls don't tell him no. That's why we were fighting on the phone before I went for my run." She looked toward her dad. "I'm so sorry, Daddy. I should have told you. I just didn't know how." Katie closed her eyes, sending the pooled tears down her cheeks.

"It's okay, Sweetie." Carl hated to see his daughter like this. "This is not your fault." He felt, though, that in a way it may be his. He had sensed Damon was bad news from the first day he met him, but tried not to interfere in Katie's relationships, whether friends or boyfriends.

"That's all the questions I have for today. Thank you, Katie. I know this is extremely difficult for you. I promise I'm working hard to solve your case. We are getting close. Very close." He knew now that he had something tangible to use against Damon that placed him at the scene of the crime. Coupled with Katie's testimony about his prior threats and his corroborating statements from the school interview, this was about to be a slam dunk.

Burns picked the bag up from the bed and exchanged it with the one still sitting on the counter. "Oh, we found something else. Does this belong to you?" He handed her the second bag.

"My jacket!" Katie exclaimed, the first glimmer of happiness she had experienced in days. She ripped open the bag, spilling the jacket out onto the bed. She frantically searched the pockets but both were empty. *Maybe it fell out on the bed.* She ran her hands across the top of the covers, flattening every fold.

"Is something wrong?" Burns inquired.

"My locket. It was inside my jacket pocket. It's missing."

Chapter 9
PRESENT

She started her day drenched in sweat before ever taking her first step. Another nightmare. Her legs glistened from the humidity as she slogged through her run, and the thick air made it hard to breathe. An unseasonable morning shower left the sidewalk sizzling and steam surrounded Katie's ankles as she splashed through the remnants of the storm. A few swollen clouds lingered above, but the threat of more rain did not keep her inside. Part of her wished the belly of the clouds would split open and their guts would wash away the three words she ran to forget.

I've got you.

Post-traumatic stress disorder was what the doctor called it. He said it was common for people who experienced a traumatic event like Katie. The nightmares, the plaguing anxiety, the inability to trust men or develop close relationships all fell under her four-letter label ... PTSD. Unfortunately, there was no known expiration date for her symptoms, and no magic cure to make it go away. So she did the only thing that ever worked to help calm her nerves and sort out her thoughts. She ran.

The anniversary of her attack was just around the corner. The most restful sleep she'd had in days was the catnap beside Ty's bed at the hospital waiting on Amanda—oddly enough—and her body was showing signs of fatigue. Her calf muscles balled up just beneath her knees, and she didn't know if her inability to get her breathing under control was from exhaustion or the high humidity. She slowed to a walk and instinctively placed her hands over her head to catch her breath. They immediately came crashing back down when a banging noise startled her from behind.

Damn it. I know better than to do that.

She turned toward the noise to see a thin woman in her late forties dressed in dark slacks and a yellow sleeveless blouse hammering a realtor sign into the front yard of the white two-story Victorian home. Katie's favorite. The engine of an unfamiliar black Cadillac hummed in the driveway, and the windshield wipers intermittently shrieked against the dry windshield.

"Did they move?"

"Excuse me?" The woman stopped hammering and looked up.

"The owners of the home." Katie moved closer to keep from shouting, but still kept her distance. "Did they move?"

"Oh, yes. Sweet couple. They decided to move to South Carolina to be closer to their daughter and two grandchildren." With one last tap on the right corner, the sign was straight. "Are you interested in the house? It is going on the market today." She dabbed sweat beads from her nose with the pads of her fingers. The sun was barely above the horizon, but the air was stifling.

"Me? Oh … no. I mean, don't get me wrong, I love the house. It's beautiful. I run by it all the time. It's actually my favorite one on the street, but I never see me living in something like this."

"I've learned to never say never, dear." People in the south loved pet names. Everyone was known as sweetie or dear. "Life has a funny way of proving you wrong."

"Life has a twisted sense of humor for sure." Katie looked toward the front door with eyes full of wonder and words began to flow out of her mouth. "This house reminds me of a place I visited once with my parents when I was a little girl. As silly as it sounds, looking at it makes me happy because it reminds me of my mom. We had so much fun on that trip, cooking together, fishing, playing cards. She passed away when I was young, so the memories I do have are extra special." An awkward feeling washed over her when she realized she was rambling to a stranger. "Wowwww, I'm not sure why I told you all of that. I apologize for the word vomit—it just kinda came out." Katie wrapped her arms across her chest, suddenly feeling exposed.

"Don't be. I'm sorry to hear about your mother. How did she pass?"

"Cancer."

"I lost my dad to cancer a few years ago. Lymphoma. It was tough as an adult, I can't imagine going through that as a child." She glanced at the gold watch dangling from her wrist and paused for a brief moment before speaking again. "What do ya say ... would you like to see the inside?"

"Really?" Katie shrieked. She looked around; there was no one else in sight. "Are, are you sure that's okay? I already told you I'm not interested in buying it. I don't have that kind of money. I would hate to waste your time."

"You're not wasting my time at all. Anyway, you'd be doing me a favor. Word of mouth is the best advertisement, and if you have stars in your eyes now, wait until you see the inside. You're going to love it!" She motioned toward driveway." Let me turn off my car and I'll give you the grand tour."

Katie closed her day planner and stuck her pen in its coiled binder. She hugged it against her chest. Freshly written inside were the details of her unexpected tour of the Victorian home, which far exceeded anything she had ever dreamed.

Still on a high from her red-carpet treatment, she sent Amanda a text and invited her for dinner. Amanda had only been inside her apartment a handful of times, and of those, Katie had only cooked for her twice, but she felt inspired to make pasta, just like she did with her mom on vacation at the bed and breakfast. She pureed olive oil, Parmesan, and a mixture of Italian spices in the blender and poured the marinade over the chicken breasts. Topped off with a dash of lemon zest, she sealed the Ziploc bag and placed the chicken on the top shelf in the refrigerator.

Katie's apartment was nothing fancy, but it was something she could afford. It had a single bedroom and bathroom and a small kitchen with barely enough room for one person to operate in comfortably. The cabinets and appliances were white, but had yellowed slightly with age. The front door opened into a tiny entryway off the side of the living room, and beside the kitchen table a set of sliding glass doors led to a covered patio. Two of the vertical blinds that hung over the door were broken on the end and resembled the jagged teeth of a Jack-o-lantern. The blinds always stayed closed, and Katie kept a broom handle in the floor track wedged between the door and the frame. She never used that door.

Katie went to the sink and squeezed a healthy amount of antibacterial soap into her palm to wash her hands. Her mother warned her repeatedly when she was young of the danger of handling raw chicken. As the soap began to lather, her cell phone rang.

Great timing, Amanda.

She quickly rinsed her hands, ran them down the side of her shorts to dry them off, and stabbed at her phone with a damp finger to answer.

"Why can't you respond through a text like a normal person? Who actually calls anymore, anyway?" She laughed and used her shoulder to hold the phone to her ear while she grabbed a towel to finish drying her hands.

"Katie?"

"Daddy?" His voice was a surprise.

"That sure is an odd way to answer the phone."

"Sorry about that, I thought you were Amanda. I should have paid more attention to who was calling."

"I'm just glad you answered. I've been worried about you."

"Worried? Why?" She dropped the towel on the table and took the phone back in her hand, letting her shoulder fall.

"You never called me back. I called you twice yesterday. I left a voicemail on your cell phone and a message on your answering machine. When I didn't hear back from you, I got worried."

She suddenly remembered silencing his call to keep from answering in front of Amanda. With the way everything unraveled afterward, she never listened to his voicemail. "Oh, Daddy, I didn't mean to make you worry." She glanced across to her answering machine sitting on the cabinet next to the wall. Sure enough, it was flashing. "I was at the hospital with Amanda when you called and I forgot to call you back."

"Hospital? What happened to Amanda?"

"Nothing. It's her brother, Ty. He was in a car accident. I was just keeping her company." Silverware rattled in the drawer when she grabbed a spoon to stir her coffee. "Did you talk to Detective Burns?"

"I left him a message, but I'm still waiting to hear back. I'm not sure why we all carry these little phones around with us. Nobody ever seems to answer them. His voicemail isn't even set up. It's that generic message that comes with the phone, which isn't very professional, in my opinion." Carl detested technology. "Did the man that came to the flower shop looking for you ever show up again?"

"No, he didn't. And to be honest, Mrs. Greyson never said he asked for me by name. He just gave a vague description of someone and she assumed he was talking about me. But maybe he wasn't? Maybe he was looking for someone else?" She begged for reassurance. "It's not like we are the only flower shop in town."

"That's a good possibility, considering he never came back."

"I hope you're right. If not, at least he doesn't seem to be trying very hard to find me." She pulled out a chair and sat down at the kitchen table with her coffee. "I'm probably being overly paranoid. Again. That seems to be happening a lot lately."

"What do you mean?"

"For starters, I cussed at Mrs. Greyson because she came up behind me and scared me. It was an accident, but I almost whacked her with a broom. Then, when I went to town to meet Amanda, I felt like someone was watching me. I kept turning around, but no one was there. And last night, I assumed this guy that is a friend of Amanda's fiancé was following me because he happened to be in the same grocery store as me. Ugh … it sounds even more ridiculous when I say it out loud. Why can't I just be normal?"

"I know this time of year is rough for you, Sweetheart, so try not to be too hard on yourself. I'm sure it's just nerves. I think we will both feel better when we hear back from Detective Burns. No news is usually good news, so I'm sure everything …"

A beep in her ear cut him off. She glanced at her phone to see an incoming call. "Daddy, I hate to cut this short, but Amanda is trying to call me. Can I call you right back?"

"You don't have to. I just wanted to make sure you were okay. I will let you know when I hear back from Detective Burns. Oh, and Katie?"

"Yes, Daddy?"

"This time, try answering the phone with a simple hello."

Katie scooped pasta into three single-serving bowls and tossed a garden salad in a homemade vinaigrette dressing before doing the same. She placed all six bowls in a brown paper sack and grabbed an oven mitt to remove the garlic bread from the oven. With no time to cool, steam puffed from the edges when she wrapped the warm bread in tin foil. She added it to the bag along with napkins and enough silverware for three. Her apartment smelled like an Italian restaurant, and tonight she was not only the chef, she was in the food-delivery business as well. Her offer to cook for Amanda had turned into dinner for three: her, Amanda … and Ty.

The sun peered from beneath a cloud on the western horizon and directly into her windshield. She dropped the visor to dampen its glare and continued driving toward the other side of town. As much as she hated hospitals, for once she hated the thought of being alone even more, so when Amanda called to decline her invitation because she would be at the hospital with Ty, Katie offered to bring the food to them.

Hands full, Katie lightly tapped on the door with the toe of her tennis shoe. Embarrassment crept in when she realized she had forgotten to change clothes before leaving her apartment. Splatters of pasta sauce dotted her sweatshirt, and her shorts showed more leg than she liked in public. Her lips vibrated when she blew out her breath. Shortly after, the door opened.

"Here, let me get that." Amanda took the brown paper bag from Katie and buried her nose inside, drawing in a big breath. "Holy cow, that smells good." She took the bag over to the counter and started pulling out bowls. She glanced back at Katie. "You and your sweatshirts—aren't you dying in that thing? It's a hundred degrees outside."

"Do I look dead?" Katie used sarcasm to hide her embarrassment. She looked at Ty. Not much had changed from the last time she saw him, other than he was awake. Same neck brace, same bandaged head, scabbed face, puffy lip. "Hi," was all she could think to say.

"You didn't have to bring food. They do feed us here, contrary to what my sister may have told you. Don't let her boss you around."

"Hey, I don't boss her around!" Amanda protested, bringing a bowl of pasta and some garlic bread to his bedside table. Beads of condensation clung to the underside of the lid when she peeled it open. "She offered to bring it because she's nice. I can't help it my friends are better than yours."

Katie stood awkwardly near the door, toes pointed in with her thumbs tucked in the pockets of her cutoff denim shorts. "It's not a big deal really. I was cooking anyway. At least now none of it will go to waste."

"You were supposed to say, 'She doesn't boss me around.' Help me out here," Amanda begged.

"I rest my case." The sutures in Ty's lip stretched with his half-cocked grin.

Amanda twirled the fettuccine noodles around the prongs of a fork, creating a beehive on the end, and placed it in Ty's hand. "Eat this and shut up. Katie, I'm going to run down and get us some drinks. What would you like?"

"Sprite, please. Or anything decaffeinated will be fine."

"Okay, I will be right back. Don't let my brother fill your head with any nonsense."

Ty spoke after the door closed. "I feel the need to apologize for her. She's so—what's the word …?"

"Extra?" Katie offered.

"That's a good word for her. Extra."

"It's okay. She has a giant heart, so that makes up for it." She noticed he was still holding the fork full of fettuccine. "Do you need some help with that?"

"No, I think I got it. You never know how much you use your stomach until you can't use your stomach." He slowly maneuvered his hand toward his mouth, keeping his torso stabilized so not to move his ribs. A groan rattled in this throat.

"What is it?" She edged closer to the bed. "Are you in pain?"

"No. I mean, yes, but no." His voice muffled by the large bite in his mouth. "That tastes good. Like, really good."

"Oh," she tugged shyly on the hem of her shorts. "Thanks."

"You made that?"

"Yes." She had seen that reaction before, each time she delivered one of Mrs. Greyson's flower bouquets. Surprise mixed with pure enjoyment. She loved that look.

"Where did you learn to cook like that?"

"My mom. She taught me."

"Remind me to thank her someday."

"She passed away when I was twelve."

Ty stopped chewing. "I'm so sorry. I didn't know. Amanda didn't …"

"It's okay." She cut him off. "Really." She didn't want the pity.

"Does that mean you've been cooking like this since you were twelve?"

"Longer, actually. But I'd like to think I've gotten better over the years. Some of my oldest memories are of me sitting on the kitchen counter helping my mom.

I would crack eggs, measure, and mix ingredients, way before I was old enough to reach the stove. I'd say I was cooking by the age of five, maybe?"

"I'm pretty sure I was eating dirt when I was five. Definitely not cooking or doing anything else productive. Would you mind getting me another bite?" He held out his fork. "I'm hungrier than I thought."

She took his fork and twisted up another hive of noodles. His skin was warm against hers when she placed it back in his hand.

"You really didn't have to cook for us, much less bring it up here. But I'm glad you did. I wanted to say thank you."

"For what?"

"Amanda told me you stayed here until she got back, in case I needed anything. That you were asleep in that chair when she walked in the door." Unable to turn his neck, he cut his eyes toward the chair. "You didn't have to do that either. But I appreciate it."

"It's not a problem. To be honest, it's the best sleep I've had in weeks."

"You're kidding, right?"

"I wish I was." She pointed toward the chair. "May I?"

"Please." His eyes followed her as she took a seat. "What happened?"

"Excuse me?" His question caught her off guard.

"That scar on your hand. What happened?"

She looked down at the pinkish-white line that streaked across the back of her hand and then turned her fist his direction. "Peach cobbler. Rookie mistake. I bumped the upper rack in the oven trying to take it out." It rolled off her tongue effortlessly because it was the same story she'd told many times before.

But it was just that.

A story.

"Chicken Alfredo, peach cobbler—I'm impressed. To this day, Amanda can't even make a grilled cheese sandwich. I hope Kyle likes takeout. Poor guy."

"What about Kyle?" Amanda bounced back into the room, carrying three cans of soda and some straws.

"Nothing. Where is he anyway?" Ty asked. "I figured he would be up here with you, stuck to your hip."

"He is helping his friend Brad do something to his truck. I'm not sure what, though. You know me and vehicles; none of that makes sense to me." Bubbles hissed when she popped the top on a can of Sprite. She pushed in a straw and walked it over to Katie.

"About Brad …" Katie took the drink from Amanda. "I ran into him last night."

"You did? Where?" Amanda asked.

"The grocery store. After I left here. He asked me out on a date."

"Well???" Amanda pried. "Don't leave us hanging. What did you say? Are you going to go?"

"I kind of told him I was already seeing someone." She twirled her straw. "I know it's a lie, but I panicked. I didn't know what else to say. And then he started talking about your wedding and all of the events we would be at together. I thought, *Great, I'm going to be alone and he's going to know I lied.*"

"Why did you lie?" Ty asked. "Is this guy some kind of jerk or something?"

"No, it's not that. I don't really know him, that's all. I just wasn't comfortable saying yes."

"Makes sense. Don't sweat it. I will be at all of those events, too. If you want to, just tell him you're with me. I don't mind and he won't know any different. Consider it my way of saying thank you for the food." He tried to shift in the bed, but the pain thwarted his efforts. "I'll be there if I can move, that is."

Katie's headlights faded into the dark when she turned off the ignition. Back at her apartment, she walked around to the passenger side of the car and grabbed the paper bag full of empty bowls from the front seat. A swift summer breeze kissed her face and she stifled a yawn.

Amanda had suggested Katie go home after she caught her dozing off in the chair next to Ty's bed. She couldn't help it. Not long after they finished eating, Ty's nurse administered his nightly dose of pain medication. When they dimmed the lights and lowered their voices so he could rest, it was as if she had morphine pumping through her veins as well. Her eyelids lagged with every blink until they lost the fight and finally closed.

And that chair. There was something about that chair.

The car honked when she pushed the button to lock the car. She slid her key into the front door and turned it counterclockwise. As it spun, there was no resistance. No thud of the deadbolt releasing its grip. No anything.

The door was already unlocked.

Plastic bowls spilled out onto the sidewalk when the bag tucked under her arm hit the ground. She pulled her key from the door and flipped the lid open on the pepper spray that hung from her key ring. Heart racing, she cracked the door, reached her hand inside and turned on the light.

Don't panic, Katie. You probably left it unlocked. You left in a hurry. Your hands were full. You even forgot to change clothes. She tried to reason with herself, but a nagging feeling kept her on defense …

… but you never forget to lock the door.

The hinges creaked as she pushed the door open wide enough to enter. "Hello?" she called. Her voice quivered.

No response.

She surveyed her surroundings as she passed through the living room and into the kitchen. Everything was as she left it. Two dirty pans on top of the stove and a baking sheet sprinkled with bed crumbs sat on a hot pad near the oven. She walked over and pressed a button on the range fan to kill its droning hum. Another creak escaped the door hinges as the wind whistled by and the blinds on the patio door swayed, feeling the touch of the current. When she separated them and looked down, the broom handle lay comfortably in its place.

She crossed the living room toward her bedroom. The door teetered, slightly ajar. "Hello?" she called again. Her chest inflated with a deep breath, and at the count of three, she forcefully shoved her way in, aiming the pepper spray with both hands like a loaded pistol. A faint click sounded behind her. When she turned around, the front door she had left open for a quick escape … was closed.

Chapter 10
NINE YEARS EARLIER

Katie sat in the bed and turned her jacket inside out. She checked the pockets one more time, hoping by some chance she had overlooked it. Nothing. She ran her hands inside the evidence bag and again through the folds of her covers. Still nothing.

"What does the locket look like?" Burns had his pad and pen ready to jot down her response.

"It is shaped like a heart." Katie made the shape of a heart with her fingers, as if that would offer a better description of the locket. "When you open it there are two pictures inside; an older picture of my mom and dad and one of me as a baby."

"What color is it?"

"The heart is silver and it's on a long, silver chain."

"And you are sure you had it with you?" Burns inquired.

"Yes. I always have it with me. I don't wear it when I run, so I took it off before I started and put it in my jacket pocket."

"Is there anything else you can tell me about it?"

"It's engraved on one side …," Katie's voice trailed off. "And it means everything to me."

"Okay. I will revisit the trail where we found your jacket and see if I can locate it for you. Maybe it fell out of the pocket when my detective picked it up. With all of the leaves on the ground, it's possible he could have missed it."

"Please find it," she pleaded. "I beg you. I really need it back."

"I will do my best, Katie. I promise." Burns knew they had already scoured every inch of those woods and the area around the trail looking for evidence, but if the locket was that important to her, he was willing to look again. He kept stacking promises on top of promises, but he was beginning to doubt his ability to keep them.

Mary had bought the locket as soon as she found out she was pregnant. Shiny and silver, it was everything she dreamed of, including the inscription she had the local jeweler engrave on the back: Three Hearts Make One Whole. She placed a picture of her and Carl on one side and left the other vacant, waiting for the baby to arrive. But the baby never came.

After her miscarriage, she held on to the locket and the promise that it stood for: that one day the missing piece of her heart would be complete. That side of the locket stayed empty longer than she had anticipated, but it made the moment of being able to place Katie's picture inside all the sweeter.

Just before Katie's twelfth birthday, on the day she gave Katie the news of her cancer diagnosis, Mary retrieved the locket from her jewelry box and placed it around Katie's neck. Katie looked down at the silver heart and back up at her mother with eyes full of fear and sadness. Mary knew her prognosis was grim, and although she had left those details out when sharing her news, she could tell Katie already sensed what lay ahead.

The next few months were difficult for the family. Carl juggled his time between the hardware store and spending time with his wife. Being the owner gave him a certain amount of freedom with his schedule, but he had a small staff and a mountain of responsibilities, which meant he couldn't disappear for extended periods of time. It was the only source of income they had, and with the influx of medical bills piling up it was important to keep things running smoothly.

Katie cooked most of the meals and did her best to keep the house clean. On occasion, she rode her bicycle to the market to pick up necessities—items like milk, eggs, toilet paper—no more in one trip than would fit in two sacks. She hung one from each of her pink handlebars and pedaled her way back to the house. After dinner was done and put away and everyone was settled in for the night, she would close her bedroom door, turn on her lamp, and begin her homework.

Mary felt her body changing, but she relished in the love surrounding her and consistently gave thanks for the time she had left with the two hearts that beat in rhythm with hers. As her lung cancer progressed and it became increasingly difficult to breathe, she spent more nights than not in the hospital. Hooked to machines and drained of every ounce of energy, Katie barely recognized the woman lying in the bed when her dad took her for a visit. Mary's once full, blonde hair was thin and brittle from her treatments. Her skin had grown pale and lost its elasticity and shine. And skinny. She was so skinny. Mary had always been thin, but her gaunt figure was proof of an illness trying hard to rob her of her life.

Amidst the physical decline, the one thing that never wavered was the sound of her voice. Even if it was a tad softer than before, she still spoke with the same angelic tone and remained positive to the bitter end.

"Easter Egg, come a little closer."

Katie took a few steps and arrived at the side of the bed. Carl lowered the bed rail and she scooted in even closer.

"I want you to know something." She brushed Katie's cheek with her hand.

"What is it, Momma?"

"I know that one day I won't be here anymore," Mary's body told her that day was quickly approaching, "but I want you to know that I will always be with you. You may not be able to see me, but I will be here." She lowered her hand from Katie's cheek and placed it on her chest. "In here." She lightly tapped Katie's heart, the veins visible beneath her translucent skin.

Katie's chin quivered. "I'm going to miss you so much."

"I know," she acquiesced. "Our time together may not have been as long as we had hoped for, but it was so full of love and we have so many incredible memories to hold on to." She covered her mouth for a wet cough and took a moment to catch her breath. "I am so proud of the beautiful young lady you are growing up to be, and being your mother has been the absolute best part of my life. You are a special little girl and I will always be watching over you."

Katie bent over and softly laid her head on her mom's chest. Crackles popped in her lungs with the ebb and flow of her breath. "I love you so much."

"I love you, too, Easter Egg. More than you will ever know." She leaned forward and kissed the top of Katie's head, which prompted another wet cough. "Please don't be sad. I know you are too young to understand, but there is power in a mother's love. If you find yourself missing me, just hold on to your locket … I will be near."

Burns' trip out to Black Bear Trail to find the locket was a bust, as he assumed it would be, but that did not stop him from spending a few hours of his day digging through leaves and sifting through dirt to try and find it. He promised Katie he would go back and look for the locket, and that is exactly what he did.

He worked up an appetite tramping through the woods and, although it was a little late in the day for lunch, he pulled into the drive-thru at the local cafe on his way back to the precinct. His squad car often doubled as a dining room, and today was no different. The hamburger, fries and large Diet Coke he ordered were gone before he pulled into the parking lot at the station, and all that remained were empty, greasy food wrappers stuffed inside a white paper sack. He backed into the parking space closest to the entrance and got out of the car. The sound of air bubbled through the straw as he sucked the last bit of soda from his cup before tossing it and the rest of his trash in the can outside the front door. A muffled belch escaped his throat as he walked inside.

It was quiet back at the station. The officers on duty were out on patrol and the lack of noise coming from the scanner was proof of an uneventful day. He glanced at the bulletin board on the way to his desk, but the only new posting was a sign-up sheet for an upcoming charity golf tournament. The other postings still the same as before: A picture of a missing teenage boy from a neighboring county; a hand-colored card from the fourth grade class, thankful for their tour of the facility; and several glossy photos, curled at the edges, from last year's company Christmas party. It was a casino theme. The picture of the guys at the craps table celebrating Wakeland's lucky toss of the dice remained his favorite.

He pulled his radio out of its holster and placed it and his keys on his desk. The dim, orange glow from the desk lamp served as a reminder of several consecutive nights of no sleep, and he rubbed both eyes vigorously as he took a seat. He tore the top page off a yellow legal pad to expose a blank sheet of paper, retrieved an ink pen from his middle desk drawer, and started to write. Everything he knew about the case spilled out on the page.

An hour passed and he was no closer to a resolution than when he arrived. Granted, Damon had no alibi or anyone to corroborate his whereabouts on the night in question, but without any witnesses or evidence linking him to the crime scene Burns still lacked probable cause to make an arrest.

Well … there *was* the toboggan.

Burns knew if he ordered forensics to run a DNA profile on the hat it would be an obvious match, but he wanted to exhaust all other avenues and leave that as an absolute last resort. Either Damon had done an exceptional job at covering his tracks, or Burns was simply missing the obvious. He decided to take one more stab at social media, hoping to stumble upon a new post or picture that might be of help. He logged in to his computer, opened a tab in Google, and pulled up Damon's profile on Facebook. No recent activity. Just as he went to close the web browser, he noticed Damon had a new cover photo. It was a picture he had taken of himself, standing in front of a bathroom mirror, wearing a backward ball cap that rested high on his head. He had one eye closed, and the hand not holding his phone was placed over his mouth, every finger tucked under except for the middle one. Burns shook his head.

He further studied the picture for anything out of the ordinary. Damon wore a dark green t-shirt with a black bear on the front that incorporated the slogan 'don't poke the bear.' The bathroom mirror was spotted with overspray from the sink, and behind him, a blue and white curtain was pushed to one side of a fiberglass shower. Eyes squinted, he leaned in toward the monitor. He clicked to enlarge the image and leaned in even further.

"Surely he's not that dumb," he mumbled.

Just above his collar was the glint of a sliver chain that disappeared beneath his green cotton tee. Thoughts raced through his head, his skin prickly with hope that this might be the ticket. *What if the victim's necklace hadn't been lost? Rather, what if it had been stolen? Better yet, what if it had been taken as a souvenir or a trophy from successfully pulling off a violent attack? And what if the assailant was dumb enough to wear it?*

He straightened his back and pulled away from the monitor, realizing that no matter how close he got to the screen, or how much he enlarged the photo, technology wasn't advanced enough to see what was beneath Damon's shirt. It didn't keep him from wondering if he were to actually poke the bear, would he be met with the resistance of a heart-shaped locket? Burns stroked his chin, still smooth from his morning shave.

Something felt off.

As much as he wanted this to be the piece of evidence that linked Damon to the victim on the night of her attack, something didn't add up. On the day of his interrogation, this kid was cunning and deceitful. He purposely orchestrated his responses to be vague, and he knew how to word things in a way to evade self-incrimination. These qualities didn't coincide with the type of guy who would slip up and post a picture online of him wearing the victim's necklace, even if it wasn't fully on display. If he did in fact take it, which was within the realm of possibility, Damon was much too smart for that.

After placing his hand back on his mouse, Burns clicked to open the photo album linked to Damon's page. He scrolled through dozens of pictures before landing on one posted a little over a year ago. It was an image of Damon wearing a grey toboggan and a plaid long-sleeve shirt, arms propped up on the tailgate of a black pickup. And around his neck … that same silver chain.

Damn it.

Frustrated with yet another dead end, he pushed himself back from the computer. Hands clasped behind his neck to support his head, the spring of his chair back was extended as far as it would stretch. The chair creaked as he swiveled slightly, mulling over his next move. Part of him felt he was so hell bent on nailing this kid that fabricating evidence ranked higher than investigating the truth. He hadn't even considered the possibility of another suspect. Based on the victim's testimony, she had spotted a red Jeep at the scene, yet there had been zero effort put into following that lead. And the young man who found the victim and called 911—outside of his initial statement, Burns hadn't even talked to the guy. No additional questioning. No verifying his account that placed him in the woods that evening. No *what if he was really the perp and not the hero?* His sole focus had been on finding evidence beyond a reasonable doubt that would implicate Damon McGregor. Everything in his gut told him that it was the right thing to do. But what if he wasn't the guy?

The grey walls felt as if they were closing in on him. He stared at the photo of his wife perched on his desk. "What am I missing?" he whispered, attempting to summon her help. Back in Tarrant County, he had gotten in a bad habit of discussing case files with Laura. Not in detail, but he shared enough information to help process his thoughts when his mental regurgitation of evidence kept him from sleeping at night. Gifted with an analytical mind, she would often interject with a fresh perspective and on occasion, something she said prompted a resolution to the case. This rocked along for quite some time, until one day she came to him and said she couldn't handle it anymore. Although he'd tried his best to shelter her from the gruesome logistics of his workload, the stories began to seep into her dreams and she told him that was it. From that day forward, he never mentioned another case.

Realizing he had not called to check on her, he pulled his cell phone from the front pocket of his uniform and dialed his wife's number. She and Sarah were in the kitchen making peanut butter and jelly sandwiches for an early dinner picnic out on the deck. He could hear Sarah squealing and laughing in the background over the repetitive yelp of a dog. The distant sound of her voice brought a smile to his face, but created an ache in his chest. When his wife informed him they had decided to stay overnight because her parents wanted to take Sarah to the zoo the next day, the ache intensified. Even though part of him was relieved, he still longed to be where they were.

As she spoke, he found solace in her words. They were a welcome break from an otherwise stressful day. She told him about fastening Sarah up in her orange lifejacket to take a paddleboat ride across the pond, and how they tossed little pieces of bread into the water to feed the ducks. How Sarah spilled grape juice down her shirt on the car ride over and then laughed because the shape of the stain looked like a giraffe. When Laura asked how he was doing and how the case was going, he responded with only a single word: fine. He knew she didn't want to hear any of the specifics, and he did not want her to worry.

"I guess I better go. I want to make sure we have plenty of time to eat and be back to the house by dark. I know she'll want to chase fireflies before we turn in for the night."

"I'm glad she is having so much fun. I miss that little toot. Please hug her for me and tell her I love her," he begged. "I miss you, too, Laura," he added, shuddering at the thought of crawling into a cold, empty bed.

"I know, but we will be home tomorrow. Try to get some rest tonight." She felt his exhaustion through the phone.

They each said goodbye and he ended the call. He tossed his phone down on the desk and went into the break room to start a pot of coffee. He replaced the old filter with a new one and peeled the lid back from the metal can. Instead of scooping the grounds into the coffee maker, he walked back to his desk, the open coffee can still in his hand. He stood there, staring at his cell phone. *Whoever was driving could have dropped their phone.* He replayed the excuse Laura had given him that morning when trying to justify the truck parked down the road from their house.

Burns set the coffee can down and grabbed Katie's file from the black mesh tray on the corner of his desk. He flipped through several pages before he found the typed report of the victim's initial interview. He read the entire thing, but did not find what he was looking for. He remembered something, though. Something about a phone call ...

How could you have missed that, you idiot? He felt accosted by his own thoughts.

While at the hospital, Burns had been so focused on the toboggan and getting Katie to confirm it was Damon's, that he skipped right over her saying that she had a fight with Damon on the telephone before she left for her run. Katie hadn't mentioned that the first time Burns interviewed her. Not only did they have a fight, it was of a sexual nature. If Damon made that call from his cell phone and was anywhere near Katie's house at the time, records from the cell provider would place Damon near the crime scene at the time of the assault.

Motive ... *check*. Probable cause ... *check.*

Thank you, Honey.

As he filled out the paperwork to request a warrant from the judge, his radio keyed up.

"406 to 401, you copy?"

"This is 401, go ahead," Burns replied.

"In response to the BOLO for the black Chevrolet pickup, license plate CCA4506, I have located the vehicle, over."

"Please advise of its location, over."

"The truck was spotted heading south on County Road 3600, over."

Shit.

Chapter 11
PRESENT

The air conditioner struggled to keep the car cool as she waited, parked in the circular drive outside of Amanda's house. It was a tan two-story brick with stone accents and more arched windows than she could count. Towering spiral junipers framed both sides of the double mahogany front doors, and three chimneys protruded from different regions of the dark-shingled roof. The house stretched across the top of a hill overlooking a private lake. Amanda's family had money, and it showed.

Katie massaged her temples. She couldn't remember the last time she'd had a decent night's sleep, and her eyes ached in their sockets. Aside from the nightmares that often visited while she slept, her insomnia had amped up a notch, driven by a fear that the cops were wrong.

The two officers who responded to her trespassing call said she must have forgotten to lock the door. They were unaware that that part of her routine came as naturally as breathing. When she mentioned that the front door closed behind her, they debunked the possibility of an intruder with a backward cliché: when one door opens, another one closes. One of the officers stood with Katie near the front door and the other officer stood just outside of her bedroom. When he forcefully swung open her bedroom door, just as Katie had done that night, she watched as the front door moved, almost as if a vacuum sucked it closed. They performed the experiment numerous times to help calm her nerves, but all it did was further convince Katie she was losing her mind.

Katie's body jerked when Amanda hopped into the passenger side and closed the door. The circulating air quickly carried the scent of her perfume throughout the car.

"Wow, you look like crap." She slung her designer bag over the back of Katie's seat and placed it on the floorboard.

"Thanks."

"No, for real. Are you okay? We can do this another day if you don't feel good."

"I'm just tired. I haven't been sleeping well. How's Ty doing? Is he glad to be home?"

"I'm sure he would rather be at his house, but that wasn't an option. At least here he has people to help him; he still can't get around very well. Did you want to go in and say hi?"

"Maybe later." Katie pressed the brake and put the car in gear. "We better get moving or we are going to be late."

Mrs. Greyson had given her the morning off. They had a ten o'clock appointment at a bridal boutique downtown to find Katie a dress for the wedding. As much as she wanted to accept Amanda's offer for a rain check, Katie knew cancelling the appointment wasn't really an option. The wedding was less than two months away, which left little time for dress alterations if needed. She'd never worn a formal gown before, and had no idea what to expect. Her wardrobe consisted mainly of athletic clothes for running, bulky sweatshirts, and a few items she could mix and match to wear to work or out with Amanda. Mrs. Greyson didn't have a strict dress code at the flower shop, another reason Katie loved her job.

When they arrived downtown, Katie circled the block looking for a shaded place to park. Everyone else must have had the same idea. The Texas heat could fry an egg on the dashboard of a car left parked in the sun for any length of time, and the only spots available were those in its direct path.

Amanda pointed to a pair of brake lights in the distance. "Over there—I think they are leaving."

Katie made her way over just in time to slide into the spot as a Ford pickup pulled away. Parked beneath the arms of an old oak tree near the courthouse, it was a short hike to the boutique. A southern breeze blew, and the snap hooks of the Texas flag clattered against the pole as they made their way down the sidewalk. They passed a man wearing a baseball cap sitting crossed-legged on a park bench with his head buried in a newspaper and two heavy-set women with grey hair who talked as fast as they fanned themselves. The morning crowd downtown was different than she was accustomed to.

"Amanda, Katie ... wait up!" They turned in the direction of the voice to see Brad, jogging in place across the street. He waited for a car to pass before crossing over to join them. "Fancy meeting you here." He smelled of an odd combination of bacon and cologne.

"You are just as bad as Katie," Amanda chimed in, "running in this heat. What is wrong with you two?"

"I didn't know you were a runner?" A slight wheeze accompanied his breath, a sign of unconditioned lungs. He continually bounced back and forth on the pads of his feet. Her calves cramped thinking about it. "I'm only a beginner, just getting started. Maybe we can run together some time and you can give me some pointers?"

"Sure, I guess." She shrugged.

His head swiveled like an owl, brows raised. "Where is your car?" he asked Amanda. "Kyle told me you finally got it out of the shop."

"I did, but we are in Katie's car. We parked back that way," she motioned with her thumb over her shoulder. "Only shady spot we could find."

"You're lucky you found one. Are you here getting stuff for Saturday? Sounds like it's going to be fun."

"No, we are shopping for Katie's dress." Amanda checked the time on her phone and then looked back at him. "Speaking of, we better get moving. Our appointment is like ... now."

"Don't be late on my account." He slowly pulled away, jogging backward. "See you two Saturday." With that, Brad turned around and took off.

Saturday's luncheon—Katie didn't need the reminder. It was one of several events in her day planner written with dread. Social gatherings weren't really her thing, but this one was to celebrate the wedding party and a few of Amanda and Kyle's closest friends. As maid of honor, she was obligated to attend.

"I guess that means Kyle invited him to come?"

"Sounds like it. I'm not surprised, though. They've been hanging out a lot lately." A buzzer sounded when Amanda opened the door to the boutique. She stepped in and Katie caught the door with her hand as it started to close behind her. Before stepping in herself, she glanced back in the direction that Brad took off jogging. He was nowhere to be seen.

Hilda, the owner of the boutique, checked the girls in for their appointment and left them to peruse the store while she finished with her last client. She worked by appointment only. The building was an original storefront to downtown, and even with its modern renovations held characteristics of its historic flair. Wooden rods suspended from the tall ceilings displayed a sea of gowns, each perfectly spaced on the racks. A series of track lighting and intricate chandeliers cast an ominous glow on the exposed brick walls and the refurbished hardwood floors sounded their age beneath each step. In the waiting area, an animal-skin rug lay beneath a glass-topped table that held a fresh flower arrangement; Katie recognized it as one of Mrs. Greyson's masterpieces and massaged a lily petal on her way by. She felt like royalty and completely out of place, all at the same time.

"You know, it's weird," Katie trailed slowly behind Amanda, staring blankly at the endless row of dresses. She had no clue what she was shopping for. "Before that night at Joe's, I had never seen Brad before. Now I seem to run into him everywhere. Don't you think that's odd?"

"Not really. You've probably run into him a million times before, you just didn't know who he was. Nor did he know you. Don't overthink it."

"I guess you're right." Katie sighed. Leave it to Amanda to give a simple yet logical explanation. "I've been doing just that a lot lately. Overthinking things. Do you remember the night I brought you and Ty food to the hospital?"

"Yeah."

"When I got home that night, I thought someone had been in my apartment. I called the cops."

"Explains why you haven't been sleeping well." Amanda stopped sifting through dresses and looked over her shoulder at Katie. "Wait, that was more than a week ago. Why didn't you tell me?"

"There was no point, really. The cops didn't find anything. It was just more of me doing what I do: making something out of nothing. I felt dumb for calling them."

"I'm glad it turned out to be nothing but I still wish you would have told me." Amanda turned her attention back to the row of dresses. "You could have stayed at the house with me." She pulled a satin slip dress from rack and held it in front of Katie. When Katie crinkled her nose and shook her head in disapproval, Amanda returned it to the rack.

"I appreciate the offer, but isn't Ty already staying there, too?"

"Yes, but there are plenty of extra rooms. Plus, my parents love the company. They always say the house feels empty. They would love to have you. So would I. Lots of wedding stuff to do." Amanda held out another dress.

"I guess that one isn't too terrible." She took the hanger from Amanda and folded the dress over her arm. "I can't believe you are going to get me in a dress."

"You definitely aren't wearing a sweatshirt and tennis shoes in my wedding. I love you and all, but that is where I draw the line."

Amanda sat on a plush white sofa outside the dressing room and flipped through a bridal magazine while she waited for Katie. "I need my something blue."

"You lost me on that one," Katie's voice strained as she fought to reach the zipper behind her back. She refused to ask for help getting dressed.

"You know, something old, something new, something borrowed, something blue. I need my something blue."

"If you make fun of me," the curtain opened and Katie walked out of the dressing room. "You'll have a pretty black and blue eye that might qualify. Well?" she held up her hands. "What do you think?"

Amanda sat without saying a word. For once in her life, she was speechless.

"Why are you looking at me like that? I told you I don't wear dresses."

Still silence.

"Say something!" Katie insisted, embarrassed.

"It's perfect." Amanda dropped the magazine on the sofa and walked over to her. "I'm not sure why you insist on hiding that body under those bulky clothes you wear. You look incredible. Here, let me try something." She reached up and pulled down Katie's ponytail. Her long, dark hair fell against her back. Amanda used her fingers to separate her locks and pulled a few strands around to frame her face. "There, that's better. You are going to blow everyone away. Turn around and see for yourself."

Katie spun around to face the mirror. The spaghetti-strap chiffon gown draped all the way to the floor. It hugged her full chest and a silk band fit snugly around her thin waist. Her dark hair popped against its champagne hue and a high slit offered a peek of her toned thigh. She didn't recognize herself. For the first time in as long as she could remember—maybe ever—she felt … pretty. The dress swooshed with her gentle sway. Layers of both visible and hidden scars melted away, and a stream of happy tears escaped the corner of her eye.

"I guess that means this is the one." Amanda pulled a tissue from her purse and offered it to Katie. "They say that when there are tears, it's the one."

"I think that applies to the bride finding her dress, not the maid of honor. If I cry, it just means I'm weird." She grabbed the tissue and tried to catch the next stream of tears before they fell.

"I am kind of disappointed, though. I thought finding a dress you liked would be much harder than this. This wasn't even a challenge. And you know me; I love a good shopping challenge."

"I think I'm as shocked as you are disappointed. Here," she handed the tissue back to Amanda. "This can be your something used."

"Ummm, gross! I take back everything nice I said about you. And that's not one of the items on the list anyway. It's something old, new, borrowed and blue."

"That's right," Katie grinned. "If all you need is something blue, what are your other items?"

"My something old is this locket my grandmother gave me," she pulled it out from underneath the neckline of her white sleeveless blouse. "My something new will be my shoes, and I'm using my stepmom's veil for my borrowed item."

Katie's heart slammed against her chest. She heard nothing after the word locket and couldn't take her eyes off the one dangling around Amanda's neck.

"May I?" she reached out her hand.

"Of course."

Katie slid her fingers beneath the chain and pulled the locket in for a closer look. Silver chain. Locket shaped like a heart. She took a deep breath and flipped it over expecting to see an inscription on the back, but it was blank. She let it fall back to Amanda's chest and slowly exhaled, keeping her gaze fixed on the locket.

"You look like you've seen a ghost."

"I feel like I have. I don't mean to stare. It's just … I used to have one very similar to yours. My mom gave it to me when I was little."

"You don't have it anymore?"

"No. I lost it when I was seventeen."

"We need to get you a new one then," Amanda smiled. To her, everything could be fixed with a shopping trip and a credit card.

"I wish it was that easy. That one can't be replaced. It wasn't only a gift, it belonged to my mother, and right before she died, she told me if I was missing her, to hold onto the locket and she would be near. As stupid as it sounds, it worked. If I was sad or having a bad day, I would squeeze it tightly, and that night I would dream about her. Or something subtle would happen that would remind me of her. It made me feel like she really was around, and it helped calm me down. It's been nine years since I lost it, and I haven't dreamed of her since."

"I don't think that sounds stupid at all. Here," she reached around to the back of her neck and unlatched the locket. "You can borrow this one until the wedding." After she fastened it around Katie's neck, she freed the remainder of her hair from underneath the chain. "I know it's not the real deal, but who knows, maybe it will help you have a dream about your mom."

Katie took her hand and placed it on the locket. No words would come, only more tears.

"Okay, ladies," Hilda returned with an armful of dresses. "I will get these added to the dressing room for you and we can get this party going."

"That won't be necessary. We've already found the one we want." Amanda pulled out her wallet. "I want to pay for the one she's wearing."

"That was fast. I will take care of that now."

Hilda took the tag that dangled from Katie's side, but Katie didn't move a muscle. Locket clenched tightly in her fist, all she could do was smile.

Less than half an hour in the store, and it already felt ten degrees warmer outside when they left than when they had arrived. "I sure hope something changes with this weather soon, or we are all going to melt at my wedding. I knew I should have gone with a New Year's Eve event. Or picked a venue in Alaska. Fall in Texas is about as predictable as the lottery."

"I'm sure it will be fine." Katie carried her new dress wrapped in a long plastic bag in one hand, and had yet to let go of the locket with the other. "I have a little bit of time before I have to be back at work, do you want to grab some lunch? We can stop at Joe's. My treat."

"You know me," Amanda rubbed her stomach. "I can always eat."

They rounded the corner and, with the car in sight, Katie noticed a piece of paper stuck to her windshield. It appeared someone had hit every car on the block. She walked up to the car and pulled the piece of paper from beneath the windshield wiper. It was a flyer for Quickie's Pizza. "Instead of Joe's, let's try something new. How does pizza sound?"

She held out the flyer for Amanda to see, and that's when she saw it. Written on the back in blue ink was a phone number and a message: *We need to talk.*

"Umm, Amanda?" Katie folded the flyer and stuck it in her purse. "Does the invitation to stay at your place for a while still stand? If so, I think I'm going to take you up on that."

Chapter 12
NINE YEARS EARLIER

By the time Burns made it outside of town, the black Chevy was nowhere to be found. The response to his BOLO indicated the truck had been spotted heading south on County Road 3600, the same road Burns lived on. He doubted it was a coincidence, since his wife had seen a truck matching that exact description parked near his place earlier that morning. Damon was either extremely brave or extremely stupid, but either way, he was playing with fire. He had no idea who he was dealing with and how easily his life could be ruined.

Burns patrolled the streets for more than an hour with no luck. It was a short drive from one end of town to the other, but covering all of the roads that webbed off the main drag took some time. They were narrow and curvy, and the county was not the best at maintaining their surfaces. The potholes served as speed deterrents, and in certain areas, two cars were unable to pass one another without one pulling off of the road and into the ditch. On a normal day, he enjoyed the slower pace that came with country living. But this was not a normal day.

Frustrated with yet another failed attempt at locating Damon, he decided to head back to the house. He had no legal premise to arrest Damon even if he did find him—not yet anyway—but he still wanted to lay eyes on him. The fact that Damon was lurking in the shadows made Burns feel uneasy. There weren't many places to hide in a town as small as Brownsboro, but somehow Damon managed to do just that.

Burns was mentally and physically exhausted. He pulled into the drive and parked his squad car behind the house, outside the garage. The place looked abandoned with his wife and daughter out of town. No lights on inside. No movement behind the windows. Coming home to an empty house was not his favorite, but it would only be for one night. Laura and Sarah would be back after their trip to the zoo with his in-laws in the morning, and the house would once again be filled with life and the giggles of his little girl. Until then, at least he had the dog to keep him company. "Atlas!" he called out, followed by a whistle. "Come here, boy!"

Atlas stayed outside during the day and usually came in just before the sun went down. Burns had adopted him from a shelter when they moved out of the city. He had tall pointy ears and brown and black fur, and Burns fell in love the moment he laid eyes on him. German Shepherds were notoriously good guard dogs, and living in the country, he served as a little extra protection—and added peace of mind—when the girls were home alone. Around people he was accustomed to, Atlas had the demeanor of a gentle giant. He was great with children, especially Sarah, and Burns had trained him to do numerous tricks. He knew all of the easy ones like sit, roll over, and shake, but Burns had also taught Atlas to ring a bell that hung from the back doorknob when he needed to go outside to use the bathroom.

"Atlas!" he yelled again and let out another whistle. It was odd for him not to be pacing at the door and wagging his tail, eagerly waiting to get inside. The sound of Burns' squad car coming up the drive normally summoned him, even if he had wandered off into the woods to chase a rabbit or a squirrel. "Silly mutt, where are you? I don't have time for this," he mumbled under his breath. The sliver of moon high in the sky didn't offer much guidance, so he grabbed his flashlight and made a lap around the house. He checked the few places Atlas would burrow down to sleep, but they were all empty, so he widened the diameter of his path and made another lap. As he walked, he waved the flashlight back and forth to survey the ground before him. His voice trailed off in the distance with each call for his dog.

He stumbled over a buckled tree root pushing out of the ground and dropped his flashlight. *Are you kidding me? I need a break. Just one break* he thought to himself. First, he couldn't find Katie's locket. Then, he couldn't find Damon, much less the evidence needed to convict him. Now, he was out fumbling around in the dark because he couldn't find his dog. He put both hands on his shoulders and dug his fingertips into the knots buried deep within his muscles. They rolled beneath his fingers and he felt a warm sensation shoot up both sides of his neck to his face. He needed this case to be over—and to get some sleep—but right now, he needed to find his dog.

When he bent down to pick up the flashlight, his eyes instinctively followed its beam of light along the ground and into the pitch-black darkness of the woods. The trees were thick and objects in their shadows were indiscernible, including the one that intercepted his light. He stood up with his flashlight in hand and walked toward the woods. Leaves rustled in the darkness. He reached down, unsnapped his holster, and pulled out his pistol. He aimed it in the direction of the noise, resting his wrist on the arm holding the flashlight. The light bounced from limb to limb as he quickly scanned the surrounding woods. He saw nothing. He aimed both the light and the gun back toward the object on the ground and continued forward in a crouched fashion. Now close enough to see, he squeezed his eyes shut and then opened them wide, trying to refocus—convinced his tired mind was playing tricks on him. That what he saw was nothing more than an illusion created by a twisted cast of shadows. He slid his gun back in its holster, knelt down, and placed his hand on his dog. His fur was wet. When he pulled back his hand, blood dripped from his palm. Atlas was dead.

He scooped Atlas up in his arms and carried him back to the house. The trip seemed to take twice as long carrying a seventy-eight-pound dog. When he reached the house, he laid Atlas and his flashlight on the dirt next to the driveway and fell onto the ground next to him. Legs in front of him with bent knees out to the side, his back went limp and he slumped forward. The pounding in his chest rocked his body.

Burns knew that living in the country posed a risk for coyotes and what that meant having an outside pet. During the middle of the night, the coyotes often howled a chorus from deep within the woods, calling on one another after a hunt. A moment of guilt washed over him, knowing he should have stopped by the house before dark to let Atlas inside with Laura out of town. It was something he always took care of when she was gone but it never crossed his mind. He was too busy chasing a phantom black truck well into the night, and because of that his dog was dead. He reached over and combed through his fur. Surprisingly, there were no bite marks. No visible cuts or gashes of any kind. He looked for the heaviest concentration of blood and traced it to its source …

That son of a bitch killed my dog.

Any energy Burns had left vanished with the last fling of the shovel. The anger that churned in his gut didn't offer enough adrenaline to find Damon and do the things to him he had vividly imagined doing the entire time he dug the hole. His white undershirt was covered in dirt and sweat and Atlas was now buried under the oak tree in the backyard, his favorite resting spot. In his line of work, Burns was used to death. It was an unfortunate part of his job. But this pained him in a way he hadn't expected. He loved that damn dog, but more importantly, so did Sarah. And now he was going to have to find a way to tell his daughter that her Atwas was dead.

Burns took the shovel back to the garage, grabbed his dress shirt and gun off the hood of his squad car, and went inside. Too tired to eat, he passed straight through the kitchen and into the bedroom. The heaviness of his pistol made a deep thud against the wood when he placed it on his nightstand. He kicked off his boots at the foot of the bed and dropped his dirty clothes on the floor next to them before heading to the bathroom. The hot water from the shower poured over his head until the entire room was engulfed in steam. After the water ran cold, he grabbed a towel from the hook on the wall and dried off. He threw on a pair of grey boxer briefs and a white t-shirt and sat down on the edge of the bed facing his nightstand. Staring at his gun, he took a few deep breaths. He knew what he needed to do. It was time. No matter that it crossed the line of justice he was sworn to uphold, it was time. Damon apparently wasn't going to stop, and Burns needed to do whatever it took to protect his family and that young girl lying in the hospital. He shuddered at the thought of what could have happened had Laura and Sarah been home. It was late, so he decided to wait until the morning to call and tell Laura she needed to stay at her parents until he could get this guy behind bars, which now would happen sooner than later. That is, if he could find him.

"Daddy!!!" Katie screamed at the top of her lungs. Panting and covered in sweat, she screamed again before he had a chance to respond. "Daddy!" Her shrill cry bounced off the walls.

The room lit only by the glow of the television, Carl rose from the sofa bed as fast as his knees would allow and hurried to her bedside in a panic. "What is it, Sweetheart? What's wrong?"

"I had a bad dream. Someone was holding me down," she gulped air between every few words, "I couldn't get away. I couldn't scream. I tried and no sound would come out." Her body trembled profusely. She latched on to his forearm with both hands and dug in, pulling his arm into her chest.

"It was just a dream. It's over now," were the only words he could muster to try to calm her down. He noticed that the sheets were wet and not just from sweat; she had wet the bed. That was something she hadn't done since she was a small child trying to potty train.

"Daddy, he had sex with me. In my dream. I didn't want him to, but he did. I couldn't make him stop."

Carl's heart sank. He felt her tears rain down on his arm. He knew she was on the brink of remembering all that happened to her in the woods, learning what the lab results had already proven. Details of an event he hoped would be erased from her memory forever. "Oh, Katie. I'm so sorry this happened to you and that I wasn't there to protect you." He put his other arm around her back and fell into her, squeezing her tightly.

"It happened, didn't it? In real life and not just in my dream?" Even with her eyes squeezed shut, tears steadily poured out.

Carl wasn't exactly sure how to answer that question. Doctor Sheffield told him she needed to remember the events of the attack on her own, without persuasion. But this was his baby girl and she was scared and searching for answers. So he did all he knew to do.

"I'm afraid so, Sweetie."

For the next twenty minutes, he held her while she sobbed uncontrollably. He wanted to give her a chance to process the information on her own terms and be there to answer any questions she might have, but she never said another word. She cried until no more tears would fall and then released her grip on her dad. Her eyes were puffy and red and her nose was swollen shut, no longer able to move air. Carl pulled a few tissues from the box on the bedside table and handed them to Katie; the indention of her hands were still visible on his arm. There was an extra gown in the cabinet, and he asked Katie to go to the bathroom while he called the nurse to come change the sheets. He didn't want her to have to suffer the embarrassment of wetting the bed on top of everything else she was dealing with.

Katie changed clothes and tossed her soiled gown into the corner. The soreness in her arms and torso made the menial task difficult to maneuver. She washed her hands and splashed some cool water on her face to calm the throbbing in her head. When she looked up, the reflection staring back at her was that of a stranger. Dark bruises covered both cheeks and encircled her right eye, while various shades of green and yellow highlighted her jawline. The scratches on her forehead were long and jagged, scabbed with dried blood. The red from the scratches matched the color of her bloodshot eyes. Her brown hair was a matted mess and hadn't been washed in days. Someone had done a number on her, and she knew her face wasn't the only recipient of their wrath. She had seen it vividly in her dream, as real as if she'd been there: a faceless man holding her down. Replaying the memory, she turned back to the toilet and threw up.

Carl tapped on the door to let her know it was okay to come out. When she didn't answer, he slowly pulled it open and found her sitting on the floor with her back against the wall and her head down on her knees.

"Katie, Sweetie, why don't you come back to bed? The nurse put on fresh sheets and I asked if she could bring you some soup and a Sprite. Are you hungry?"

"Not really." The taste of bile coated her teeth. "But I could use something to drink."

He reached out his hand and helped her off the floor and back to the bed. Her knees were weak and she relied on him for the strength to make the trip. It wasn't long before the nurse returned with some chicken noodle soup and the Sprite Carl had requested. She also brought something for anxiety, which Carl had not mentioned when he asked her to come back to bed. Katie placed the pill on her tongue and took a drink of the Sprite. When she swallowed, she felt the cool, bubbly sensation race to the bottom of her empty stomach. She took another drink, swished it around in her mouth to wash off her teeth, and swallowed it as well. The smell of the chicken soup was tempting, but she hadn't been able to keep anything in her stomach so she passed on eating. Instead, she rolled over on her side with her back to her dad and pulled the covers up to her chin. She didn't want to talk—or think—she just wanted this to go away. She reached for her locket, just as she did every night she wanted to dream of her mom, but it wasn't there. The medicine eventually kicked in and she went back to sleep.

"Laura, I know you're ready to come home, but I need you to stay a little while longer," he pleaded with his wife over the phone.

"I didn't bring enough clothes to stay. For me or Sarah. Plus, you said you never found the truck that I saw. The one that may or may not have anything to do with the case you're working. I don't understand. Why can't we come home today?"

"You're right, I didn't physically see it. But Deputy Todd did, last night, and he said it was leaving town headed this way again."

"Well, did he follow him? To see if he stopped at our house?"

"No." His patience was growing thin with her naïveté. "He was en route to a call when he saw it. But he did confirm the plate number."

"Our place is not the only stop on that road. Maybe he was going …"

"He's dead, Laura," he interrupted her. "Atlas is dead."

There was a moment of deafening silence.

"How … what …," she searched for words, unable to formulate a sentence.

"Listen, I didn't want to tell you this over the phone, especially with you being out of town. And please don't tell Sarah. I will tell her when you get home. But this is why I need you to stay at your parents."

"Because of Atlas? How … how did he die?" she was almost afraid to ask.

"He was shot. I knew something was wrong when he wasn't waiting for me when I got home. I found him in the woods out back. It was dark, and honestly when I saw that he was bleeding, I assumed coyotes had gotten hold of him. I didn't see the bullet hole until I brought him back to the house."

"Where is he now?"

"I buried him under his favorite tree in the back yard." Standing in the kitchen in full police attire, he peered through the window blinds at the fresh mound of dirt. A storm of sadness and anger brewed in his chest. "Now do you see why I need you two to stay out of town? This is serious."

"Yes. Whatever you need us to do," she conceded, worried. "But … what about you?"

"Don't worry about me. I know it is Sunday, but I'm going to try to get the judge to sign an arrest warrant so I don't have to wait until Monday to pick this guy up. I have what I need, and as soon as I know he's behind bars you can come home."

"Oh, good. So you found proof that he's guilty?" she sounded hopeful, although she knew no details of the case.

"Like I said, I have what I need." It was the best way to summarize the situation without completely lying to his wife.

He finished his second cup of coffee and then emptied the remainder of the pot into an insulated mug to carry with him. He put the cream cheese spread he'd used on his bagel back in the refrigerator and put his dirty dishes from breakfast in the bottom of the sink. It was eight in the morning, on what was once again supposed to be his day off, but he headed into work anyway.

When he got to the office, he found the paperwork he'd started the night before on his desk. It was an unfinished requisition to subpoena cell phone records from the night of Katie's attack. She had stated that she and Damon had argued over the phone before the incident. The phone records would indicate if he was near her home when he made the call, placing him at the scene of the crime just before the attack. Knowing how long it often took to obtain those records, he pushed that requisition to the side and started on his written affidavit for arrest, including a subpoena for DNA. He wrote down all of the information he had to implicate Damon McGregor on the charge of aggravated sexual assault of a minor, Katherine Upton; his most damning piece of evidence being a grey toboggan that belonged to the accused, found at the scene of the crime.

The only thing she had to do was concentrate on doing nothing—to be perfectly still and occasionally hold her breath. The room was cold, and the repetitive tapping and thumping of the MRI did nothing for the dull pain that had taken up residence in her head. It never seemed to fully go away any more, it only varied in intensity. They offered her earplugs before the test began to help block the noise, but she refused. The last time her hearing was obstructed, someone snuck up behind her and changed her life as she knew it.

The MRI lasted about forty-five minutes. She stared at the top of the circular tan tube and wished that the magnets and radio waves looking inside her brain could somehow permanently erase everything that had happened—like a mini frontal lobotomy—taking her back to a time when deciding what to wear to school was her biggest concern of the day. A time well before that night in the woods. A time before Damon McGregor walked into her life.

Dr. Sheffield ordered the MRI to see if the swelling visible in the images from her initial assessment had diminished, and he said that if the test yielded good results she would be discharged to go home within the next few days. He was pleased with her progress, and although he explained that it could take weeks to fully recover physically, he felt it was unnecessary for her to remain in the hospital to do so. He had yet to broach the topic of mental recovery—at least not with her—and she thought maybe that came later. As far as he was concerned, she still had no memory of what happened in the woods. Neither she nor Carl had mentioned her dream, or the events that followed, when he stopped by her room for a visit that morning. She knew divulging the truth would open a new round of questioning she wasn't ready to deal with. And it wouldn't change anything. What had happened, happened, and talking about it wouldn't make it any less real. The thought of having such an intimate discussion with a complete stranger, especially a man, made her painfully uncomfortable. At seventeen, that was a conversation she wasn't even comfortable having with her father—the reason she had yet to ask him any further questions. The dream revealed more than she wished to know, and she was content keeping those details to herself.

She tried to remember what day it was. *Saturday? Sunday, maybe?* With random sleep patterns and losing an entire day somewhere at the beginning of all of this mess, time had grown elusive—not that time held any relevance at this point anyway. Whatever day it was, she was certain she'd missed her cross-country meet, and even if she hadn't, she was not in any condition to run. This was going to be the year they made it to state competition, and Katie was the team's golden ticket. She wondered what Coach Fletcher and her teammates had thought when she didn't show up to run at the district meet, and then it hit her … people were eventually going to ask what happened. Or worse, what if they were already talking about it? Suddenly the thought of going home lost all of its appeal.

Her initial reaction when she received the news of her impending release was one of relief. She was ready to sleep in her own bed, surrounded by her own things, to wear something other than a bulky hospital gown that constantly wadded up around her anytime she changed positions … but most importantly, she was ready to escape the strange looks and the secret conversations that took place at the hospital. Everyone who came into her room looked at her like she had a horn protruding from the center of her forehead. She couldn't tell if it was her battered face that everyone pitied or if there was a bulletin posted somewhere in the hospital letting everyone, down to the janitor, know the details of what happened to her. Either way, everyone looked at and treated her as if she were a piece of tempered glass that might spontaneously shatter at any moment.

And then there were the secret conversations. The whispered words in the corner of the room and the ever-popular 'Mr. Upton, would you please step outside for a moment?' all of which she hated. She believed that if they were talking about her, they should be talking to her, not behind her back. At some point between the thumping and the tapping of the MRI she realized all of the things she wanted to run away from at the hospital were going to be a million times worse once she got out. The strange looks. The whispering behind her back. It was an inescapable reality, and she was about to be sucked into the vortex of small-town hell.

She remembered back to when Damon first moved to Brownsboro and how that vortex swallowed him when numerous rumors circulated about the real reason he came to town. The more benign accusations included habitual drug use and that his parents didn't want him around because he was out of control and constantly in trouble. Another rumor said he had knocked a girl up, and when she didn't concede to his demand for an abortion, he roughed her up a little in an attempt to take care of the situation himself. He claimed it was an accident, but her accusations got him expelled from school and shipped out of town. But of all of the outlandish stories that circulated, Katie's favorite was the rumor he served time in juvie for setting a convenience store on fire for no reason other than he was bored. And that he roasted hotdogs on the edge of the blazing inferno while he waited for the fire department to arrive. People in small towns had wild imaginations, and his personality did nothing but fan their creative flames. Part of her thought he enjoyed the attention because he had a tendency to go along with whatever was being said, but Katie didn't buy into the hype. She assumed his jaded attitude was a defense mechanism for a troubled past, which is why she conceded to his request for a date. She had a soft spot for anyone who didn't quite fit the mold … like her. And now ironically, because of him, she was about to be the focus of eccentric story-telling time. A level of attention she assuredly did not enjoy.

The test was over and she watched the squares on the floor pass one by one as the nurse wheeled her down the hall. She kept her chin tucked in toward her chest, doing her best to avoid the horrified stares that inadvertently paralyzed the faces of anyone who saw her. Her chair came to a halt and the nurse pushed the up arrow on the wall to summon the elevator. When the large silver door slid open, an older gentleman carrying a teddy bear stepped off and the couple who remained on the elevator shifted to the side to make room for Katie's wheelchair. The door closed and the woman nudged the man standing next to her and nodded her head toward Katie, directing him to take a look. Katie closed her eyes at the sound of his audible gasp. She may not have witnessed what happened, but she didn't have to. She knew.

The elevator stopped and the nurse pushed Katie past the nurse's station and down the hall toward her room. Her gaze shifted from the floor to her hands, which were folded in her lap. She opened them up in front of her and studied the signs of her struggle, evident by the abrasions scattered against her bruised skin. She thought about Damon and how he used to hold those hands at lunch or when they walked down the hall between classes. And how, even at his worst, she could never have imagined him doing this to her. Yes, he was arrogant and occasionally had a foul mouth, but he wasn't a monster. At least she hadn't thought so before now. Maybe the seemingly fabricated stories that circulated when he came to town held some underlying truth and he was a bad person after all. Or maybe all of this was the result of something she had done to provoke him. Making out behind the school, the way she placed her hand snugly on his upper thigh when they sat close to one another, the way her body fell into his when they hugged—maybe she had asked for this. Blame trickled in with the belief that this was somehow her fault.

When they arrived at her room, the nurse spun the wheelchair around and used her back to push open the door, wheeling Katie in backward. She heard a man's voice coming from the other side of the room. Once the nurse turned her chair back around to face the bed, she raised her head to find Detective Burns standing next to her dad.

"He did it!" Carl exclaimed, a smile on his face that had been absent for days. "He arrested Damon. He's in jail!"

Chapter 13

PRESENT

Katie sat on the bed in the guest room and stared at the piece of paper, the creases thin and ragged from opening and closing it so many times throughout the day. She didn't tell Amanda what was written on the back of the flyer. Nor did she tell her dad when she called him after work to say she would be staying at Amanda's. When he assumed it was to help plan for the wedding, she didn't argue. He mentioned he had gotten no response to the two voicemails he left for Detective Burns and assured Katie he would call the sheriff's office in the morning for some answers. She hoped the next time she heard from her dad it was good news.

The random visitor at the flower shop no longer appeared to be random.

She opted not to call the police department for fear of not being taken seriously. After they dismissed her report of an intruder, she doubted a call about a random note on her windshield would be well received. There was nothing threatening in the message, and her name was nowhere on the piece of paper. If they called the number, whoever answered more than likely would play dumb when they realized they were talking to the cops. That is, if the number was even real.

Nothing out of the ordinary happened at work after she found the note. She spent most of the afternoon packing up homecoming supplies and retrieving boxes of Christmas decorations from the storage room. Although the store itself would soon be splashed with the rich colors of fall, the window displays would tell a different story. The few months leading up to Christmas were some of the busiest outside of Mother's Day and Valentine's Day. Mrs. Greyson would spend her nights and weekends transforming the place into a winter wonderland that would rival any storefront in Manhattan. Her Christmas Bazaar, held on the weekend after Thanksgiving, brought in record-breaking crowds each year and normally Katie's excitement would be building for the event. But lately, nothing had been normal.

Katie folded up the piece of paper one more time and tucked it under her pillow. The door didn't make a sound when she peeked out into the hallway. Complete silence. The sun had yet to rise, and everyone else appeared to still be in bed. She padded down the stairs in her socks and made her way to the kitchen, hoping to find a box of leftover pizza in the fridge. Lunch with Amanda was the last time she had eaten. When she got off work, she stopped at her apartment long enough to call her dad and throw a few things in a duffle bag to take to Amanda's, watching carefully to make sure she wasn't being followed on the way. She got a quick tour of the house and before everyone sat down for dinner, she told Amanda she had a bad headache and wanted to turn in early. Amanda had gotten good at not questioning Katie's aversion to socializing.

"I thought I was the only one who liked cold pizza for breakfast?" He watched her from the doorway.

She flinched, surprised by Ty's voice. "You scared me. Are you supposed to be out of bed?"

"Probably not. I didn't figure I would get caught. Nobody in this house is usually up this early."

"I hope I didn't wake you."

"No, I'm always up early. Is there enough for two?"

She looked at the pizza and then back at him, propped against the doorframe. "Sure. Need some help?" She walked around and pulled out a seat from beneath the bar and then over to him. "Give me your hand." He limped his way to the chair, using her as a crutch. She felt his weight through her core to her toes. Once he sat down, she walked back around to the other side of the island.

"How are your ribs?"

"Sore as hell, but at least they finally quit moving. I can deal with the pain. Feeling the bones rub together, not so much."

"Shouldn't you still be wearing a neck brace?"

"Are you the medical police?" He pulled a slice of Canadian bacon and pine-apple pizza from the box. "Good choice."

"No, sorry." Her nose crinkled. "I'm not the best at small talk."

"I'm just messing with you. But to answer your question, yes. I'm not the best patient. Even took my own stitches out last night, which is probably frowned upon as well." He puffed out his bottom lip, surrounded by the beginnings of a beard from lack of shaving. "Not bad, huh?"

"Impressive."

"I doubt I can manage these on my own though. Amanda is taking me to get these out this afternoon." He ran his hand through his hair, fully exposing the staples high on his forehead. The muscles in his arm stretched the sleeve of his t-shirt.

She blushed at the fact she noticed and looked down at her pizza.

"You okay?" he asked, oblivious to what had happened.

"Yeah, weak stomach. Staples freak me out." Her fingers barely poked out of the cuffs of her sweatshirt. She picked a piece of pineapple off her pizza and stuck it in her mouth. "Are you going to be at the party Saturday?"

"By default. I will be here anyway. I heard that you would be staying here for a while, too, that you had quite the scare recently."

How do you know about the note? I didn't tell anyone.

Confusion contorted her face.

"Amanda told me you thought someone broke into your apartment?"

"Wow, there are no secrets with your sister." She rolled her eyes. "It was nothing. I did think someone had been inside, but I was wrong. The cops came and checked everything out for me. Nothing was missing or broken, which was good, but I have had a hard time sleeping since then, so," she shrugged her shoulders, "here I am."

He threw the crust back in the box after he took his last bite and dusted off his hands. "Whatever the reason, I'm glad you're here. I like having someone to share cold pizza with in the morning."

Ty was the only man she had ever been alone with who didn't intimidate her. Even with comments like that, she never felt threatened or took it as an advance. The thought of those same words coming from someone like Brad made acid bubble in her stomach. But not Ty. There was something comforting about the deep tone of his voice and his slight southern drawl. His eyes never begged for more. It was a welcome change from what she was used to.

"I never thought I would say this, but me too. Thanks for joining me."

"Anytime." He used the countertop to push himself up and then held the edge to gain his balance. "How about we meet back here in the morning. Same time?" He leaned forward and brushed a crumb from her chin.

"I would like that," she smiled. A tingling sensation remained where his hand touched her face.

She finished her piece of pizza and put the box back in the refrigerator with one slice remaining. Hardly seemed worth it, but she was full. She wiped off the countertop and washed her hands, draping the towel she used to dry them over the handle on front of the oven. On her way out of the kitchen, she flipped off the light and glanced down the hall in the direction of Ty's room. He had already disappeared behind the door.

Back upstairs, she closed the door to her room, plopped down on the bed and pulled the folded piece of paper from underneath the pillow. "Let's get this over with." She didn't need the flyer—the phone number was burned into her memory—but she stared at it intently as she dialed the numbers on her phone. Her fingertip hovered in hesitation over the green call button. Pulling every ounce of courage from within, she finally pressed it. She put the phone to her ear and waited.

But nothing happened.

"No signal? You've got to be kidding me."

The call failed. She walked over to the window, holding her phone close to the glass. Still no signal.

"Maybe if I go back downstairs …"

She crammed the note back under the pillow and headed for the stairs. The door across the hall opened and Amanda walked out, blonde hair piled in a ratted mess on top of her head. She had crease marks across her cheek from her pillow and eyes that were only half-open, yet she still looked like a million bucks.

"Where are you headed?" She yawned.

Katie held up her phone. "I was going to try to call my dad, but I didn't have service in my room. I thought I might try outside."

"I forgot to tell you, if you have Sprint, it won't work out here. Downside to living so far out of town. Feel free to use mine, it's on my dresser, or you can use the phone in the kitchen." Amanda stumbled toward the bathroom in her red silk pajamas.

"It's okay. I will call him on my lunch break later today. It's not important."

Amanda closed the bathroom door and, just like that, the courage Katie had mustered to call the unknown number was gone.

Katie dug through the papers in the drawer at the front counter. She looked under the register and scoured the desk near the telephone, even combed through the display of deflated Mylar balloons on the table in the corner.

"Mrs. Greyson, have you seen my day planner? The one with the yellow flowers on the front?"

"I haven't seen it, Dear," she called from the back. "Did you leave it at home?"

"I looked for it last night, but I couldn't find it. I was in a hurry, though. Maybe I overlooked it." At night, it lived on the table next to her bed, but most days she carried it with her. When she stopped by her apartment to grab things to take to Amanda's, she didn't see it. Her search of the bottom shelf of her workstation left her empty handed, too. "Where is that thing …" she mumbled, crouched on her knees.

Katie kept everything in that day planner. Her entire life bound by a plated aluminum coil. At the end of each year, she often found it hard to part with a book so full of personal details about her life—pages that overflowed with colorful ink and doodles in the margins—but there was something hopeful about beginning a new year with a blank canvas and stark white pages. Each book had something in common, a picture of something yellow on the front.

"When was the last time you had it?" Mrs. Greyson walked up, pruning the leaves off the stem of a purple hydrangea.

"That's a really good question. I normally write in it every day or two." She remembered having it the morning she took the tour of the Victorian home because she wrote about her experience and drew a house with a heart around it that day. Nothing after that rang a bell. "I guess it's been longer than I thought." No real surprise with everything that had been going on.

"Have you looked under the seat of your car? Maybe it worked its way down there. You've made a lot of deliveries lately."

"Good thinking! Do you mind if I go check?"

"Of course not, Dear." Mrs. Greyson turned and walked towards the back of the store, humming a Christmas tune.

Katie walked out the front door and around to the side of the building where she parked her car. About one in the afternoon, the sun baked everything in its gaze. When she opened the car door, a wave of heat singed her face, the temperature inside well over a hundred degrees. She spotted something she didn't even realize she was missing sat in the front passenger seat: her cell phone. It must have missed her purse when she tossed it that direction leaving Amanda's house that morning. She picked up her phone and had a missed call and voicemail from her dad, but continued to look for her planner. She ran her hands under both front seats, looked in the console, the glove compartment, and checked the floorboards in the back—no planner.

Katie locked her car and headed back to the store. On her way in, she listened to her voicemail. *"Sweetheart, it's Dad. Listen, I called the sheriff's office this morning like I said I would. I wanted to let you know why I haven't heard back from Detective Burns. He no longer works there. I'm not sure why, but I spoke with an Oliver Speights and after I explained who I was and what I needed, he said he would get back with me promptly. I expect to hear back from him soon. Okay. I love you. Let me know you got my message. I really wish you would answer your phone. Bye-bye."*

It wasn't odd for detectives to move around. She knew he came to Henderson County from the big city and probably left there to go work somewhere else. Katie sent her dad a text to let him know she got his message and thanked him for calling, followed by *I love you.* About that time, a car honked. It was Amanda and Ty. She remembered he had an appointment to get his staples removed and they were likely headed to the doctor. She smiled and waved as they slowly drove by and couldn't help but feel a little warm inside when he waved back.

"Good morning." His first words of the day were raspy in his throat. Ty hobbled over to the bar and took a seat. "What smells so good?"

The timer beeped as if on cue. She grabbed a hot pad and pulled the pan from the oven. "Blueberry muffins." Satisfied with their appearance, she transferred the piping-hot muffins from the muffin pan to a plate. Steam billowed from their golden-brown tops. "Careful, those are hot."

Tiny sprinkles of flour dotted the front of her Old Navy sweatshirt. Her blue eyes sparkled and he watched her maneuver the kitchen effortlessly, like it was her very own. She poured a cup of coffee and placed it on a saucer in front of him.

"I'm not sure how you take your coffee, so there's cream, half and half, sugar, sugar substitute," she motioned to each respectively. "Or I can get you some milk from the fridge. I actually like mine with a little dash of cinnamon if you would like to try that." She talked like she was on her fourth cup when in reality she had yet to have a single drop. They didn't have decaf.

"Black is fine." An inviting aroma of French vanilla rose from the cup. He picked it up and took a sip; the hot liquid warmed his stomach. "How long have you been awake exactly?"

"Not long. I figured I would come down a little early to see if there was anything I could make for breakfast so we didn't have to fight over that one slice of leftover pizza."

"You didn't have to cook anything. I wasn't looking forward to this morning for the food." He winked at her over the rim of his glass as he took another drink, his eyes the same rich color of the coffee. "But since you went to all the trouble, let's eat."

Ty inhaled three muffins in a matter of minutes, leaving a pile of crumb topping on the plate in their wake. He wiped his mouth with a napkin and then used it to cover his mess. "So, tell me something about yourself. Other than that you're a damn good cook. That's obvious."

"That's a loaded question," Katie professed. "What do you want to know?"

"Anything." He fell into the back of the barstool. "Tell me something my sister doesn't know about you."

She thought for a minute and then blurted, "I'm adopted."

Ty's eyes widened. "Wow, you came out swinging."

"Was that the wrong thing to say?" her shoulders fell.

"Not at all. I expected something like your favorite color or that you have a hidden tattoo."

"Yellow and no—no tattoos."

"Noted," he smiled. "How old were you when you found out you were adopted?"

"I was eleven. Right before my mom died." She leaned over on the bar and propped herself up with her forearms. She picked at her cuticles to avoid eye contact. "I remember the day vividly. I was sitting next to my mom's bed and she was bundled up to her neck in a white quilt. I remember because it was unseasonably warm and I didn't understand why she needed such a big blanket. I was wearing shorts and still burning up. At this point, I knew she was sick but hadn't fully grasped the toll it was taking on her body. We talked at length about her illness. I asked her questions about cancer and if she was afraid to die. I asked her if it was hereditary and if she thought I might get cancer too one day. Man, thinking back I must have been super annoying with all my questions," she admitted and stood back up. "Anyway, Mom told me that some types of cancer were genetic but not to worry, even if her type was, I didn't have any of her genes so I would be okay. Then she explained why to me, and that's how I found out I was adopted."

"Do you know who your real parents are?" he asked carefully.

"My mom and dad are my real parents. They are the only parents I've ever known."

"I know, but still. Are you curious?" he wasn't trying to be nosy; he was genuinely intrigued.

"Not really. I asked Dad more about it once when I got older. He told me a woman showed up at their church and gave me away." Katie replied bluntly and then drifted away in thought.

Ty was at a loss. He stared at her for a moment. "You've never told anyone that story before, have you?"

"Nope, I haven't. You're the first."

"If you don't mind me asking, why me?"

"That's a really good question. You're easy to talk to? You asked?" she shrugged. "I don't know." And that was the truth. She had no idea why she chose to share that with him.

"In that case," he leaned back, trying to brighten the mood, "tell me something else. What else do I need to know about you?"

"I'm not sure I can top that one."

"Why do I have a hard time believing that?" he smirked.

The list of things to share was endless, most of which she would never discuss with him, but she couldn't help but feel the need to think of something else to say. Something that he wouldn't expect.

"I have a nickname," she offered shyly, hoping he would find it interesting. "Want to try and guess what it is?"

"Depends. If I guess correctly, do I get to start calling you this name?"

"Sure," she laughed. "Because there isn't a chance in hell you will ever get it right."

"Sounds like a challenge," he put his hand on his chin and stroked his jaw. "Let me think …"

She watched his proverbial wheels spin. He was giving this some serious thought.

"I've got it!" he exclaimed. "Kit Kat. Your nickname is Kit Kat."

"Really? That's the best you could come up with over there?"

"Yeah, this was harder than I thought. I'm not ashamed to admit defeat though. So," he shifted to find a more comfortable position, "lay it on me. What's this mystery name you speak of?"

"I guess if you want to be technical, Katie is my nickname. My actual name is Katherine."

"That's cheating," he protested.

"Let me finish," she held her finger in the air. "Yes, I go by Katie. But my mom had another name for me. She called me Easter egg."

He studied her face, his head cocked to the side, eyes at a squint. "Huh, I see it now. At just the right angle, your head is somewhat shaped like an egg."

Katie waded up her napkin and threw it at him. "Oh, shut up. She didn't call me that because I looked like an egg, you dork."

Getting a rise out of her excited him for some reason. "I'm just messing with you. That's a cute name and you're right, I would never have guessed. Why did she call you that?"

"For the longest time, I thought it was because my birthday occasionally fell on Easter, so I never really questioned it. She finally told me the true meaning when we had the conversation about my adoption. Mom and Dad tried for years to get pregnant. They did once, but Mom couldn't carry the baby, and they had a miscarriage. When the opportunity came to adopt me, she called me her little Easter egg because I represented new life for her and my dad. She used to say I was the perfectly designed egg she had been searching for, I had just been hidden in someone else's womb."

"Wow, Katie," he let out a deep breath. "You definitely win at this game. What a great story."

"I'm glad you liked it," she said, pleased with herself for not coming across as lame. She glanced at the time. "I should get this mess cleaned up before everyone else wakes up and go get ready for work. Thanks for hanging out with me again this morning. This was fun."

"My pleasure; I enjoy your company. I can honestly say I've never met anyone like you before, Katie." He stood up and steadied his balance. "The homemade muffins were just a bonus."

Before he ever turned around to leave, she spoke up. "Hey, Ty, before you go, can I show you something?" She reached into the pocket of her shorts and pulled out the folded piece of paper she'd been hiding under her pillow. "I found this on my windshield the other day when Amanda and I were downtown shopping."

He took the piece of paper and unfolded it. "A flyer for Quickie's Pizza?"

"Turn it over."

He studied it for a moment. "Was this intended for you or Amanda?"

"We were in my car, so I assume me. I didn't tell her about it."

"Have you called the number?"

"Not yet."

"Do you have any idea who might have left it?"

"No. None." Well, that wasn't entirely true. She had a suspicion.

"Does this have something to do with that guy you're trying to avoid? Kyle's friend?"

"I honestly hadn't thought about that. But maybe? He was there that morning. We talked to him. He had every opportunity to write that while we were in the store looking for dresses."

"Guys do strange things when their egos get crushed. If he feels like you're avoiding him, this may be his little cry for attention. I'm assuming he will be at the party tomorrow?"

"Yes."

"If I were you, I would toss it. If someone thinks they need to talk to you—him or anyone else for that matter—they should have the nerve to walk up to you and talk. We are all adults. This," he waved the paper in the air and tossed it down on the counter, "is nothing more than a child's game."

Everything he said made sense. She had automatically assumed the message came from someone from her past. It never crossed her mind it might be Brad playing a silly game. "You know what? You're right!" She took the paper, wadded it up, and tossed it in the garbage. "Thank you. That makes me feel better."

"That's my girl. And remember, I will be here tomorrow. If he makes an ass out of himself, I will take care of it."

She believed him, too. He didn't speak in a narcissistic or arrogant tone. He wasn't waving a macho flag or puffing his chest out like an alpha male. It was a sincere promise to take care of her and she felt it.

Katie waited upstairs as long as she could, dressed in an outfit she borrowed from Amanda: a fitted white scoop-neck t-shirt tucked into a pair of black knit shorts that were tied with a matching bow for a belt, Amanda's locket visible against her chest. She wore her hair down with a slight natural wave and her makeup consisted of only mascara and a tinted lip balm.

She could hear the sound of laughter and a rumble of voices coming from downstairs. It sounded like a herd of people. The view from her guestroom overlooked the front of the house so she strolled over to the window to count the cars.

There weren't as many as she anticipated based on the level of noise, but she could see two more coming up the drive.

Her stomach flipped.

The only thing that kept her going was the thought of Ty being downstairs among the crowd. She felt safe with him around. Large groups of people caused her anxiety to flair, especially in a setting where everyone mingled. The noise made it hard to know when someone was coming up behind her, and she had a tendency to jump when they did. The fear of causing a scene—such as screaming or throwing a punch—only made that anxiety worse.

Fifteen minutes into the party, she finally slipped into a pair of Amanda's black wedge sandals and went downstairs. When she walked into the great room it was empty, so she headed to the kitchen. Also empty. Through the French doors leading to the backyard, she could see that everyone had moved outside. She scanned the crowd. She recognized Amanda and Kyle, Amanda's parents, and that was it. No Ty. Most importantly, no Brad.

"Hey, Katie."

Or so she thought. She shuddered at the sound of his voice. "Hey, Brad. What are you doing inside? The party is out there."

"I just got here, running late." His eyes traveled from hers to her feet and back again. "Wow, you look great."

"Thanks," she wrapped her arms around herself.

"There's no need to be shy." He took a step closer to her.

"There you are." Ty came around the corner wearing a pale green button-down shirt, starched jeans, and boots. The dimple in his chin was visible on his cleanly shaven face and he did well at hiding his limp. It was barely noticeable. "I got worried when I couldn't find you." He put his arm around Katie and kissed her on top of the head. "Hi, I'm Ty," he extended his right hand to Brad. "And you are?"

"Brad. I'm a friend of Kyle's."

They shook hands, knuckles white from the tight grip, neither wanting to be the first to let go. Katie felt Ty's weight heavy on her shoulders. She had felt that weight before. He was using her for a prop.

"Thank you for coming, Brad. I know Amanda and Kyle appreciate you being part of their celebration. The party is outside, just through those doors," Ty nodded the way in a cordial and respectful manner. "I'm sure you'll find Kyle somewhere near the horseshoes."

"I see." Brad finally picked up on the fact he was being given the brush off. "Guess I will make my way outside then. Katie, it's always nice to see you. Ty," nothing followed the mention of his name.

The door closed behind him.

"Are you okay?" Ty looked down at Katie, his arm still around her.

"How did you know that was him?"

"I didn't. It was a guess based on how uncomfortable you looked."

"Good guess." Her head fell onto his chest. She quickly lifted it back up when she realized what she had done. "I should be asking how you are. You feel pretty unsteady."

"I took an extra pain pill, I will be fine." His arm dropped from behind her back and he took her hand in his. "Don't worry. He isn't going to bother you. I won't let that happen." He looked down into her eyes. "Are you ready?"

Lost in his gaze, she nodded.

When they walked outside, they parted ways. The rumble of water cascading down the rocks behind the swimming pool was barely audible over the blaring music and bellows of laughter. Each seat at the bar wrapped around the outdoor kitchen was occupied, as were all of the lounge chairs by the pool. This was a far cry from the image Katie had in mind when Amanda told her about the party and called it a quaint luncheon. Drinks were raised in every direction, and Katie wondered if she looked as out of place as she felt.

"Katie!" Amanda's curls bounced as she made her way across the lawn. She looked the part of a bride, dressed in a white romper. "Did I just see you holding hands with my brother?"

"He helped me out with something. It was nothing."

"That's just like him, always playing the role of protective big brother. Is everything okay?"

"Yes, everything is fine."

"Good! I'm so glad you're here. Come on, I want to introduce you to some people."

She towed Katie by the hand toward two girls sitting next to the pool, almost jerking her out of her sandals. Katie frantically looked around and immediately spotted Ty, who already had eyes on her. He sat in a wooden rocker next to his stepdad, who flipped burgers on the grill. Ty smiled and, with his slight nod a wave of calm washed over her. For whatever reason, that's all it took.

Even with numerous guests to entertain, Amanda never abandoned Katie. She pulled Katie around from one group of people to the next, snapping pictures with her phone and proudly introducing her as her best friend and maid of honor. The only person not receptive to Katie's charm was Amanda's aunt, who still believed her daughter should have been asked to fill the role. Katie tried to commit each new name to memory, knowing she would see these people again at the wedding, but after the first dozen faces, she gave up.

Afternoon turned to early evening and, for the first time since their trek around the backyard, Amanda and Katie were alone. Standing next to the pool under the shade of an umbrella, they watched as Kyle's brother and Amanda's cousin lobbed a volleyball back and forth across the net.

"Everyone seems to be having a really good time." Katie spun the pole, causing the umbrella to twirl overhead. "And by everyone, I mean me, too. I've had a lot of fun."

"It took me, what, roughly two years to get you out here? Proof or it didn't happen." Amanda opened the camera on her phone and held it up in the air. She put her other arm around Katie. "Say cheese!"

Looking at the picture, they realized they had been photo bombed.

"Here you go, ladies." Kyle stood behind them with two glasses of wine, one in each hand.

"Thanks, butthead. You ruined the picture." Amanda took one of the glasses. "You better be glad you brought this," she took a sip.

He held out the other glass for Katie.

"I'm good, thank you," she declined.

"Oh, come on, it's a parrrrty." He raised the glass for a toast, his words loud and slightly slurred. "One drink won't hurt." It was apparent he'd already had way more than one. He wasn't quite hammered, but definitely feeling no pain. Kyle got carded every time he went into the liquor store. His baby face and pouty lips made him look years younger than he really was.

For the sake of arguing, and to keep him from downing the wine himself, Katie took the glass.

"That's better. So, I gotta know," he slung an arm around Amanda and lunged forward toward Katie, his breath reeked of beer. "When are you going to give my boy a chance? He sure is dying to talk to you."

"Who, Brad?"

"Yes, he never shuts up about you." He hiccupped. "He said you were seeing someone, though. Is he here?"

Katie froze, not knowing how to answer that question. If she said yes, Kyle would ask to meet him. If she said no, he would surely tell Brad she was alone, giving him the green light to come talk to her.

"Yes, he's here. You must be too drunk to notice," Amanda piped in, remembering her conversation with Katie at the hospital.

"Maybe I am. Because I swear Brad said he saw Ty kiss you." He hiccupped again and stumbled forward even further. "Surely you're not dating Amanda's brother. Not after …"

"Okay, cowboy, looks like we need to cut you off." Amanda put her hand on his chest and pushed him back upright. "I don't need you making an ass of yourself and pissing Dad off this close to the wedding." She took a bigger sip of her wine, more like a gulp, and handed Katie the glass. "Excuse us. I'm going to go splash some water on his face, get him some coffee, maybe tie him to the bed or something," she laughed. "He never has been able to hold his liquor."

"Do you need any help?"

"No, I can handle him. You stay and have fun." The next words that came out had no sound. She simply mouthed, *You kissed my brother?* and walked away.

Katie brought the wine glass to her nose and breathed in its fruity aroma. She avoided alcohol or anything that made her feel like she wasn't in control, but she decided to try a sip. Kyle was right, one wouldn't hurt. It was a party. Just as the rim of the glass touched her lips, a hand on her lower back caused her to jump and red wine sloshed from the cup down the front of her white shirt.

"I'm so sorry," Ty apologized. "I didn't mean to scare you. I saw Amanda drag Kyle inside and I wanted to check on you." His eyes widened at the bright red dribble down her chest. "Oh wow, I hope that comes out."

"It's not a big deal. It's your sister's shirt anyway," she joked, deflecting her skittish nature.

"In that case, I'm not worried. She probably has ten more just like it."

"Her closet does look like a department store." She shook her hand, shaking off droplets of wine.

"You were quite the social butterfly today."

"No, that's Amanda. She just tucked me under her wing and pulled me along for the ride. I enjoyed it, though. More than I thought I would. Everyone has been really nice. Well, except your aunt, she kinda gave me the stink eye."

"Aunt Charlotte? Don't pay any attention to her. She's that way to everybody. Did anyone else give you any trouble?"

She knew what he implied. "Nope, not at all. I don't think I said thank you for that, by the way."

"Good." With his bad knee bent, he kept all of his weight balanced on the other foot. "Did you want to come over and sit with me until Amanda comes back? I'm not good at standing for very long right now, especially in these boots."

"I would love to," she looked down. "But I should probably go try to save this shirt first. Save me a seat?"

"I will be waiting."

In the kitchen, she poured out the rest of the wine from both glasses and left them in the bottom of the sink. She wet the tip of a towel with club soda and dabbed the red blotch on the front of her shirt. A shiver rocked her shoulders when the cold liquid soaked through to her skin, but it worked. The red faded to a light shade of pink, but she needed to get the shirt off and soaking as quickly as possible.

On her way by the French doors, she glanced outside to look for Brad—wanting to put eyes on him before she went upstairs. He stood alone in the shadows next to a tree at the edge of the yard, holding a beer in one hand and his cell phone in the other. Shoulders drawn forward and his chin tucked in toward his chest, he looked as out of place as she had felt at the beginning of the party. He swept the toe of his shoe back and forth across the grass. The cold, wet shirt clinging to her chest begged her to go change clothes, but she found herself unable to walk away. She thought back to the note she had tossed in the trash the day before. *What if Ty was wrong?* Other than bumping into Brad in the kitchen, he hadn't made an attempt to speak to her. For hours they had been in the same place, yet not once did he try to approach her. But maybe that was because of Ty? His eyes hadn't left her for longer than a few minutes, Brad didn't stand a chance.

Curiosity got the best of her. She picked up the telephone from the kitchen counter and dialed the number written on back of the Quickie's Pizza flyer from memory. It rang. She eyed Brad, still standing by the tree, expecting him to answer his phone at any moment. Or at least look to see who was calling. If he recognized the number, she could hang up and blame it on Kyle. After all, he was inside … and drunk.

It rang again. He shifted from one foot to the other and took a drink of his beer, but he never looked at his phone.

After the third ring, the phone clicked. "Hello?"

Katie sat in silence.

"Hello?" the woman spoke again.

Katie hadn't expected a female. "I'm sorry, I - I must have the wrong number," Katie apologized.

"Katie? Is that you?"

Her knees threatened to buckle at the sound of her name. "Who … is this?"

"You don't know me. My name is Laura. Laura Burns. I would really like to talk to you."

Chapter 14
NINE YEARS EARLIER

The video camera mounted on a tripod in the corner of the room pointed directly at Damon. He sat in an armless, straight-backed chair with his wrists cuffed and resting on the cold metal table in front of him. A single light hung from the ceiling directly above his head, and the walls were void of any décor. Burns studied him through the one-way glass for nearly half an hour, relieved to finally have him in his grasp. Serving the arrest warrant had proved to be way easier than he had anticipated. When he showed up at Damon's house, although his truck was nowhere in sight, Damon was home. Strangely, he did not put up much of a fight when Deputy Wakeland placed him under arrest. He exercised his right to remain silent and simply glared at Burns with a smirk on his face.

Damon sat alone in the soundproof room, and his apathetic demeanor left Burns scratching his head. There were no signs of fear, surprise, concern, or remorse—no fidgeting or shifting in his chair, no paranoid glances around the room or tension in his stature, no anything—he was completely void of all emotion. This would be Burns' second attempt to talk to Damon, and he had no clue what to expect. Sitting in an interrogation room, facing felony assault charges at nineteen—at any age for that matter—should evoke some type of reaction. Yet there he sat, motionless and indifferent, oblivious of the severity of the charges. Burns was certain he'd done the community a great service by getting this sociopath off the streets—and he wanted nothing more than to take his head and smash it repeatedly into the table for killing his dog.

The door creaked as Burns finally made his way into the room. Rage pinged every nerve ending in his body, looking for an escape. Being in close proximity to the guy who taunted him for days conjured a wrath deep within that begged to get out. The folder he carried in his hand slapped against the table when he dropped it next to the pitcher of water and single drinking glass sitting near Damon's hands. Damon didn't flinch.

"Thirsty?" Burns asked. He picked up the pitcher and filled the glass before taking a seat. Instead of offering the drink to Damon, he put the glass to his lips and drank the entire thing himself. He returned the empty glass to the table and sat back in his chair. Damon didn't budge. He continued to stare forward with stoic resignation.

A battle of wills, the air grew thin as the two sat in silence. Burns' previous attempt at planning a conversation with Damon had failed, so he tried a different approach. An egotistical personality would eventually want credit where credit was due, and Burns figured Damon itched to brag about the things he'd done. He just had to provide him the right opportunity to start scratching. Damon played excellent defense and knew how to successfully navigate a conversation to his benefit. He made that very clear during their earlier encounter at the school. He effortlessly danced around Burns' line of questioning and accusatory remarks. This time, although the sole purpose of the meeting was to elicit a confession, Burns opted out of the typical Q&A, knowing it would get him nowhere. Damon knew what he was doing, and was much too clever to fall for that.

Time continued to pass without a single word being uttered. Both men sat on their respective side of the table in silence. Burns opened the folder he brought into the room and shuffled through the photographs inside. He intentionally dropped one of Katie's bloody, swollen, and barely recognizable face in Damon's line of sight. For the first time since Burns entered the room, Damon moved. The muscles in his face flared as he clenched his jaw, and when he locked his fingers together, the scratching sound of his handcuffs against the metal table broke the silence. White-knuckled and visibly agitated, Damon still never spoke a word. So Burns dropped another photo. And another. And another. The last one on a pile of many was of Atlas, his dead dog. Of all of the images that flashed in front of him, the photos that piqued Damon's interest the most were the one of a grey toboggan, sitting on a table near a ruler, with a yellow number three in the upper right-hand corner … and the one of the dog. The other photos made sense to him, those two did not, but they didn't create enough curiosity for him to speak. He knew that's what Burns wanted, and assumed that those extra pictures were added to the mix to purposely confuse him. Damon refused to take the bait.

Burns gathered his things and left the room; the only word between the two during their entire encounter was *thirsty*. It wasn't from lack of interest, they both had plenty to say, but neither of them was willing to fire first. The more Burns thought about it, the less he cared. Damon was in custody with no alibi, and he had done himself no favors, alluding his guilt by sitting in silence and refusing to plead his case. Bail had not yet been set, but Burns assumed that given the heinous nature of the crime, and with Damon's criminal history and lack of ties to the community, it would be denied by the judge. If not, it would likely be set unattainably high, which would yield the same result: Damon sitting in jail waiting on his trial.

At least now, with him no longer an imminent threat, Burns' wife and daughter could come home and Katie would not have to fear a repeat attack or constantly look over her shoulder once she was released from the hospital. If only it could bring Atlas back as well.

"Dad," Katie mindlessly dragged her spoon through her apple cinnamon oatmeal. "Can I ask you something?"

"Of course. You can ask me anything," Carl replied, sitting on the sofa bed reading the newspaper.

The words were on the tip of her tongue, but she hesitated to let them escape.

"What is it, Sweetheart?" He folded up the newspaper and set it next to him on the sofa. "Are you okay?" He braced himself for what may come next.

"Yeah, I guess. Well … no, actually. I'm not." She continued to draw rows in her oatmeal with her spoon. "Do you think Mom is disappointed in me?"

"What? Good heavens, no!" he exclaimed. The question caught him completely off guard, not at all what he had expected her to ask. "Why on earth would you think that?"

She put down her spoon and rested her head back on the bed. She turned to face the door, which was the opposite direction from him. "Because I think all of this is my fault."

"Katie, no," Carl's knees cracked when he stood and shuffled toward the bed. "This is not your fault."

"I think maybe it is. I think I led him on. Some of the things I did probably made him think I was ready to … to … be with him." She struggled to use the words *have sex*. "I knew I wasn't ready, but I don't think he saw it that way."

"Oh, Katie …"

"I should have been able to stop him, too," she continued rolling through her self-blame, not giving him an opportunity to speak. "I'm pretty strong. I should have stopped him. Maybe I did want it after all. Or maybe had I not broken up with him, he wouldn't have done it. I don't think he meant to hurt me."

"Look at your face, Katie. Those bruises didn't happen at the hands of someone who didn't mean to hurt you. He's a monster." It killed him that not only was she blaming herself, she was attempting to defend Damon. "If it's anyone's fault, it's mine. I don't care for Damon. I never have. I could tell from the first time I met him that he was no good for you. I didn't like the way he looked at you. Or talked to you. And for the last few days, I've sat on that sofa by the wall wondering if I had said something in the beginning, if I had kept you from hanging around him, this would not have happened to you." He reached out and brushed the hair back from her face. "I'm so sorry, Katie. Please look at me."

She rolled her head his direction.

"Do not blame yourself for this. What happened to you should never have happened. Period. And it's definitely not your fault. You did absolutely nothing wrong."

She heard the words coming out of his mouth, but it was as if she lacked the ability to comprehend them. They bounced off her ears and floated away in tiny little bubbles, randomly popping in the air. Her eyes were dry and she couldn't have forced a tear if she tried. She rolled her head back toward the door, too ashamed to look at her father.

"My locket is gone, Dad. The one she gave me before she died. It was my only link to her. If I was sad or having a bad day, I'd hold the heart in my hand when I fell asleep and it would always make me feel better. Just like she said it would. It almost always made me dream about her, too. And now that's gone. I need her, bad, and she's not here. I think she knows what happened and she's disappointed."

"Honey, I know you cherished that locket, so did your mother. And I know you're sad that it's gone. But that isn't what made you dream of her. It's just an object. Your mom lives in your heart, your *real* heart, just like she does in mine. Not one that hangs on a chain around your neck." He placed his hand on hers and gripped it tightly. Her hand lay limp, not reciprocating the gesture. "You've been through a lot in your short amount of time on this earth. More than most people go through in a lifetime. You are strong, just like you said. I know you don't feel that way right now, but you will someday. And those dreams of your mom will come back to you. I promise. Just give them time. I know I'm not near as good at this kind of stuff as she was, but one thing I do know for a fact is she would never, ever, be disappointed in you. And neither am I."

His attempt to console her failed to penetrate her numb ears. She realized after she asked him the question that she didn't really want to hear his answer. She had her answer already. Her truth. And it was something she was going to have to learn to live with.

Burns sat at his desk and stared at the pile of paperwork that had accumulated over the last week. He had taken a few days off to mentally decompress and to spend some much-needed time with his daughter. When he told Sarah about Atlas, she didn't quite understand why she would not be able to play chase with him anymore or share her ice cream with him if he was only sleeping under his favorite tree. Burns did his best to explain that Atlas would never wake up again, but at her age, death was a difficult concept to understand. He was happy she still exuded the innocence that came from the lack of exposure to the harshness of reality. And he did not look forward to the day he could no longer shield her from the ugliness that lurked around every corner. An ugliness he witnessed daily that gnawed at his insides and left him questioning his ability to remain in law enforcement.

As he sorted through the pile, he placed all of the documents and evidence related to Katie's case into a box for the prosecutor. Damon's bail request had been denied by the judge, which meant he would spend his time waiting for trial tucked safely behind bars. Not for the purpose of his own safety—even though Burns wanted to kill him—but for Katie's safety.

He picked up the folder that contained photos from the case and, before he added it to the box with the rest of the evidence, he opened it. The photo on top was one of Katie's freshly mangled face. The swelling erased her age and Burns knew that the internal damage not visible with the eye erased her age as well. She was no longer a carefree teenager with big plans for her future. He had seen it before. An incident like this would force her to have to scratch and fight every single day to win the battle against her demons, however those chose to manifest within her. She would have to learn to do and experience things people her age took for granted, all while juggling anxiety and hellacious trust issues. He stared at the picture, at the tiny slits where her bright blue eyes should be, and he saw Roxie.

Roxie was only fourteen when Burns arrived at the apartment she lived in with her mother to find her crumpled in the corner of the bathroom floor. The room was damp with steam and her hair still wet from a shower, her skin crimson red from the vigorous scrubbing. Any evidence that remained from Roxie's assault trickled down the drain. In Tarrant County, being assigned this case added one more to an already bulging workload. With no leads and a lack of evidence, the case grew cold. Time passed, but her wounds never healed, and Roxie struggled to cope with the fear of another attack and the deepening depression that lingered within. One Monday afternoon while her mother was at work, Roxie's demons finally got the best of her and she took her own life at the age of fifteen. Burns carried the weight of her death on his shoulders from that day forward and vowed to do whatever it took for something like that not to happen again— not on his watch.

He closed the folder and placed it in the box. Cases like these never got easier and he didn't know how many more it would take to completely break him. He had grown numb to visions that would traumatize the average person and caught himself walking a fine line between right and wrong to seek justice. He thought about Roxie and Katie and Sarah and what each of those names represented in his life. He rehashed everything that transpired to land Damon in jail and prayed that the truth he'd bent to seek justice for Katie would keep her from ending up like Roxie, and Sarah from ending up like Katie. It was a truth he needed for himself as much as he needed it for each of them.

He got to the bottom of the pile and the requisition to subpoena Damon's cell phone records stared him in the face, unfinished. He knew the ramifications of sequestering the records at this point, but any decent defense attorney would ask to see them and he didn't want any surprises. As much as he wanted to toss the requisition in the trash, he didn't. Instead, he took a pen from his desk drawer and finished filling it out.

Over the next few months, Katie struggled to find her new normal and where she fit in. She was discharged from the hospital with a slew of pamphlets and literature on how to cope with surviving a sexual assault and countless resources about the steps to take toward healing and recovery, but all of the paperwork sat on the kitchen counter, untouched. At least by her. Carl read and studied every piece of information available to him, but he quickly learned that even though the words may sound good on paper, they were just words, and implementing their actions did not prove to be successful. Not with Katie.

Everything he read indicated it was best not to leave Katie by herself during her readjustment phase, so he asked Brenda, one of the ladies from church, to sit with Katie a few hours a day while he worked and ran errands. Appalled at the thought of needing a babysitter at seventeen, Katie locked herself in her room for two straight days in protest, only coming out to use the restroom. She finally surrendered when her hunger pangs superseded her desire to prove a point. Brenda cooked Katie homemade chicken and dumplings, and from then on the arrangement was no longer an issue.

Therapy appointments were twice a week on Monday and Thursday afternoons. Carl sat in the car for the entire hour while Katie visited with her psychologist, and on the drive home he never pried into what they discussed. Katie didn't want to go, but she knew putting forth the effort would make her dad happy, so she did. She'd had enough counseling after her mom died to last a lifetime, and honestly was tired of people telling her what to do or asking her how she felt. She felt like shit. Like a useless, giant pile of shit. And she didn't feel the need to broadcast that to the world.

Over time, her ruddy complexion returned as the physical remnants of her attack faded into memory. The abrasions healed and the bruising diminished, and to an outsider looking in, it appeared that nothing had ever happened. But to Katie, everything was still very real and very fresh and she had no idea how long that would take to pass. Dreams of her mom were replaced with horrifying nightmares of her attack, to the point she dreaded going to sleep at night. She never told Detective Burns, or her psychologist, that the portion of her memory she had lost alongside her innocence that night in the woods had returned. All of it. Telling anyone she remembered what happened would require her to relive her experience on the stand at Damon's trial, out loud and on display in front of a room full of people. Every detail down to the shape of the rock he used to bash her over the head. The images came back to her one by one and snapped together like a puzzle until the entire picture was clear and in focus—minus the one piece missing from the center of the puzzle—the one that showed the face of her assailant.

She finally mustered enough courage to go back to school, but her return was short-lived. Contrary to what everyone told her, settling back into her normal routine did not help. She had done her best to mentally prepare for the rumors and all of the elaborate stories that she knew were coming, but what her psychologist and Dr. Sheffield failed to mention was that the slamming of lockers between classes and the horde of teenagers coming up behind her in the hall would trigger panic attacks. Her head constantly swiveled to keep an eye on her surroundings and her heart rate never dipped below that of a marathon runner in action. She would sweat when it was cold, she trembled at the mention of her own name, and when the guy sitting behind her in statistics class innocently tapped her on the shoulder to borrow a pencil, she screamed. She ran out of the room, down the hall into the bathroom, and locked herself in a stall. That's where she stayed until her dad came to pick her up from what turned out to be her last day of school. She never went back.

At Katie's follow-up appointment with Dr. Sheffield, Carl held her hand while the nurse placed a tourniquet around her arm. Katie flinched at the sting of the needle going into her vein and she looked away as the nurse filled two vials with blood that would be used to check for sexually transmitted infections. All of the tests came back clear and, just when Katie thought the poking and prodding had come to an end and that she could move on from this phase of recovery, Dr. Sheffield referred her to a gynecologist. He didn't go into details as to why he made the referral, but her father did. It was the first she had heard of the potential damage to her womb and the possibility she might not be able to have children. Just like her mother.

On the cusp of her eighteenth birthday on a dreary winter day, she and Carl headed to the city for her appointment. Katie had never been to the gynecologist before and she had no idea what to expect. The lobby resembled any other doctor's office she had been to before—a random pattern of chairs scattered about the room, magazines piled on the table, strange art on the wall—the only major difference was that most of the people in the waiting room were pregnant. If her dad felt uncomfortable being the only man in the room, he never let on, which was good since he insisted on coming with her. She checked in, filled out her new-patient paperwork, and took a seat in a chair next to the wall in the corner of the room, where no one could sit behind her. When the nurse opened the door and called her name, Katie stood to walk toward her, but Carl remained in his chair.

"I'll be right here waiting for you when you are done, Sweetheart," was all he said. He knew what happened behind those doors.

Katie was confused why he didn't go back with her, he always went back with her, and she was even more confused when the nurse stopped in front of the restroom and asked her to go inside and urinate in a cup. She didn't know why they needed her urine, she wasn't pregnant, but she did what she was told to do. Once she finished, she washed her hands and used the marker on the counter to write her name on the lid. She placed the cup of urine inside a tiny door on the wall that opened into another room from the other side. *Well, that's different* she thought.

After stopping at the scale to be weighed, they finally made it back to the exam room. It, too, resembled every other doctor's office she'd seen before ... except for the silver things at the end of the bed. Those were new. The nurse took her vitals and handed her what looked like a pink paper tablecloth. She instructed Katie to take off all of her clothes and to put the paper gown on like a jacket with the opening in the front—to sit on the table and drape the sheet over her lap— and that the doctor would be in to see her soon.

She waited alone, uncomfortably nude, covered only by a thin piece of crepe paper. The air was chilled but she began to sweat, just like at school. Ankles crossed and dangling off the edge of the bed, she looked at the silver things to each side of her. She assumed by their shape that they were armrests for the doctor. It wasn't until the doctor came in the room and explained that those silver things were stirrups and meant for her feet that it all started to make sense. She didn't like where this appointment was headed. After a lengthy conversation about what was going to happen, the doctor asked Katie to lie down and place her feet in the stirrups. She rolled her stool to the end of the bed out of Katie's sight and when she placed her hand on Katie's knee to make her presence known, her reflexes took over and Katie kicked the doctor directly in the face ... hard. Embarrassed and afraid, she hurriedly changed into her own clothes and ran back out to the lobby to find her dad. They left the gynecologist's office without an exam, and just like school, she never went back.

Chapter 15
PRESENT

She snuck out of the house without saying a word after her morning run. The run wasn't to escape a nightmare—she hadn't had one of those since staying at Amanda's, even with her looming anniversary. Rather, she ran to settle her thoughts. At breakfast that morning, she didn't tell Ty that she called the number on back of the Quickie's Pizza flyer, or that she had agreed to meet Laura Burns, because when she wadded up the flyer and threw it in the trash in front of him, the matter seemed closed. But as she sat in her car, staring out her windshield at this woman—a complete stranger—she regretted that decision. Nobody knew where she was or what she was doing. What if things went south?

The woman who claimed to be Laura Burns sat on a park bench, legs crossed with an oversized tote bag in her lap. Katie recognized her based on the description she had given over the telephone. And the fact that Laura was sitting on the bench in front of Joe's, exactly where Katie told her to be. Short black hair poked out from beneath a New York Yankee's baseball cap, her thin frame was covered in a baggy dark blue shirt and white shorts. With sunglasses so large they swallowed her face, she looked like a poster child for the witness relocation program. Laura was restless and unable to sit still. She searched the face of every woman who walked by, unsure of which one might be Katie. Other than Katie's age, Laura had nothing to go off of. Katie had not given a description of herself.

What am I doing here?

All Katie knew was that Laura was the wife of Anthony Burns, the detective who worked her sexual assault case when she was seventeen. The urgency in Laura's voice dripped heavily through the phone when she said she wanted to talk. She claimed to have important information pertaining to what happened to Katie nine years ago. Something that Katie needed to know.

Laura had called an acquaintance of hers in Tarrant County a few weeks ago. Everyone called him Sully, but she wasn't sure if that was his real name or a nickname. She had only met him in person once before, and that was when Burns introduced them at his captain's retirement party at the Stockyards in Ft. Worth. They had shared a table at Eddie V's where she learned all about his career as a private investigator over steak and beer. When Laura called Sully, he informed her he had retired from the business, but given the circumstances he agreed to help her find Katie.

After minimal searching, Sully had tracked Katie down. He knew she lived in an apartment in Victoria and that she worked at a flower shop downtown. Although Katie did well at keeping a low profile and blending in with her surroundings, she technically had no reason to hide from anyone and always used her real name. It made her easy to find, especially for someone like Sully, someone who knew how to look.

Laura gave him strict instructions to be discreet and not to approach Katie directly. All she wanted was for him to leave Katie a message. Whether she acted on it or not needed to be her choice. He knew from the DMV records what car she drove and roughly what she looked like, as best he could tell from an old driver's license photo. He drove by the flower shop a few times, but she was never there. Out on deliveries, he supposed. That was the nature of the business. He followed Katie the morning of her shopping trip with Amanda, watched from behind a newspaper until they went into the store, and then left a note on her windshield on Laura's behalf. The message was written on the back of a flyer for a local pizza joint, the same flyer he had strategically placed on the windshield of every other car on the block. This was a common method for businesses to promote themselves or offer coupons, and it worked as the perfect disguise. The flyer included a temporary telephone number linked to a pre-paid phone Laura had paid cash for and intended to destroy after she spoke with Katie—if she ever called.

Katie found herself counting each crack in the concrete as she forced her body toward the bench, trying to suppress the anxiety building inside over what was about to happen. The plan was to let Laura do all the talking—she would hear what she had to say and then leave—nothing more. It's not like this lady knew any details about what had happened that night in the woods. The basics probably, but not the details. Those had never been shared and remained locked away in Katie's memory.

Her clammy hand gripped the pepper spray on her key ring, her pulse hard and quick in her throat. She tried to swallow but nothing would go down. "Mrs. Burns?" she croaked when she stopped in front of Joe's. "I think you're looking for me."

Laura looked up at Katie, but never removed her sunglasses. "Please, call me Laura." She slid to one end of the bench. "Have a seat."

The steel slats were warm against the back of Katie's thighs when she sat down.

"Thank you for meeting me. I drove most of the night to get here. I wasn't sure if you would come. Do you mind if I smoke?" When her head dropped to look in her bag, a piece of blonde hair popped out from beneath the black. She was wearing a wig.

Katie noticed but didn't say a word. She simply shook her head no.

Laura pulled out a pack of cigarettes and tapped it on the end, freeing one from the opened corner on the top. "I'm sure you are probably wondering what I'm doing here. Before I start, I want you to know my husband was a good man." She put the cigarette in her mouth and lit it. The end glowed like the fuse of a firecracker when she inhaled. "He may have done some questionable things during his time as a detective, but they were all done with good intentions. He's seen some very ugly things over the years and I watched as those things changed him." She took another drag and blew out a cloud of smoke, away from Katie. "The wheels of justice don't move very swiftly, and sometimes they don't move at all. I know that doesn't give him the right to take matters into his own hands, but when lives were at stake, he did what he needed to do."

Katie listened as the woman rambled, not sure what any of this had to do with her.

"What I'm about to tell you I will deny until the day I die. It's why I didn't want to talk over the phone—too much liability. But you deserve to know the truth. A truth I didn't know myself for several years." Another long drag. Another cloud of smoke. "When my husband worked your case, he did something he shouldn't have done. We have a daughter who is almost sixteen now, and when I look at her, I know why he did it. He looked at you back then the way I look at our daughter now. As the detective on your case, you were his responsibility and that meant taking care of you, no matter what it took." Her words sounded rehearsed.

Even more confused than before, Katie finally spoke up. "So, exactly what did he do?"

"He worked a case before yours, very similar in nature, before we ever moved to Brownsboro. A young girl was ra …," she couldn't make herself say raped, "… assaulted. He wasn't able to find the guy who did it, and that little girl lived in fear her attacker would come back and do it again. She couldn't handle it, and eventually Roxie took her own life." Laura cringed. She didn't mean to use the girl's real name. "Since Anthony couldn't get her justice, he felt responsible for her death."

Katie rubbed the scar on the back of her hand. She understood all too well the desire to escape fear; she had almost done the same thing herself. "You still haven't told me what he did. What does any of that have to do with me?"

Laura bent over, scrubbed the lit end of the cigarette butt on the sidewalk, and left it on the ground. She then hugged the tote bag in her lap. "There was certain evidence in your trial that brought about the conviction of Damon McGregor."

The sound of his name made Katie queasy. "I remember. They found that stupid toboggan of his in the woods, next to where I …," Katie trailed off, unable to say the word either.

Laura stared at her from beneath pitch-black lenses, willing her to connect the dots so she did not have to say it aloud. Katie didn't bite, so Laura finally continued. "The only reason his toboggan was found in those woods was because my husband put it there."

Katie's head reeled. "What? I don't understand. Why would he do that?"

"Because he needed to. To get the arrest warrant. He needed proof Damon was in those woods. Without witnesses or any DNA from your rape kit, he had nothing."

"Yes, he did," she shook her head. "There was other evidence. There were phone records that put him near my house right before it happened. My dad told me."

"Damon was already behind bars awaiting trial when those phone records came back." Laura retrieved another cigarette from her bag and lit it. "During Damon's appeal, his new attorney argued those were circumstantial. Brownsboro is a small town. He argued that Damon simply used his phone to make a call from his house, which fell within a ten-mile radius of the tower closest to you, and that living in the same small town didn't make him guilty. All of which I'm sure Damon knew when he did it. But during your trial, his court-appointed attorney never questioned anything. Damon didn't have the best representation."

"Wait," Katie closed her eyes and pinched the bridge of her nose. "Are you trying to say Damon wasn't the one who did that to me? Is that why you are here?"

"No, that's not what I'm saying at all. I just wanted you to know the truth. In case …"

Katie stood up and looked around. "The truth? Why now? Is your husband here, too? Or did he send you to deliver the news by yourself?"

"Katie, I thought you knew." Laura dropped her cigarette and smeared it into the concrete with her tennis shoe. "My husband is dead."

Katie fell back on the bench—hard—and stared at Laura in disbelief. Surely she had misunderstood what she just heard. *Dead? How could he be dead?* "How …? When …? Wha …?"

Laura put her hand on Katie's knee. "Car accident. His brakes failed. And to be honest, had Damon already been out of prison, I would have assumed he was somehow responsible. Katie, Damon did things while you were in the hospital recovering that you may not know about. He toyed with my husband. Posted taunting pictures on social media and drove up and down our road. He even killed our dog. He's sly, and handles himself in such a way that he knows he won't get caught, acting just out of the reach of the law. Had my husband not planted that evidence, he probably would have walked away and done the same thing to someone else. He's dangerous and ..."

"Wait ... go back. What do you mean if Damon had already been out of prison?"

"That's why I'm here. The judge finally granted his appeal. Katie, Damon was released about three months ago. My daughter and I have been hiding with family out of town in fear he might seek revenge. And word has it he's been asking around, trying to find you."

Katie could barely see the lines on the road through her swollen eyes. Cars whizzed by in a blur as she headed away from town toward Amanda's house. She should have listened to Ty and not called the number. Nothing good had come from it. Life was hard enough without having to fear that Damon wanted revenge. And for something she had no control over. If he had asked around about her, did he already know where she lived? Laura had been able to find her. Had Damon been the one that stopped by the flower shop? Had he been by her house in Brownsboro?

"Oh my God ... Daddy," she gasped.

She jerked her wheel and slammed to a stop on the shoulder of the road; her wheels squealed against the pavement. Her purse fell to the floor, flinging its contents out on the way down. She unbuckled her seatbelt and scrambled through the mess to find her cell phone. Close enough to town to still have a signal, she called the house first.

"Pick up, pick up, pick up," she chanted, trying to think of the last time she actually spoke to her dad. With each unanswered ring, the ache in the pit of her stomach grew stronger. It felt like someone had ripped her guts through her skin when she heard the sound of his voice on the answering machine.

He didn't answer.

Her hands shook uncontrollably, making it hard to dial his cell next. After the first ring, he picked up. "Daddy, thank God. Are you okay?"

"Yes, but I need to tell you something. I've tried to call you several times, but it goes straight to voicemail and I didn't want to leave a message. Not about this. Honey, I finally heard back from the sheriff's office. Damon is out."

She looked up at her icy blue eyes staring back in the rearview mirror. "I know. And Detective Burns is dead."

Katie's feet dangled off the edge of the dock and her toes lightly brushed the water. Several hours had passed, and too much time alone with her own brain had made her numb. She stared into the ripples in the water as they pulsed their way out onto the lake, watching how one thing, something as small as the tips of her toes, could create such a disturbance. Like making a simple phone call. Dialing the number on the back of that flyer caused a tidal wave of emotion she didn't know how to handle. Burns was dead, Damon was out of prison, and he might not have been the one with her that night in the woods. Planted evidence had landed him behind bars, and despite the fact that Burns was responsible, Katie was not upset. Not about that. Based on the letter Burns had written her years ago, she should have suspected something. Like Laura said, Damon needed to be locked away, and Burns did what it took to make that happen. Unfortunately, now she had a decision to make: what to do next.

Carl had spent half an hour on the phone begging her to come home, but Brownsboro was the last place she wanted to be. For now, she agreed to stay with Amanda and not go to her apartment alone, or anywhere else for that matter, at least not for a while. She gave him Amanda's cell phone number for emergencies, since hers didn't work well out at her house, and promised to text him every morning when she got to work. He offered to come and stay with her in Victoria if she needed him to, as soon as he was released to drive, but she wasn't sure what she needed. Nothing in her wanted to move and start over again somewhere else, but with all of the recent weirdness going on, staying in Victoria didn't seem like the smartest thing to do either.

"Want some company?"

Lost in her own thoughts, she hadn't heard Ty approach.

"Sure," she ran her palms over her face, a failed attempt to erase the redness in her cheeks. "Do you think you can get down this far?"

"Getting down isn't the issue." He fell to the deck with a thud. "It's getting back up that's the problem." The ripples grew larger when his feet dipped into the water next to hers. "I used to come out here a lot when I still lived at home. It's a great place to think. Except at night, the tree frogs get a little rowdy. Makes it hard to concentrate."

His comment didn't elicit a smile.

"Hey," he bumped her shoulder with his. "You okay? You disappeared on me today."

Part of her wanted to tell him everything that had happened, but she was still processing it herself so she didn't. Instead, she asked, "Do you like living here? In Victoria, I mean?"

"It's not bad. Why?"

"Just curious." She straightened her knee, and droplets of water fell from her toes.

"It's close to the coast. Never gets too cold. It has a certain charm, I guess," he shrugged. "After growing up here, I will say I never thought I would be a lifer."

"Why not?"

"I don't know. I think everyone secretly wants to run away from where they grew up. Didn't you?"

"I couldn't get away quick enough," she admitted.

"See what I mean? I had planned to join the military after I graduated with two of my buddies. It was going to be our ticket out of town. Didn't work out too well for me though," he slapped the side of his knee. "Couldn't pass the MEPS physical. They got in. I didn't."

"Amanda told me you hurt your knee playing football. I didn't know about the military though. I'm sorry to hear that." She knew what it was like to have your dreams pulled out from underneath you. "So what did you end up doing?"

"After my chance at the military got shot to hell, I thought I would take a stab at college. Packed up and moved to Arkansas, but that didn't go so great either. My head wasn't in the right place and I got mixed up in some things I shouldn't have. I ended up dropping out after a few semesters."

Her head tilted in confusion, seeking explanation.

"Young and dumb, let's leave it at that. That was a long time ago. I've changed a lot since then. Anyway, I took a few jobs here and there before moving back to Victoria, but nothing stuck. It seemed like no matter what I tried, life always brought me back here. I finally quit fighting it and went to work for my stepdad. I already knew the business and it's what he had wanted me to do all along. I had worked for him on and off during high school doing grunt work."

"Grunt work?"

"Yeah, you know, heavy lifting, banging hammers, construction—the physical stuff. But now I have my own crew and get to focus more on the design side of building, so it's not so bad. What about you? Did you grow up around here?"

"No, I'm from a small town up in east Texas. When I say small, I mean small. Like a thousand people small. My dad still lives there, but I moved right after high school."

He picked up a small rock he had found sitting on the dock and skipped it across the top of the water. "How did you end up here?"

"By picking a random town on a map," she answered quickly. She remembered the day well. It made her think of Burns and her heart stung.

I can't believe he is dead.

"That's one way to do it. Are you glad you picked this one?"

"Yes. Although when you walked up behind me on the dock, I was thinking about moving." She stared blankly across the lake. Her gaze not fixed on any one object. "Ty … there's something you should know about me."

"You don't have to tell me. I already know."

"You already know what?" She snapped.

"I know that someone did a number on you."

"What makes you say that?" she was almost embarrassed to ask.

"I can tell. The way you jump at loud noises or jump when someone comes up behind you. The fact you have pepper spray on your key ring. How someone like Brad makes you uneasy, and makes you feel the need to lie about being in a relationship already. When I watched you at the party the other night, you never put your back to the crowd, intentionally or not. I noticed." He reached over and rubbed his finger across the scar on the back of her hand. "And if I had to guess, this didn't come from making peach cobbler. Listen, you don't have to tell me anything you don't want to. We all have our skeletons. There is no need for details. It doesn't matter to me one way or the other. No judgment here."

Without her ever having to say a word, Ty knew.

"You are much more observant than your sister. We've been friends for quite some time now and she hasn't picked up on any of that," Katie spoke in a defeated tone. "Have you told her yet?"

"No. It's not my story to tell."

"Thank you," she whispered. "I've started a few times, but the time never seems right. I will tell her someday."

"Whenever you're ready and only if you want to. That's nobody's business but yours. But if you need someone to talk to, I don't mind lending an ear."

Her head fell over onto his shoulder. Everything about him was a safe place to land. He expected nothing from her, and it was refreshing.

"Maybe someday."

"Hey, how do you feel about a distraction? I have something I want to show you. You'll have to drive, of course. I still don't have any wheels."

"I would actually love a distraction," she sighed. Katie pushed herself up on the dock and held out her hand to help Ty. "I'm not sure where you are taking me, but do you mind if we stop by my apartment on the way? I need to get some more clothes and I really don't want to go alone. I think I'm going to be staying here a little while longer, if that's okay."

Back on his feet and standing more than six feet tall, he looked down at her and brushed the side of her cheek. "Stay as long as you need."

She followed the winding driveway carved out between the trees. On the ride to his house, Ty cringed at the scene of his accident, seeing it for the first time since it happened. The tree he collided with stood naked, missing half its bark. Black skid marks stretched from one side of the road to the other and intertwined with streaks of white paint where the police did their best to mark the path of the accident. He replayed what happened the best he could remember and told Katie how thankful he was someone stayed with him until the ambulance arrived. Especially since the person who hit him fled the scene. His body was recovering quicker than anticipated, but the graduation present he had received from his mom when he was eighteen wasn't as lucky. It now lived at an impound lot waiting for the insurance claim to be settled, hardly worth its weight in scrap.

They emerged into a clearing at the end of the driveway and Katie's jaw dropped. "You built this?" The car leaped when she threw the gearshift into park. She jumped out without waiting for a response.

Logs notched at the ends, stacked one upon another, framed his cabin in the woods. More glass than cedar, the front of the house pulled the sunlight from the sky. The steep pitch of the roof pointed toward the heavens and a natural-stone stacked chimney ran up the side. The multi-level deck protruding from the front extended like a welcoming hand. Everything else visible from where she stood was in pairs: two Adirondack chairs on the porch and two bicycles parked near the steps. A twinge of disappointment pinched her heart. It appeared that he did not live alone. Of all the morning conversations over breakfast, they never once discussed if Ty was seeing someone. Since a woman had yet to visit or check on him, she assumed he was single.

"If I was Amanda, I would want to get married here. Don't get me wrong, your parents' place is beautiful, but this …" her arms opened wide in explanation, replacing her lack of words to describe what stood before her.

"Don't think she hasn't already asked," he hobbled across the rock pathway to where Katie was standing and put his hand on her shoulder for balance. "I might have agreed had I not already seen her guest list. I don't really want that many people crawling around my place."

"Can't say I blame you on that one. I'm not very big on crowds myself. But I guess you already knew that, too," she said shyly, knowing that he was able to read her like a book.

"I might have picked up on it," his hand lightly squeezed her shoulder. "Would you like to see inside?"

"Is that a serious question?" she smiled.

With no railing for support, she helped him up the steps and didn't let go of him until they reached the front door. She questioned whether he actually needed that much assistance or if she offered as an excuse to get to touch him. Either way, she didn't feel guilty.

He turned the knob and pushed it open. "After you."

The rich scent of cedar and fresh paint rolled out the door before she ever stepped in. Surrounded by wood, she slowly made her way around the cabin examining his handiwork. The place hardly looked—or smelled—lived in. Natural light poured in through the windows, bouncing off the shiny hardwood floors, and the head of a ten-point buck stared down at her from high on the wall. With a throw blanket folded neatly over the edge of the brown leather sofa and hunting magazines stacked at precise angles on the coffee table, everything appeared staged. The only thing out of place was a muddy pair of tennis shoes just inside the front door.

"Sorry. Those must be Shaun's," Ty grabbed the shoes with a grunt. Bending over still required extra effort.

"Who is Shaun?"

"A buddy of mine. He's been keeping an eye on the place since the accident."

He. Thank goodness.

"Looks like he did a great job. I may need him to look after my apartment."

"Don't be fooled. He paid someone to come clean it for me as a get-well-soon gift." He held up the shoes. "And then he leaves these behind? Pretty typical Shaun."

"Muddy shoes or not, he sounds like a great friend."

"He is. My oldest friend, actually. We've been thick as thieves since we were teenagers."

"Is that his bike out front?" she continued her slow pace around the room, hoping the answer to that question was yes as well.

"One of them is. The other is mine. We ride a lot. Hence the muddy shoes." They landed with a thud on the front porch and he shut the front door. "He probably hit up the trails out back while he was here."

Ty gave Katie free reign to explore on her own, but she never ventured too far from the great room. She leaned into his bedroom for a quick glance, but was out as quick as she went in. No sign of a woman. Standing near the stairs that led to a loft above, she ran her fingers down the curves of the wall, her face filled with awe like a kid at Christmas.

"How did you learn to do all of this?"

"There's nothing to it, really. Just hammer and nails."

She threw a sly look at him over her shoulder. "Just hammer and nails, huh?"

"Pretty much." He made his way around the sofa, sat down, and propped his leg up on the coffee table. "Like I said, I've been on the construction side of the business pretty much since high school. I figured if I'm going to be building things, I might as well build something for myself. So, I put what I learned to good use."

"And that you did. It's beautiful." She slid off her shoes and took a seat cross-legged on the other end of the sofa, facing him, a throw pillow clutched in her lap. "You know, it's funny. This is the third house I've gotten to tour lately. All much nicer than where I come from. I feel like I'm on the Parade of Homes or something."

"This one and Mom's place I know. Where was the third?"

"It's kind of random, really. I run a lot and there's this Victorian home on one of the roads I go down. You've probably seen it before in town. Giant two story on Main Street with a wrap-around porch? I absolutely love it. The other day, a realtor was banging a For-Sale sign in the yard and offered to give me a tour, so I took it."

"That is random." He sank a little further into the sofa and clasped his hands behind his head. "Did you ask to go inside?"

"Kinda? Not really, though. We got to talking about my mom. I told the real-tor how the house reminded me of mom because we stayed in something similar on a family vacation we took when I was little." She cleared her throat. "This all happened the same day I brought food to the hospital for you and Amanda. The whole reason I cooked pasta that night was because I went inside that house. That's one of the things I cooked with Mom on that vacation."

"Things tend to happen for a reason," he dropped his hands and rubbed his stomach. "Reason being I like to eat and you are a damn good cook," he laughed.

"That was also the night I thought someone had been in my apartment. Explain the reason for that."

"That was the same day?"

"Yes. I remember because I dropped the empty food containers I brought home from the hospital all over the sidewalk. I'm glad that turned out to be nothing, but it sure didn't feel like nothing at the time. I was pretty freaked out."

"Wait, how many days after you thought someone was in your apartment did you find that flyer you showed me?"

Katie ran the seam of the pillow back and forth between her fingers. "Ty, about that flyer …," she paused. "I have a confession to make. I called the number."

"When?"

"Yesterday. At the party."

"I thought you threw it away?"

"I did. But I stared at it so long before I ever showed it to you, I had the number memorized."

"Was it Brad?" he cracked his knuckles. "Is that why you had been crying earlier when I found you sitting on the dock?"

"No. I really thought it was going to be him. I even watched him from inside the house when I called because I expected him to answer his phone, but he didn't."

"Who answered then?"

"A woman."

Ty patiently waited for her to elaborate, but she didn't. Her last words hung in the air like a thick fog. "Someone you know?" he fished.

"No. But related to someone I know, yes. That's where I was this morning. I went to meet her." She unfolded her legs and drew in her knees, sandwiching the throw pillow between them and her chest. Her socks squeaked when they slid against the leather. "On the dock, you said you could tell someone did a number on me …"

He dropped his leg from the coffee table and turned to face her, a million questions funneling in his brain.

"… well, that was an understatement. It's not like I was cheated on or dumped or even physically abused in a relationship. I was raped," her voice quivered as she choked on the word. "Brutally attacked from behind and left in the woods. The guy responsible was in prison and the lady who answered the phone—that

I went to see—was the wife of the detective who worked my case. She wanted to tell me he had gotten out. And that she heard he had been asking about me." Katie dropped her chin down on her knees.

"Good Lord, Katie. We should go to the cops."

"And tell them what? I called them when I thought someone had been in my apartment. They didn't find anything. And the person who left the flyer on my car was just trying to give me a heads up. I've been back and forth over it in my mind a million times, trust me. I sadly know all too well how things like this work. I have no basis to call. He hasn't done anything. The worst part about it is I found out that the detective who worked my case, Detective Burns, tampered with evidence."

"What did you say his name was?" Ty raised a brow.

"Detective Burns. Which is irrelevant now—his wife said he passed away in a car accident." She raised her head and looked toward the window. "What is it with car wrecks and hospitals and people dying in my life?"

Ty studied her for a moment. Her long brown hair, the curve of her cheekbone, the scar on her hand. "Where did you tell me you were from again?"

"Brownsboro. You've probably never heard of it before."

"Vaguely," was his only response, which was a lie. He knew it well. So did Shaun. "Listen, how about we stay here tonight? I will take the couch and you can have the bed. We can figure all of this out tomorrow."

"But I have to work tomorrow." Katie finally looked toward Ty.

"I guess you'll have to call in then."

Chapter 16
NINE YEARS EARLIER

Katie entered the courtroom and walked over to the bailiff. She placed one hand on the Bible and the other in the air and swore to tell the truth, the whole truth, and nothing but the truth, so help her God. When she took her seat on the stand, she found herself face to face with Damon for the first time since before her attack. It was a moment she had dreaded for months leading up to the trial, yet he looked nothing like she had imagined. She expected him to be cuffed, with shackles around his ankles, and wearing a dirty orange jumpsuit. Not because anyone told her that would be the case, but because that's what she had seen once in a movie. Instead, he wore a navy-blue long-sleeved shirt that buttoned down the front, tucked into a pair of belted khaki slacks, and brown leather shoes. His wavy black hair had been cut short, his face cleanly shaven, and for the first time since she'd known him, the diamond stud was missing from his ear. He looked … normal. Not like a criminal. And definitely not like someone capable of the crime he was on trial for.

She gnawed on the inside of her cheeks as her eyes darted around the room, unable to focus on any one object for more than two seconds. The Xanax she had taken before arriving at court was no match for the anxiety caused by a room packed full of unfamiliar faces. Outside of her dad and Detective Burns, she didn't recognize anyone in the crowd. *Why are all of these people here?* The heat from their leering stares burned holes in her skin and her muscles quivered from being exposed to the elements. She bit down harder on her cheeks, hoping the pain caused by the pinch of her teeth would supersede the pain that gurgled in the pit of her stomach, and wondered if it was too late to drop the charges and walk away.

Her attorney approached the stand and systematically fired off a series of questions, walking her through her account of that dreadful September night. Doing her best to ignore the judgment she felt being cast by the crowd, she recited every answer exactly as they had practiced before the trial. She detailed her fight with Damon on the phone, her run at Black Bear Trail, and how Damon attacked her from behind in the woods. Using Damon's name in the last scenario was a slip of the tongue, and his attorney latched on to the mistake. He objected on grounds of speculation, as Katie had not been able to positively identify her attacker. Records indicated her memory from that evening stopped with the sound of the three words *I've got you*, and resumed when she awoke in the hospital the following day. Everything in between had all but vanished from her memory. Or so they thought. She wondered if omitting that her memory had fully returned violated "the whole truth" portion of the oath she took when she entered the courtroom, not that it mattered. Nobody, especially a room full of strangers, would ever hear the gruesome details of what she endured that night. And if that meant violating some silly oath, then so be it.

Katie stayed in a holding area during the remainder of the trial, but Carl provided a recap of what happened inside the courtroom each night over dinner. The prosecuting attorney put Burns on the stand. He testified to finding evidence at the scene that provided a DNA match to the defendant, which Katie already knew. Burns had brought the evidence bag containing the toboggan by the hospital for her to identify. The prosecutor also entered into evidence cell phone records that placed Damon near the scene of the crime just before the incident occurred. Burns confirmed those records were the result of a subpoena issued after Katie's testimony of a heated conversation between her and the defendant had occurred moments before the attack. This piece of information was news to Katie. Burns never mentioned anything about the cell phone records to her, but it served as the missing piece to her puzzle. Snapping it in place with the rest of the picture erased any sliver of doubt about his guilt that she'd let seep into her thoughts. Damon had done this, and there was plenty of evidence to back it up. He was guilty. When Carl started to tell her about Damon's testimony, she cut him off. She no longer wanted or needed to hear anything he had to say.

The jury shared her sentiment and it only took three days of deliberation after closing arguments before they returned a guilty verdict. Damon was sentenced to ten years in prison with no chance for parole. She assumed there would be some sense of relief or vindication that came with receiving the news. Oddly, she felt exactly the same. Borderline numb even. The verdict meant Damon would pay for the crime, but it didn't erase the damage he had done. He remained in custody until his transfer to prison, and Katie never saw him again.

Burns came by the house to check on Katie about a week after the trial. She watched his squad car pull up the drive from her bedroom window, but she never came out of her room. Dressed in starched blue jeans and a black knit polo, he walked lightly toward the door carrying a bouquet of fresh flowers wrapped in translucent cellophane. Tucked inside was a white envelope. The droning mumble of his voice penetrated the wall as he conversed with her dad in the kitchen, but she was unable to make out the words either of them said. Later that evening, long after her dad had gone to bed, Katie opened her bedroom door and found the bouquet of flowers on the floor at her feet. Next to them was an envelope with her name on it and a message that said: Open when you're ready. *When I'm ready? Ready for what?* She picked them up, went back into her room, and closed the door. The vibrant bouquet of yellow tulips smelled slightly of honey, and a hint of a smile tugged at the corner of her mouth. She folded up the sealed envelope and tucked it under the secret flap in the bottom of her jewelry box, then placed the flowers on the nightstand next to her bed. She crawled back under the covers and pulled them up to her chin, then stared into the yellow petals until she fell asleep.

The next morning, she opened her eyes to the same splash of yellow she'd fallen asleep to and, for the first time since the attack, she felt an urge to run. She put on a pair of spandex leggings and slid one of her cross-country sweatshirts over the tee she had worn to bed. She grabbed a pair of socks from her dresser drawer and went to the closet to get her favorite pair of shoes, but they were nowhere to be found. *Maybe I left them by the door.* A few steps outside of her bedroom it dawned on her ... nothing she wore the last time she ran made it home from the hospital. Her clothes. Her favorite pair of shoes. Her locket. None of it.

With less ambition in her step, she continued barefoot toward the front door, stopping at the picture of her mom on the mantle in the living room. She picked up the photo and carried it outside with her. No clouds in sight, the warm morning sun peeked through the trees and kissed her on the face. She took a seat on the steps leading off the porch and placed the picture in her lap, her mom's face looking back at her. *I wish you were here, Mom. You would know what to do.* She rubbed her thumb across the locket that hung from her mother's neck in the photo and a tear dripped from her cheek, splashing when it hit the glass below. Pulling the picture into her chest, she raised her head to face a swath of trees that once held her path to mental clarity, a place she visited for a temporary escape from reality. Now, those very trees were tainted with tragedy and represented the one reality she would never be able to escape.

The sun traveled across the sky until it disappeared over the house. Hours passed, and the only thing that changed were the position of the shadows cast about the yard. Katie never moved. And she never let go of the picture.

"It's well past lunch. Do you want to come in and get a bite to eat?" Carl spoke to her back, holding the front door open.

She flinched at the unexpected sound of his voice behind her, but didn't respond.

"Katie, honey …" He walked over to her and saw her clutching the picture of Mary. Gripping the porch rail tightly, he bent his knees and took a seat beside her on the step.

"I don't think I can stay here, Daddy. In Brownsboro." Her blank stare was lost in the trees. "I know you won't want to leave the memories you have here with Mom. And that's why I want you to stay. Here, in the house y'all built. Plus, you have the hardware store to take care of. I'm old enough to go somewhere on my own. If none of this had happened, I'd be moving off to college soon anyway." She hugged the picture a little tighter. "I know you really want me to go to college, Daddy, but I don't think I can. Not right now. Maybe I can at least get my GED and find a job. Somewhere without a lot of people and where nobody knows who I am or what happened to me. I can use the money from my savings account to get started until I get my feet on the ground. I just need a place I can go to move past all of this because I can't do that here. I hope you're not disappointed in me."

"I've already told you, I could never be disappointed in you, Katie." He leaned his arm into hers. He was surprised by how much thought she'd already put into the decision. Being forced to grow up so quickly after the loss of her mother, she had always been wiser than her age. But he never expected her to want to leave. Not now. "We will do whatever is best for you. Always. If this is really what you want to do, I will support you. Have you thought about where you want to go?"

They didn't have any relatives nearby for her to stay with. Katie had two aunts, both married, and a few cousins, but none of them lived in Texas. All but one of her grandparents had passed away when she was little, and her only remaining grandfather, Carl's father, lived in an assisted living facility for veterans in a town less than an hour from Brownsboro.

"No, not yet. Honestly, leaving town, and this house, none of it crossed my mind until today. It's weird. For the first time since all of this happened, I actually woke up wanting to run." She wiggled her bare toes. "And then I couldn't find my running shoes. At first, I was sad when I remembered why I couldn't find them. But then I came out here. Sitting here, I realized that not finding them was a good thing. I was kidding myself to think I could ever go back out there alone. To the trail. But running is the only thing I've ever been able to do to keep my mind straight when something is bothering me. And I've got a lot bothering me."

He felt the unhappiness behind her words and listened sympathetically as she continued.

"And you've seen the way people look at me in town, Daddy. Everybody knows what happened. Nobody treats me the same anymore. It's hard enough for me to be around people, but when they act weird around me, it makes it that much worse. I'm not exactly sure if moving is the answer, but I think it's what I need to do. Or at least what I need to try."

"We will figure this all out together." Carl wrapped his arm around her back and rested his head on top of hers. "Me, you, *and* your mom."

Katie lowered the picture from her chest and they both looked down at Mary, her approving smile as bright as the sun in the sky.

"Hey, Daddy?"

"Yes?"

"Will you do something for me?"

"Anything, sweetheart."

"Will you help me go look for my locket?"

Katie stood in the bathroom of her Austin apartment, mascara streaming down her face. How could she have let this happen? She knew better than to get close to anyone. Not that he meant anything by it, it's what friends did, she just wasn't able to handle hearing those three words. If she had only told him about what she'd been through in the past, then maybe her reaction would have made more sense to him, or the misunderstanding could have been avoided all together. Having known each other for almost year, there had been ample opportunity to come clean. But she hadn't. Now, he was probably at the hospital getting stitches in his head, and she would undoubtedly lose her job.

Working the reception desk at the Eye Care Clinic had many benefits—and not the monetary kind. The pay was decent considering her lack of experience and only having a GED, but more importantly, her desk was situated in a way that kept her eyes on the door and people out from behind her. It was always quiet and, since everyone needed an appointment, there were never many people in the lobby at once. It was a welcome change from her previous job as a cashier at Kohl's.

She had spent the last five years bouncing around from place to place. Even the slightest bother kept her on the go, but none of her moves took her more than a day's drive away from her dad. Carl kept himself occupied at the hardware store and, in the beginning, texted Katie almost every day. He wasn't fond of that particular form of communication because he could never get a true feel for how she was doing without hearing her voice, but it was how she wanted to keep in touch so he went with it. The only time Katie actually called was the morning after a treacherous nightmare or when she needed help settling her nerves. He learned quickly that not hearing her voice meant she was doing okay.

Austin was the seventh town she called home since leaving Brownsboro, and meeting Ethan made her feel this might actually be where she grew some roots. He worked for the local courier service that delivered packages regularly at Katie's office. He had an unparalleled passion for life, and she found herself drawn to his flamboyant demeanor and eccentric sense of style. She'd never met anyone quite like him before. Each time he bounced in the door, he would say "What's kickin', little chicken?" making light of her skittish tendencies, and he normally followed that with some corny cliché. He loved clichés. She took to him instantly and, when he invited her for dinner, saying she looked like someone who needed a little spice in her life, she accepted. She met him and his boyfriend Sebastian at an Oyster Bar on Sixth Street, making sure to take her anxiety medication an hour before they went, and from that moment on, they bonded. He became her first friend in five years.

During her midday run through of the lobby to tidy up, she picked up a magazine left behind in a chair and returned it to the wooden rack on the wall. Ethan came in the front door of the clinic and quietly placed the brown package in his hands on the reception desk and tiptoed up behind her with a mischievous grin on his face. "Ah-ha, I've got you!" he exclaimed as he goosed her in the sides. Instinctively, she grabbed the first object she could get her hands on: a lamp from the table next to her. She spun around and caught him across the forehead with the black metal base. Blood spewed from his head and he fell to the floor, landing on his face. When the room stopped spinning, she realized what she'd done.

"Oh my God ... Ethan! I'm so sorry!"

That image replayed in her mind as she stared at the blue bottle of prescription pills next to the sink on the bathroom counter. The ones prescribed to her when she was diagnosed with PTSD. The end of her suffering lived at the bottom of that tiny plastic container. Temptation to unscrew the lid and swallow its contents taunted her like it had done before. It spoke to her in a calm voice, assuring her that everyone would be better off if she was no longer around, that the path to finally being free from anxiety, to silencing the nightmares, and to no longer being a burden to others, was only a handful of pills away. One swallow. That's all it would take.

The pills rattled when she picked up the bottle. She stared into the desperate blue eyes in the mirror in front of her and unscrewed the lid. The final crack of her broken heart throbbed inside her chest as it ripped completely apart. She wanted to end it all. It was time. She was ready.

But then …

It felt like someone pushed their finger in the empty space where her locket used to hang.

Pills scattered everywhere when she turned and threw the opened bottle at the door. In a fit of rage, she swept both arms across the countertop, sending everything on top crashing into the floor. The shower curtain rod bounced violently against the tub after she yanked it from the wall. She kicked and screamed and punched at the demons toying with her head until she collapsed onto the floor, suffocating in a hurt so intense she thought her ribs would snap.

The rage finally evaporated along with the last ounce of her energy, leaving a trail of tears in its wake. Blood trickled from a shard of glass stuck in her foot. "I can't do this anymore," she pleaded, looking up at the ceiling, searching for answers. "I just can't do it. It hurts. Everything in me hurts. I'm … so … broken," she cried, each word enunciated by its own syllable of defeat, but there was no one there to listen. She melted into a puddle of sorrow and, when her face hit the floor, she noticed something white poking from the fractured corner of her jewelry box. Pieces of glass slid from the top as she reached over and pulled the tattered white envelope toward her from beneath the mess.

"Open when you're ready," she whispered. Something told her that time was now. She peeled opened the sealed envelope and pulled out a handwritten letter:

Dear Katie,

I've written these words to you in my mind at least a million times, and now that I put them on paper, I still don't know if I have them right. I hope when you're reading this letter that you are doing well and if you're not, please know that's okay, too. You have a bumpy road ahead of you, I've witnessed it before, and that is to be expected with what you've been through. Never be afraid to ask anyone for help, including me. I don't have all of the answers and I'm not going to pretend that I know how you feel, but I do know what it's like not to be able to escape certain images in your head. What it's like to feel alone and like nobody understands. It's important to know that loneliness is a liar. It will try to tell you things that simply aren't true.

I moved my family to Brownsboro to run away from the things I saw where I used to live. Sometimes you just need a fresh start. If you start to feel the same way, then pack up and go, because eventually you'll end up where you are meant to be. I know I did. When I walked into your hospital room on that first day to do your interview, I finally knew why I picked this random small town in the middle of nowhere. You, Katie. It was because of you.

I have done some things in my career I'm not necessarily proud of, but I will never regret a single thing that helped see justice be served. I pray I did you right in the investigation of your case. Nobody should ever have to endure what you went through and I wish I could explain to you why that kind of evil exists in this world, but I can't. I don't understand it myself. But know that you can triumph over evil and that happiness is waiting for you, I truly believe that in my heart. Whatever happens in the meantime, please continue to fight. If you need to run, run. Trust in the direction you're being led. Just don't ever stop fighting.

Sincerely,

Detective Victor A. Burns

Katie's face was stuck to the tile when she woke with a jerk. The light from above shimmered across the shattered glass on the floor, an unfortunate reminder that the last twenty-four hours weren't just the product of her dreams. It actually happened. She pushed herself up to survey the damage and the unfolded letter crumpled under the weight of her hand. Patches of dried blood stained the bathroom rug and little pink pills peppered the floor, a few stuck to the skin of her bare legs. Her jewelry box lay smashed to bits and its contents were wadded in a tangled mess. There were dents in the sheetrock the shape of her fist and a gash in the fiberglass shower from when the curtain rod came tumbling down. *Another security deposit down the drain.*

She rolled up the rug and moved it to the side. She used the opened envelope as a dustpan and swept the broken glass up with a hand towel the best she could and dumped it and the towel in the trash can. The pills from the floor were flushed down the toilet, and the contents of the jewelry box stacked into a pile to be untangled later. The entire time she cleaned, she thought about the letter and how Burns said to follow the direction she was being led. She limped from the bathroom to the sofa and fell backward into the cushions, grabbing her cell phone from the coffee table on her way down to call her dad. Instead of dialing his number, she found herself pulling up a map. She closed her eyes and took in a deep breath, "Show me where to go, Detective Burns—where my happiness waits." She exhaled skeptically, but tried to release the remnants of doubt from within her body. When she opened her eyes, in bold black letters, his name stood out above anything else.

"Victoria."

Chapter 17
PRESENT

"Are you sure? You'll be more comfortable in the bed." Ty handed Katie a set of tan cotton sheets and a down pillow. "I can sleep out here."

"The couch is just fine. I promise, I don't mind."

The sheet popped when she fanned it out, letting it fall over the leather sofa. She tucked it snugly into the cushions before covering it with the second sheet. She topped them off with the grey cashmere throw hanging on the back of the couch and then placed the down pillow Ty had given her near the armrest.

"See? I will be quite comfortable out here." She patted the couch like an old friend.

"If you're sure," he stepped around her and opened the drawer on the coffee table. "Here is the remote if you want to watch television. I also put clean towels, some soap, and toothpaste in the guest bathroom if you want to shower." He surveyed the room with a quizzical look on his face as if mentally marking boxes on a checklist. "Am I missing anything?"

"Umm, I know we stopped at my apartment for more clothes, but it was mainly stuff to wear to work. I didn't get anything to sleep in. All of that stuff is at your parent's house."

"I'll get you something from my closet."

He disappeared into his room and returned with an old George Strait t-shirt. "I hope it doesn't swallow you. It's the smallest one I've got." He spoke as he walked into the kitchen to make himself a glass of water. "I saw him in concert when I was sixteen. Great show." He paused long enough for the ice to stop dropping from the freezer door; it rang loudly in the bottom of the glass. "That's where that shirt came from."

"I've never been to a concert before."

"Never?"

"Nope."

"I guess that makes sense, if you don't like crowds or loud noises. That's pretty much all a concert is—noise and people." He swung open the fridge and glanced inside. "Help yourself to anything you can find if you get hungry, although there's not much to choose from. We probably should have stopped at the store." Ty walked back over to Katie, his water in hand. "Glasses are in the cupboard by the sink and the plates … hell, it's a kitchen. I bet you can find what you need."

"I'm sure I can manage, thank you," she smiled. "You know, you're getting around much better. That has to feel good."

"I doubt I'll be pedaling down the trails out back anytime soon, but I'm getting there." He took a drink of his water. "Can I get you anything else?"

"Actually, yes," she hated to ask. He seemed a little different. Not agitated, not upset, just different. Preoccupied was the best word she could think to describe it, but she had just dropped a huge bomb on him. Maybe he didn't know how to act around her anymore. "Do you mind if I borrow your phone? I left mine at your parent's house. I want to call Amanda and tell her I'm staying here. I don't want her to worry."

"Sure." He took his cell phone from his pocket and handed it to her. "I'm going to take a quick shower. Make sure Amanda knows you are sleeping on the couch, please."

With no password required, Katie plopped down on the couch and browsed his contacts. When she came to Amanda's, she dialed her number.

Amanda answered, frantic. "What did you do, kidnap her? There's no way she would have gone with you alone, not willingly. And what is this I hear about you kissing her? Didn't you learn your lesson last time? I thought we had a deal. What is wrong with you?"

"I'm pretty sure you just exceeded the most number of questions asked without allowing a response," Katie laughed. "Are you finished?"

"Oh my God!" Amanda gasped so hard that Katie swore she felt a breeze cross her chin when Amanda sucked wind through the phone. "Why on earth do you have my brother's phone?"

"I left mine at your house. I didn't realize when we left earlier that we wouldn't be coming back tonight."

"You're not coming back? Where are you?" she demanded, almost hysterical.

"At Ty's house. Calm down. That's why I am calling, to let you know. I didn't want you to worry."

"Are you sure you're okay with that? Staying there? With only him?"

"Yes, I'm sure. And FYI, your brother didn't kiss me. Not kiss-kiss anyway. He kissed the top of my head in front of Brad, but it was just for show. That's it." Even though she kind of wished it wouldn't have been.

"I guess that makes me feel a little better. I haven't seen you all day. Where did you disappear to this morning? I came to get you for breakfast and you were nowhere to be found."

Nobody in the house knew Katie and Ty met for breakfast in the kitchen each morning before anyone else woke up.

"I had a meeting in town. Listen, there have been a few things going on lately I haven't told you about."

"Other than you thinking someone had been in your apartment?"

"Yes, other than that."

"So much for not worrying. What's going on?"

"I will fill you in tomorrow. Remember at Joe's a few weeks ago, I told you I wanted to tell you something, but we got interrupted when Kyle and Brad stopped by?"

Amanda thought before answering. "Yes. Damnit. With Ty's accident that night, I totally forgot we were supposed to finish that conversation the next day."

"It can wait one more day. But what's going on now has a lot to do with that." Movement out of the corner of her eye caught her attention. Through the crack in Ty's bedroom door, she saw him walk by in just a towel. Her heart slammed against the wall of her chest. "Listen, I have to go."

"Okay, but you better be ready to spill the beans tomorrow. I'm not going to forget to ask about it this time."

"I will, don't worry. Oh, and for whatever reason, Ty wanted you to know I was sleeping on the couch. Talk to you soon."

She ended the call and put Ty's phone down on the coffee table. In exchange, she picked up a picture frame lined in seashells, with the words Lake Days written across the bottom. The picture inside was a candid shot of Ty and Amanda, in what looked like their early teens, standing on the edge of Saxet Lake. Amanda wore a proud smile on her sunburned face, her blonde curls floating in the wind above her head. Her braces glistened in the sun. She stood tall with her shoulders back holding a fishing pole and Ty kneeled next to her, his thumb in the lip of a shimmery large-mouthed bass.

"She never would touch a fish. Still won't. But man, she sure loves to reel them in."

His voice caught her off guard. Katie turned to see Ty leaning on the doorframe that led into his bedroom, his eyes on her. The khaki cargo shorts he wore hung to his knees and the waist rested just below the band of his boxer briefs. He was not wearing a shirt. His freshly combed hair had a natural wave and looked almost black when it was wet. Her eyes were drawn to his chest and the fading bruise around his ribs. Given the impact he sustained, she was surprised that was the only sign of a wreck she could see on his body. Her heart fluttered once again.

"That doesn't surprise me. Amanda doesn't strike me as one to get her hands dirty." She turned and placed the picture frame back on the coffee table, trying to break her stare.

"No. Not at all. Unless you count the time she tried to free the bait. She dug each worm out of the Styrofoam container one by one and then ran and hid them. When her dad went to get bait and the container was empty, she tried to deny it, but her fingernails were packed with black dirt. Not to mention, I watched her do it. I didn't care; it was less work for me. I always had to bait her hooks and take off the fish she caught. She just did the fun part."

"I wish I had a sibling growing up. She said you've always been her protector. I can see that about you. Especially with how good you've been to me. And in case I haven't told you … thank you. For everything."

"Don't go making me out to be a saint. I'm definitely not." He reached for the doorknob, the vein in his forearm protruding. "You know where to find me if you need anything. Goodnight, Katie."

"Goodnight, Ty."

Katie changed into the George Strait t-shirt, washed her face, and did the best she could to brush her teeth with her finger, using the toothpaste Ty left for her in the guest bathroom. The minty flavor was refreshing. On her way through the kitchen, she turned the light on over the stove. It offered enough visibility to get around if she woke up in the middle of the night. She turned off the rest of the lights and crawled into the bed she had made for herself on the couch. The sheets were cool, which sent goose bumps across her skin. She pulled the blanket up to her chin and let out a deep breath. A symphony of tree frogs and crickets played just beyond the walls, sounds she couldn't hear living in an apartment in town. Sounds that reminded her of being back home in Brownsboro.

Sounds that, unfortunately, made her think about Damon.

Whether it was Amanda's locket still hanging around her neck or the fact she hadn't spent a night alone since the day Amanda loaned it to her, Katie had not had a nightmare since. Coincidence or not, it was nothing short of a miracle. Given everything that had transpired over the last few weeks and the fact that tomorrow marked nine years since that dreaded day, her nights would normally be haunted by memories she desperately wanted to forget. After this morning's conversation with Laura Burns, and with those very memories raw and on the surface, she was reluctant to close her eyes.

So she didn't.

Instead, she imagined being at a concert—listening to the band of critters playing outside—and counted the cedar planks on the ceiling.

The flower shop crawled with customers. When Katie tried to report off for work that morning at Ty's request, Mrs. Greyson asked that she please try to make it in unless it was an absolute emergency. With more orders to fill than hours in the day, Mrs. Greyson wanted all hands on deck, and seeing as there was no emergency—not an explainable one, anyway—Katie went to work.

She stood behind the counter waiting on customers while Mrs. Greyson constructed flower arrangements in the back. Deliveries were on hold until the end of the day, or at least until the walk-in traffic thinned out. Even then, deliveries would depend on the severity of the storm that was brewing in the Gulf. When Katie pushed the tender button on the cash register, the bell above the front door rang, announcing the arrival of another customer. She couldn't get one out the door before another one came in. The flower shop hadn't been this busy since the last Christmas bazaar, and for no particular reason. September typically wasn't a stellar month for sales and normally served as the calm month before the Christmas storm.

"Here you go, Mr. Henderson. I hope your wife enjoys her surprise fortieth birthday party tonight." A dozen black and gold helium balloons bounced off one another when Katie carefully handed him the group of attached strings. "You may want to tie those to your wrist before you walk outside. It's a little windy with the storm coming in. You don't want them to get away."

"That's a good idea. Thank you," he nodded.

She tightened her ponytail as she watched the floating bouquet make its way to the front of the store, tensing slightly when it passed a display case full of china. One bump would have created a mess she didn't have time to clean up. Thankfully, Mr. Henderson and the balloons made it out unscathed, but when the door opened, she couldn't help but notice the dark, angry sky swirling in the distance. The storm was coming quicker than the weatherman had predicted on the news this morning. In that moment, she found herself wishing she were with Ty at his cabin in the woods, not at work.

Katie pushed her thoughts of Ty aside and, one by one, she helped every customer until she finally reached the end of the line. Using the cuff of her sweatshirt, she blotted sweat from her nose. The air conditioning couldn't compete with the muggy air that flooded in each time the front door swung open. She straightened the bills in the register and wiped down the counter top, cleaning it of dirt and foliage left behind from the plants that crossed its path. She put the ink pens that customers used to sign credit card receipts back in the jar where they belonged, and when she stepped around the corner to grab the broom to sweep the floor the bell on the front door rang again.

"I'll be right with you," Katie called out.

"No rush, take your time. I'm just going to look around for a bit," a woman happily replied.

Katie rounded the corner with the broom and saw the woman thumbing through a jewelry stand covered in charm bracelets. Katie couldn't see her face, but caught a glimpse of her dress. It was red and covered in tiny white daisies, a pattern she'd seen before.

"Is there something I can help you with today?" Katie asked while doing a quick sweep of the floor behind the counter. She spoke loudly enough for the woman to hear her across the room.

"Yes, I'm looking for an anniversary gift," the woman continued to peruse the inventory, shifting from the jewelry display to a table full of succulents.

"We don't have a wide variety of gifts for men. But there are a few items on the table by the window, if you would like to check those out."

"It's not for my husband."

"Oh, I apologize. Is the gift for a friend?"

"No. It's actually for my daughter."

"How long has she been married?" Katie strained to get a better look at the woman. From what she could see, the woman hardly looked old enough to have a married child.

"Oh, she's not married. It's not that type of anniversary." The woman picked up a candle and breathed in its scent of vanilla. "It's … complicated."

"Well, you've come to the right place. I know all about complicated," Katie laughed and propped the broom up in the corner, the pile of dirt she swept up resting beneath its bristles. "Did you have anything specific in mind?" She brushed her hands together and then ran them down the sides of her pants.

"Not particularly."

"What kinds of things is your daughter interested in? That will help give me an idea of where to start with suggestions."

"Well, she loves to bake. Do you have any cookbooks by chance?"

Katie walked around the counter and in the direction of the woman who now stood with her head down, looking at a table of figurines. "No, ma'am, I'm afraid we don't. Is there anything else she might be interested in?"

"Flowers," the woman answered. "My daughter loves flowers."

"A girl after my own heart. Do you by chance know her favorite type?" Katie stopped a few feet shy of the woman. A familiar scent piqued her interest. Face cream. A particular brand Katie hadn't smelled in quite some time. "I can run to the back and see if we have any in the cooler."

"Tulips," the woman's red dress and her blonde hair flared when she spun around to face Katie. "Her favorite flower is a yellow tulip."

Katie froze in disbelief, mouth open and eyes wide.

"Mom?" her voice quaked.

"Of course it's me, Katherine. Who did you think it was?"

"But you're …"

"But I'm what? Standing right in front of you?" she flashed a wink and a smile.

"Hhh … how … ?" Katie stammered. "I thought you were gone?" She stared in awe at her mother's skin—radiant and supple, her cheeks a rosy shade of pink. Nothing like Katie remembered from the last time she saw her.

"Let me let you in on a little secret, Easter Egg." She leaned forward, put her hand up to her mouth, and whispered, "I never left."

"Oh, Mom!" With open arms, Katie eagerly rushed toward her, accidentally bumping the edge of the display table with her hip on her way by. The tabletop teetered just enough to send all of the ceramic figurines crashing to the ground in a roaring boom. Katie instinctively pinched her eyes closed to protect them against flying debris as the ceramic shattered against the concrete floor. When the broken pieces finally quit skittering across the ground, she opened her eyes, only to be rattled again by another boom. But this one was different. It was thunder—and it was close.

The storm is here.

Slightly disoriented, Katie blinked her eyes hard several times. When the cedar planks overhead came into view, she knew …

It was a dream.

It was the first time she had dreamed of her mother in nine years. Something she convinced herself would never happen again after she lost her locket. She sprang from the couch, wearing a smile from ear to ear, eager to share her news with Ty, but his bedroom door was still closed. She considered knocking. She got as far as raising her fist to the door before she chickened out. *Let the man sleep, Katie*, she told herself. Remembering that Ty said he always woke up early, she padded into the kitchen to check the time. The clock on the stove let her know she still had about an hour before sunrise. Reeling with excitement over the vision of her mother, Katie knew exactly how she would pass the time waiting on Ty to wake up.

She decided to cook.

Ty stumbled out of his bedroom, partly due to his stiff knee, but mainly because he was half-asleep. The smell of bacon and coffee had pulled him from bed before he was quite ready to emerge. His nose followed the scent into the kitchen like a hunting dog and he took a seat at the bar—hair a mess, eyes barely open, and still … no shirt.

"I thought you said you were always up early?" Grease popped as Katie used a fork to flip the bacon in the frying pan.

"Normally I am. I guess I missed my bed more than I thought. I would probably still be in it if it didn't smell so good in here. Who can sleep through bacon?" He yawned big and rubbed the back of his neck.

"That was my master plan. When the thunder didn't wake you up, I had to try something."

"Did you go to town?"

"Nope, I found all of this in the fridge."

"Are you sure that bacon is still good? I haven't been to the store in a while."

"The jury is still out. If you don't get sick, you'll have your answer," she laughed.

"Someone is in a good mood this morning."

"Yes. Yes I am. Because I …," she drug out the word I as she slid him a cup of coffee—black, just the way he liked it, "… had the best dream ever last night."

"Oh yeah? What about?" He took a sip of coffee, both hands curled around the cup, his eyes still puffy and tired.

"My mom!" she squealed, unable to contain her excitement. Her cheekbones rose with her smile and her high ponytail swayed when she bounced up and down on the pads of her feet. "And it wasn't sick Mom, either, which is how I normally see her in my dreams. Well, back when I used to dream about her. But not this time. She was young and beautiful and healthy." Katie's face beamed as the words spewed out of her mouth. "Oh, Ty, you should have seen her. She had on the same dress she wore to my Christmas program in elementary school when I played the role of Rudolph."

"Now that I would like to have seen." He watched her. No makeup, hair a mess, wearing only his t-shirt, so big that it hung to her mid-thigh.

He could see it now where he couldn't before. It was definitely her.

"I was a sight for sure. The antlers on my head were too big, and each time I hopped up and down with my hands out in front of me, they fell down over my face. Thankfully, I had a giant red nose to catch them on the way down." Katie flipped the bacon again and then turned toward Ty, the fork in her hand pointing his direction. "I'm certain I looked more like a kangaroo than a reindeer. But it didn't matter to my mom. I will never forget the look on her face when the program was over. She was so proud. She stood taller than anyone in the audience, clapping and whistling and calling my name. She was my biggest fan."

Katie pulled the last two slices of bacon from the pan and added them to Ty's plate next to the fried eggs she had already prepared. After she turned off the stove and put the empty pan on the back burner to cool, she handed him his breakfast.

Ty looked at the plate of food and then up at Katie. "If you keep cooking for me like this, I may take her spot as your biggest fan." He instantly regretted his choice of words.

For multiple reasons.

"Don't speak too soon. You may be hugging the toilet later," she winked.

"Are you not going to eat?" He asked, speaking around the piece of bacon that already hung out of his mouth.

"I'm not hungry."

"Then why did you cook all of this food? Please don't tell me you did all this for me."

Katie walked around to his side of the bar and used her hands to slide up on the counter. Ankles crossed, her legs dangled toward the floor. He was close enough to touch, but she kept her hands to herself. "Actually, yes. I did."

Ty put his fork down and finished the bite in his mouth. "Katie, listen …"

"Can I go first?" she cut him off.

He nodded, reluctantly.

"I've had nightmares for years. Not every night, but more than I want to admit. When those started, I stopped dreaming about my mom. Until last night … then there she was. Don't laugh," her shoulders fell forward timidly. "I think it's because of you."

"Why do you think that?" his eyebrow arched, pushing the fresh scar on his forehead up toward his hairline.

"Like I said, don't laugh." She looked down, watching her ankles sway back and forth. "Remember when you were in the hospital and I fell asleep beside your bed? Stuff like that doesn't happen. Not to me. I can't even sleep in my own bed most nights, much less in a strange place next to a man I don't know. I never told you, but I was on the edge of a full-fledged panic attack before you woke up and talked to me. Afterward, I slept hard. I didn't think anything about it at the time, but then it happened again the night I brought food. Amanda had to wake me up to go home. The point is, I didn't have a nightmare in either of those instances. When I started staying at your mom's, they stopped completely. And trust me, they were in full force. They always are this time of year." She cut her eyes toward him. "Today is the day, ya know?"

"I know," he whispered, and closed his eyes for a long blink.

She looked back down at her feet. "Last night I had a dream about my mom—for the first time in nine years—and it happened here. That has to mean something. The only common denominator in all of those things … is you." Those last two words choked her up.

Ty knew he needed to tell her. He pushed himself up and stood in front of Katie although she never looked up. "Katie …," using his finger, he lifted her chin until her eyes met his. When he saw a single tear fall from the corner of her eye, he didn't say another word.

Katie unlocked her ankles and he stepped between her knees. She wrapped her legs around his hips and let her forehead fall into his bare chest. Caught between right and wrong, Ty put his arms around her and pulled her in. When she did the same, he winced under the pressure of her embrace, not wanting to remind her that he was still recovering from fractured ribs. Lost in the sound of his beating heart for what felt like an eternity, she didn't move. She had never been held by a man like that before.

Ever.

Chapter 18

The back porch ran the length of the cabin, its roof lined in the same tongue-and-grove cedar planks as inside. A wood-post railing encased all but one opening that allowed access to the ground. With a slight elevation change, it took six steps to reach the grass, which needed to be trimmed. It was a short distance from the house to the edge of the woods, which made it easy to see a path winding between the trees. Heavily worn and nothing but dirt.

A light rain fell just beyond the comfort of the porch, the parched soil thirsty for every drop. With Tropical Storm Javier brewing in the Gulf, heavier rainfall was expected soon, the brunt of which would be felt on the Louisiana coast. Javier was only a precursor of what was surely to come, with September being the most active month in hurricane season.

A swing bed, with a Tuscany finish and an upholstered twin mattress for a seat bottom, offered a dry place for Ty and Katie to sit and listen to the rain. They'd hardly spoken since breakfast in the kitchen. She wasn't sure if it was because of her awkward confession over bacon and eggs or because they had stayed so busy that morning. Katie cleaned the kitchen and loaded the dishwasher while Ty got dressed and, when it was her turn to change out of his t-shirt, Ty did his best to fold the sheets and blanket Katie used for a bed. She then used his phone to make a few calls, the first to Mrs. Greyson. When she asked for the day off, Mrs. Greyson did not even question why. She expected a slower than average day—the total opposite of Katie's dream—and told her that with the storm coming, she planned to close the shop early anyway. Katie also called her dad. She didn't want to text him from an unknown number and had promised she would let him know when she made it to work. She contemplated withholding the truth for fear he may worry, but after she told Carl where she was, he seemed relieved. His initial shock waned quickly. The thought of her being hidden away in the woods for the day with someone she knew managed to calm his nerves, given the circumstances. Contrary to Ty's suggestion the night before, her phone calls did not include one to the cops. There was no point, really, and after she explained her reasoning, Ty didn't bring it up again.

They sat in the swing bed propped up opposite one another, Katie's legs tucked between Ty's and the back of the swing. She attempted to make small talk to break the silence.

"Is that where you and Shaun ride?" she asked, pointing to the trail entrance at the edge of the woods.

"Yeah, when we can. We aren't as fanatical about it as we used to be, but we still enjoy it."

"I have a bike, too." She cringed at how corny that sounded and wondered why she suddenly felt like a teenage girl with a crush. "I ride it to work sometimes. I've never ridden trails before, though."

"Feel free to bring it over sometime and give it a try if you want. Be careful, though. We've added some obstacles to make it a little more interesting."

"I will probably stick to pavement for now. I'm still not fond of being in the woods."

"Understandable." He treaded lightly with his next question. "Do you ever talk about that night?"

"No. I've always been too embarrassed to, ashamed even, like people were going to look at me differently or think I was gross. You're the first person I've ever told." Her head tilted in confusion. "But then again, I didn't really tell you, did I? You told me."

"Like I said, it wasn't hard to figure out. What about guys you've dated over the years? Surely one of them noticed something was up like I did."

"I've never dated anyone before. Not since high school. Heck, you're the first guy I've let sit this close to me who wasn't gay."

He coughed. "Excuse me?"

"I had a really great friend when I lived in Austin. His name was Ethan. We hung out a lot and I absolutely adored him. Super funny and always made me laugh, but totally gay."

"Do you two still keep in touch?"

"No. I don't think he ever wants to speak to me again."

"Why's that?"

"He came up behind me at work one day and surprised me. I'm not sure if it was what he did or what he said that caused me to react the way I did, but I grabbed the lamp sitting on the table next to me, spun around, and clipped him upside the head. He fell to the floor like he'd just been knocked out by Mike Tyson."

"Ouch," he winced.

"Exactly. Not one of my finer moments. The last time I saw Ethan he was covered in blood and being loaded up in an ambulance. I'm lucky he didn't press charges."

"It's not like you hurt him on purpose. I mean, he kinda had it coming."

"He didn't know any better. I never told him anything about my past." She rubbed the scar on the back of her hand. "What about you? Have you ever been married before?"

"Came close once.

"What happened?"

"Her job ended up getting in the way."

"Why, what did she do?"

"Her boss."

"Double ouch." Katie put her hand on Ty's leg. "I'm sorry."

"I'm not," he shrugged. "Better to know before the vows than after. The only thing I regret is it ruined a friendship between her and Amanda. They were good friends, and once we split up it made it too awkward for the two of them to hang out, so they also went their separate ways."

"I can see how that would be weird. You and your sister are pretty close."

"Now you know why I had you tell Amanda you were sleeping on the couch. I promised her I would never get involved with one of her friends again." He looked away and mumbled, "A promise I'm struggling to keep."

For several moments, the only sound that could be heard was rain trickling through the leaves of the trees and an occasional rumble of thunder. Neither of them commented on his promise to Amanda, and the unspoken words created a tension in the air so thick it could be cut with a knife. Katie's mind flashed to his shirtless body, standing in front of her, and for the first time ever, she wanted more from a man. But not just any man. From Ty.

Her heart threw the next two words from her mouth before her mind could stop them. "Kiss me."

Taken by surprise, Ty whipped his head back her direction. "Katie … I don't think that's a good idea. It's only going to complicate things and it's not fair to …"

"Please?" she pleaded, too caught up in the moment to think about the repercussions.

He clenched his jaw and his temples flared. "Are you sure that's what you want?"

"I've never been more certain about anything in my life."

He could hear the need in her voice and knew it was about more than a kiss. Against his better judgment, Ty swung his legs around until his feet were planted on the porch. The swing bed wobbled against its supporting chains when he pushed himself up. He turned and held out his hand for Katie. With a slight tug, she rose from the swing and stood directly in front of Ty. He placed his hands on the sides of her face, tilting her head back until he was looking directly into her eyes.

"You are absolutely sure?" He asked, needing to see the certainty in her eyes as much as hear it in her words.

She nodded.

"Close your eyes," he whispered. He took a moment to study her face. The freckles across her nose, the oval curve of her chin, two tiny white scars that were undoubtedly nine years old.

Her breath quickened, the anticipation of his lips touching hers almost more than she could handle. She felt them first on her forehead. And then on the tip of her nose. He lightly kissed one cheek … and then the other …

"I'm about to kiss you," he whispered into her ear. "Stop me at any time if it's too much."

He gently pressed his lips to hers, parting them slightly, reaching for her tongue with his. When they collided, a warm sensation flooded her lower body. He ran a hand underneath her hair up the back of her neck and chill bumps raced down her arms. She stepped into him until there was no room for air to move between their bodies, his arousal now as evident as hers. Her knees weakened when a slight moan escaped his throat and, once again, she found herself wanting more. She wanted him in every way a woman could want a man. He wrapped his arms around her and she melted into his embrace. When their lips finally parted, their eyes met, both searching the other for reassurance. With the slightest nod, he consented to what her heart was asking him for, and they went inside.

Amanda shook beads of rain from her umbrella and dropped it in the stand next to the door. "Good afternoon, Mrs. Greyson," her voice carried freely throughout the otherwise empty store. "Man, it's nasty out there."

Wearing a green apron with the words, *Life's a Garden, Dig It* embroidered on the front in yellow, Mrs. Greyson worked to fluff a Christmas garland that would soon be adorned with red and silver balls. The increased humidity from the storm had made her hair extra frizzy.

"What are you doing out in this mess? If you're looking for Katherine, she's not here today. She called in."

"Did she say why?" Amanda popped the lid on a cinnamon pecan-scented candle and took a whiff.

"I didn't ask. She's a grown woman. I'm sure she had good reason."

"I guess you're right." After another sniff, she put the candle back down, trying to ignore the fact that Katie was probably with her brother. "That's not why I'm here, though. I wanted to show you a picture of something and see if you could make it for the wedding." From boutonnieres to bouquets and everything in between, Amanda had hired Mrs. Greyson to handle all of the flowers for her big day.

"Have you been on Pinterest again, Dear?"

"What do you think?"

"What I think is you need to stay off the Internet, or your father is going to have a stroke when he sees my bill."

"Ugh, I know. I just want everything to be perfect."

Amanda reached inside her Kate Spade satchel. Beige with black straps, it was color coordinated with her outfit: a beige blouse with three rows of chunky, deep-plunging pearls draped around her neck, black Capri pants, and heels to match. She fished out her cell phone and opened the photo library, searching for the picture of the floral table runner she had found online.

"Aww, look," she stopped on a photo and held her phone out for Mrs. Greyson to see. It was the selfie she had taken of her and Katie at the party Saturday.

Mrs. Greyson took the phone for a closer look and slid her glasses down to the tip of her nose. "Katherine is such a beautiful girl. Just look at that smile."

"Wait until you see her at the wedding. We picked out her dress and jaws are going to drop. Who knew she was hiding that body under those baggy sweatshirts she wears all the time?" Amanda motioned with her finger. "You can scroll left to see the rest of the pictures from Saturday if you want. We had a lot of fun."

After a few swipes to the left, an incoming call interrupted the screen.

"Oh, here, you're getting a call." Mrs. Greyson handed the phone back to Amanda. "But now I know why Katie's smiling so big."

"Hello?" Amanda held her finger up to pause the conversation while she took the call. "No, I'm at the flower shop, why?" she spoke into the phone as she turned and walked away.

Mrs. Greyson went back to fluffing her garland, separating each strand, and humming a Christmas tune, happy that the man looking for Katie had finally found her. She recognized his face in one of the photos.

Ty lit two candles and placed one on the table on each side of his bed in case the power went out during the storm. Although the rain was still light against the roof, a flash of lightning followed quickly by a clap of thunder signaled how close Javier was to arriving.

Ty pulled off his shirt and dropped it on his bedroom floor. The soft glow of candlelight danced on his skin. He held Katie's gaze and ran the back of his fingers down her cheek. Still drunk from his kiss, her face was flushed and tingled beneath his touch. Instinctively, her eyes wanted to close, to drink him in, but he stopped her.

"Keep them open. I need to be able to see that you're okay," his deep voice was tender and caring.

She didn't try to speak, knowing her words would have been incoherent had she tried. At twenty-six, she'd never been touched by a man—not willingly—and the tornado of emotions circling inside made her borderline dizzy. She wanted him without question, but a brief moment of panic tried to slither in. *What if I can't handle it? What if he's disappointed?*

What if I don't know what to do?

Ty reached for the bottom of her sweatshirt. She raised her arms and he slowly lifted it over her head. He never looked down, rather kept his brown eyes locked on hers. Katie pulled the rubber band from her hair and let it fall against her skin. She noticed a twinge in Ty's jaw and how his chest heaved when he took a deep breath. In that moment, her storm of innocence and desire struck him. He reached behind her back and unclasped her bra. She felt it release its hold on her as he slid the straps down her shoulders. He pulled her into him to introduce their bodies and she wrapped her arms around him. With her face nestled in his neck, he lay his head down on top of hers and they both closed their eyes, breathing in rhythm with one another. One of his hands held the back of her head while the other traced up and down her spine. The tickling sensation made her acutely aware of her bare chest pressed against him. Overwhelmed by the warmth of his body, she felt all of the worry that tried to creep in dissipate. She was ready.

Katie took a step back and focused once again on his eyes, letting him know it was okay. She slid off the remainder of her clothing and stood naked in front of Ty, exposed and vulnerable, yet confident in her decision. For the first time, Ty looked down. His eyes traced every curve of her body, committing them to memory, and of all the places for his hands to land, he brought them back to her face. He tucked a piece of hair behind her ear and whispered, "You are absolutely stunning."

Katie turned to pull back the covers on the bed and Ty watched as she crawled beneath the sheets. He undressed the rest of the way and removed a small, square package from the nightstand before joining her. Although he tried to ignore the pain in his ribs as he supported his body above hers with his arms, he couldn't keep his shoulders from trembling. Katie sensed his discomfort and pulled him down on top of her, his weight comforting her like a heavy blanket. Ty kissed her for the second time, more sensual than the first, and when she finally felt him inside her, their bodies becoming one, she gasped. Her fingernails clenched into his back.

They spent the next hour wrapped up together—never rushing, never talking—just appreciating what they had to offer one another. When he brought the woman in her to life, she cried, but not because she was sad. Nine years of repressed emotions—of feeling damaged and unworthy of love—released its foothold on her heart. It bubbled to the surface and poured out her eyes. He never questioned her tears, rather wiped them from her cheeks as they fell. He couldn't even begin to imagine what she was processing mentally, and allowed her to work through the train of emotions. After their energy was spent on that rainy Monday afternoon, Katie curled up under Ty's arm with her head on his chest and dozed off. He held her while she slept and stared at the ceiling, wondering how he was going to tell her.

A violent clap of thunder rattled the walls and jarred Katie from her nap. It sounded as if lightning had struck a tree directly outside the cabin. Sheets of rain slapped against the window, blowing in sideways with the raging winds. Javier had arrived.

When she woke, Ty's side of the bed was empty, but she could see a glow of light coming from around the closed bathroom door. The sound of the shower running was almost completely drowned out by the sound of pouring rain. She pulled the covers up to her chin and smiled, thinking about everything that happened beneath them, and wondered if he would ask her to stay with him again tonight or if they would go back to his parents' house. If they would settle back into their secretive meetings over breakfast or if things would forever be changed. Her smile waned slightly when she wondered how they were going to tell Amanda.

Katie rolled over on her side and watched the flicker of the candle on the bedside table; its wick barely sticking out of a pool of melted wax. The air held the cinnamon scent of its perfume mixed with Irish Spring soap. Next to the candle was a picture lying on the tabletop, not in a frame and slightly tattered around the edges. She reached over, grabbed it, and fell back on the bed. It was of two guys, Ty and someone she presumed to be Shaun, both straddling mountain bikes and covered in mud from head to toe. Neither of them had on a shirt, but both of them had on knee guards and black riding gloves. She laughed, wondering what the point of the protective gear was if they weren't even going to wear shirts.

The water in the shower stopped running. Katie contemplated getting dressed, but decided to wait for her turn to clean up. There wasn't any part of her he hadn't seen at this point anyway, a thought that made her blush. She rolled over again to put the picture back on the table and underneath where it had been sitting was a necklace. She hooked the silver chain with her finger and as it unraveled, the weight of a heart-shaped locket caused it to swing like a pendulum. With each pass by her face, an inscription hypnotized her into a paralyzed trance: *Three Hearts Make One Whole.*

Oh my God …

Chapter 19

Katie heard the faucet running and the intermittent tap of a razor against the sink. Ty was shaving. She pried open the locket to find a faded picture of her parents on one side and her baby picture on the other. All of the blood drained from her face and her pulse drummed in her ears. She sat naked in his bed, connecting all of the pieces.

With the final tap of the razor, the faucet turned off. She hopped out of the bed and scrambled to find her bra. Nothing in her wanted to be naked when he walked out of the bathroom, and she was running out of time. Skipping the bra, she threw on her sweatshirt and then stepped into her shorts, tripping in feverish haste as she heard the knob turn on the bathroom door. It opened just as she fastened the button on her shorts and then she scooped up her locket in her hand. Ty walked out, greeted by the horrified look on her pale face.

"Katie, what's wrong?" he hurried toward her.

"Don't you dare take one more step," she threatened in a deep growl, her voice quivered in fear.

Ty stopped and held his hands up, surrendering to her demand.

"Why do you have this? Why?" She held her locket out in front of her. Her hand shook uncontrollably. "It was you, wasn't it? That night in the woods—it was you?" She picked up the picture from the bedside table and threw it toward him. It sliced through the air and then floated to the floor, flipping repeatedly before landing at his feet. In the photo, parked behind Ty and Shaun, was a red Jeep. The same red Jeep he had just totaled. And the same red Jeep she remembered seeing in the parking lot on her final run at Black Bear Trail. "That's how you knew it happened at night. Yesterday, on the porch, you asked me if I ever talked about that night. I never told you what time of day I was attacked." She willed her legs to support her trembling body. "That's how you knew everything about me. That whole *I could just tell* story you came up with was a bunch of shit. Why?" she screamed, begging to understand. "Why did you just sleep with me? Is this some kind of sick fantasy for you?" Her chest bounced as she began to sob, pissed at herself for giving him the pleasure of seeing her cry.

"Katie, let me explain," Ty pleaded. "I wanted to tell you ..."

At the sound of his confession, she felt the sides of her stomach slam together and held her hand in front of her mouth. "I think I'm going to be sick." She darted out the bedroom door, escaping his hand as he reached to stop her.

"Please don't leave. It's pouring outside and you're too upset to drive. Can we at least talk about it?"

There was nothing to discuss. She snatched her car keys from the kitchen counter and flew out the front door, not bothering to close it on her way out. Rocks ripped through the bottom of her bare feet, shredding her skin as she pounded toward the car. The torrential downpour soaked her to the bone, her hair matted to her face. Not once did she turn around to see if he was behind her. Luckily, he was in no condition to run.

Nature screamed on Katie's behalf. The A bolt of forked lightning webbed across the sky, followed by a rumbling so ferocious it shook the earth. The wind whipped fiercely, curving the tops of the trees. Water flew from the windshield in sheets as the wipers worked hard to clear a path for her to see. White-knuckling the steering wheel with both hands, she leaned forward, trying to find the driveway between each pass of the blades.

"Why, why, why?" she echoed nature's wrath, releasing her grip long enough to slam her hand into the steering wheel repeatedly. Damon was innocent. It was Ty. A feeling of disgust washed over her, knowing that everything that happened between them was at her request—starting with the kiss. He never initiated anything. When he finally agreed to what she asked him for, he still requested her approval at each step. This time, at least. Nine years ago was a completely different story. Maybe this was his way of reconciling what he had done in the past.

She reached the end of the driveway and turned toward town, headed in the direction of her apartment. Most of her things, including her cell phone, were still at Amanda's, but she sure as hell didn't want to go back there. Ty had more than likely already called his sister. Katie understood why Amanda made him promise not to ever get involved with one of her friends again. He had ruined everything. There was no way she could be in Amanda's wedding, not now, and not only had Katie lost the first man she'd ever fallen in love with, she just lost her best friend too.

The roads couldn't disperse the rain as fast as it fell from the sky and sections of pavement disappeared beneath the flooding, causing her car to hydroplane when she barreled too fast into one of the pools of water hidden in the night. She regained control and slowed her speed, even though a nagging voice inside urged her to press the gas pedal to the floor. To get her speed up so fast that the next time she hit a flooded area in the road, there would be no recovering. It seemed like a better alternative than returning to the one place she swore she would never see again—Brownsboro—but she had nowhere else to go. She conceded to throwing as much of her stuff into boxes as she could, and leaving town before anyone knew she was gone.

Rain pelted her bathroom window, drops the size of gumballs. It sounded like hail. The lights flickered on more than one occasion, likely from an intruding limb brushing hazardously against the power lines. She pulled a towel from the cabinet and scrubbed it over her hair, but drying off seemed pointless with Javier still wreaking havoc outside, her clothes still drenched from his fury.

Throwing her life into a series of boxes was something she had done numerous times before, and she had it down to an art. She ran a roll of packing tape across the bottom seam of a moving box and tore it at the end. Her arms felt like noodles, her adrenaline waning. She emptied the medicine cabinet and the three drawers from her vanity, leaving just enough room for the jewelry box she had bought when she moved to Victoria. It had replaced the one she smashed right before leaving Austin, and she couldn't help but see the irony. Her last jewelry box led her to Victoria, and now a piece of jewelry was sending her away. She taped the top of the box closed on that memory and jumped at the sound of a knock on the door.

He's here.

Katie ran into the kitchen and ripped opened the box on the floor packed full of her dishes. She pulled a butcher knife from inside and scrambled toward the door. "I've already called the cops," the lie spilled effortlessly out of her mouth. When she got to her apartment, she had picked up the phone to call, and her heart sank at the absence of the dial tone. The lines were down.

There was another knock at the door, this one more aggressive than before.

"Please go away," she begged. "Why are you doing this to me?"

"Katie?"

A man's voice came from the other side of the door, but not the deep, southern drawl she expected to hear. Confused, she eased in closer and peered through the peephole. There stood Brad, shoulders hunched forward, wearing an oversized raincoat with a hood, his left arm tucked inside.

"I'm just returning your phone and some other stuff you left at Amanda's." He pulled a brown paper bag from beneath his raincoat and held it in front of the peephole to offer proof. "Amanda gave me your address."

Amanda did what?! Katie's forehead fell into the door and she closed her eyes. Nothing made sense to her anymore. *Why would Amanda give him my address?* She knew from day one how uncomfortable Brad made her feel and couldn't fathom the idea of Amanda telling him where she lived. A sea of betrayal swallowed her. *First Ty, now Amanda?* Maybe they were tangled up in one giant web of lies together. Maybe the locket Amanda let her wear was an inside joke between her and Ty, knowing he had hers all along. Doubt ran rampant in her mind and erased everything she had known to be true over the last few years.

"What's going on in there?" Brad called out.

She sat in silence, wishing she had never said a word. Pretending not to be home was no longer an option. Brad knew she was there.

"Hey, I'm drowning out here. Will you please open the door?" He knocked again. "You can have your stuff and then I'll leave."

She debated asking him to leave it on the ground, but on the chance Ty showed up before she was done packing, she didn't want to be alone—even if it was Brad. Her gut instinct had steered her wrong on everyone else, why would Brad be any different? The locks clicked one by one as she turned the knobs and, after sliding the last chain that kept her from the outside world, she opened the door.

"Whoa, what's going on?" he caught a glimpse of the blade pointed his direction.

"I thought you were someone else."

"Obviously," he gave her the once over. "You look like you just crawled from the grave."

With red-rimmed eyes, soggy clothes and hair, and muddy bare feet, it's not like his statement was misguided. "Rough night," she turned and set the knife on the hutch before walking over to the couch to sit down. The cushion sucked water from her shorts like a sponge.

"Looks like it." Brad followed her in and shut the door behind him. He put the brown paper bag on the hutch next to the knife. "Are the cops on the way?"

"No. That was a lie."

"Are you moving or something?" In a short period of time, she'd already assembled and stuffed six moving boxes, which sat scattered about her apartment.

"Yeah."

"Where are you going?"

"I'm not sure, honestly. I'm just not staying here."

"Understandable. It's not that great of a town," he offered, sweeping water off his raincoat with his hands.

But it was a great town. Or at least she had thought it was, until recently. It was her home. "Yeah, whatever. I guess."

"Do you mind? I'm making a mess here."

"No, go ahead. There's a hook on the wall."

Brad slid off his coat and hung it by the front door. He used his hands to tame his hair, messed up from the hood of his raincoat. "Why the sudden urge to move? You were totally fine the other day. Did something spook you?"

"Let's just say I'm learning people aren't who I thought they were." She dropped her elbows to her knees and put her head in her hands.

"Oh yeah? How so?" He studied her.

Staring into her palms, she suddenly wondered why Brad didn't ask why she lied to him about where she lived. The day she ran into him at the market, she told him she lived on the other side of town, near the airport.

She looked up at Brad who was still standing between her and the door. "Why did Amanda send you with my stuff and not bring it herself?"

And how did she know I was home? Ty must have called her.

"I'm sure she didn't want to get out in this mess. In case you haven't noticed, there's a tropical storm parked on top of us."

Made sense. Maybe she was just being paranoid. "It could have waited. You didn't have to get out in this mess either." Katie got up from the couch and walked over to the paper bag Brad put on the hutch. She unfolded the top and looked inside. Her phone, a bottle of perfume, and her day planner. She reached inside and pulled out the perfume. "This isn't mine," she said. The hair on the back of her neck stood on end.

"Amanda must have put it in there by mistake. You know, wedding jitters and all. I'll give it back to her the next time I head over."

"I don't mind giving it to her. I'll probably see her tomorrow anyway. Actually, I'm glad you brought up the wedding. I need to call her right quick and tell her I thought of what she could use for her something blue." Katie didn't really want to call Amanda; the phone lines were down. She wanted to gauge his reaction.

And grab her key ring.

On her way to the kitchen, she stubbed her toe on a box full of books, causing her to trip. Brad leaned in and caught her before she fell.

"It's okay. I've got you," he assured her.

I've got you.

Katie's blood ran cold. That voice. How could she not have recognized that voice? It had only haunted her dreams for the last nine years. She had heard his voice that night in the woods.

Ty.

"Wow, thanks." She did the best she could to steady her voice in the face of her attacker. "I need to be more careful next time. I'm just going to run into the kitchen for a minute. I will be right back."

Brad wasn't dumb. "You're not going anywhere."

The room went black.

Katie opened her eyes. Her head throbbed. Not like she'd been hit, more like a hangover from a night of drinking too much tequila. As she tried to make sense of her surroundings, it was like déjà vu, but instead of a hospital bed, she was tied to one of her kitchen chairs in her own living room. Her ankles shackled to the legs with packing tape, her arms bound at the wrists behind her back.

Brad sat smugly on the couch, directly in front of her, eyeing his handiwork, fingers clasped behind his head and his feet propped up on the coffee table. His wet pants clung to his calves, a bulge above his ankle. The tread of his shoes packed with mud and rock. "Chloroform," he said as if answering her unasked question. "Works every time."

Katie stared at him intently through hazy eyes, straining to force him into focus. The unknown man in the woods now had a face. A blurry one, but a face nonetheless. She had heard his voice. She had felt the brute force of his hands.

And even though the details of what he did to her were seeded vividly in her brain, he had always lived as a faceless ghost in her memory—until now—and she couldn't make herself look away.

"You know, I don't remember seeing this the first time I was here." He dropped his hands, leaning forward to pick up a mirrored glass vase from the coffee table. It once held a bouquet of yellow tulips Mrs. Greyson had given Katie for her birthday. "That's pretty cool." He checked his reflection and then set the vase back down. "FYI, your maintenance man can be bought with a thirty pack of Keystone Light. In case you were wondering."

That's how he got my day planner.

Katie blinked hard, her stomach in knots, but feeling slightly vindicated. She knew those cops were wrong. There was no way she had forgotten to lock the door that night.

The fog around his face continued to lift and she noticed tiny things about him she hadn't seen before. She'd always done her best to avoid looking at him until now. His eyebrows hung heavy over his sinister brown eyes and he had a slight dimple in his chin, the stubble on his face the color of sand. The hair just above his ears and around the back of his head was cut short, fading into longer locks on top that whipped up in different directions. He carried tension in the deep lines etched across his forehead. She flipped through her memory of faces, trying to decide if she knew him from somewhere, but she came up with nothing.

He walked over to Katie, leaving a trail of red mud on the carpet. Like an old scab, he picked at the corner of the tape over her mouth. "Don't try anything stupid." With one yank, he ripped it from her face. Certain her lips were still stuck to the tape, she opened her mouth wide, stretching through the pain. Her instinct was to scream, but she knew that with the storm still thrashing outside, nobody would hear. She wasn't in a position to chance her cries fading into the night. He'd already warned her not to do anything stupid, and he clearly had the upper hand.

"Why are you doing this to me?" Her face contorted, trying to calm the sting.

"Don't take it personally. You're just collateral damage." He walked back over and sat on the arm of the couch. Arms crossed over his chest, he surveyed the room. "Damon McGregor was my real target. But killing him would have been too easy. He needed to suffer for what he did to my sister. I've heard they really like pretty boys in prison."

Katie thought back to the stories she had heard when Damon moved to Brownsboro. Apparently, one of them had been true. Rumor had it he got a girl pregnant and then roughed her up when she wouldn't get an abortion. She ended up losing the baby and almost died herself, but Damon walked away unscathed. That girl must have been Brad's sister.

"So to get back at him, you did the same thing to me?"

"Do you think I wanted to do those things to you? No offense, but you're not my type. It was the best way of getting back at Damon. He goes down for rape and murder, which is basically what he did to her, and my sister gets justice."

"Justice? Where's my justice?" she felt rage building in the pit of her stomach. "He went to prison for nine years. You got what you wanted, why won't you leave me alone?" Surprised by her lack of tears, she fought hard not to scream.

"I was hoping for a sentence of life without parole for that douche bag. You were never supposed to make it out of those woods. Now that he's out of prison, I have to clean up my mess. That crooked cop screwed me over on this one. But don't worry, I took care of that already," Brad nodded with a half-cocked grin.

"You're the one who killed Detective Burns?" The bile creeping up in her throat burned like battery acid. She swallowed thickly.

"No," he snarled sarcastically. "Driving off an embankment during a high-speed chase killed him. I simply drained the fluid from his brake lines. There's a difference. They ruled it a mechanical failure. See? I'm innocent," he shrugged. "Now his dog was a different story. That was definitely me. I shot him point blank." With one eye closed as if staring down the barrel of a gun, he aimed a finger toward Katie and jerked his thumb, pulling the trigger. "I needed to get that detective's attention, and it worked. I had him so snowballed. Every redneck in East Texas drove a truck like Damon McGregor. I borrowed one from a friend, slid into McGregor's place in the middle of the night, and swapped license plates with him. Nobody ever had a clue. Then, all I had to do was pop up in the right place at the right time without getting caught, and bam, Damon got arrested. Poetic justice at its finest." He rose from the armrest, walked over to the patio door, and peeked outside, making a gap in the blinds with his hands. "You can shoot animals because nobody is going to investigate. Shoot a human, and there are all kinds of questions," he turned and looked at Katie, "which is why you are still breathing." He reached down and pulled up his pant leg, exposing a gun strapped to his calf. "I could shoot you, but then who are they going to think did it?" He dropped his pant leg and tapped his head with his finger. "You have to be smart about this stuff. Think it all the way through."

Everything started to make sense. "It was you who came to the flower shop that day, wasn't it?"

"Of course it was me. I always do my homework. Just like I did in Brownsboro. It's how I knew you were Damon's girlfriend, that you were a runner, and all about that trail you took through the woods. You should really pay better attention. I lurked out there more than once, you just never saw me. I'll tell you who did notice me though, that sweet little old lady at the flower shop. We had a lovely chat the day I stopped by, looking for you. Maybe I should go by and pay her another visit."

I will kill you, asshole. Katie cringed at the thought of him being that close to Mrs. Greyson. He was ominous, yet calm and methodical. She could see why Mrs. Greyson was deceived by his charm.

"I followed you on your deliveries that day. I watched you when you were waiting for Amanda after work. When you went inside that coffee shop, I called Kyle to see if he wanted to hang out. I only wanted to ask him questions about you, but the damn fool led me right back to you." He walked back toward her, stopping a few feet away. "That was just a bonus. I didn't plan that one."

"I don't understand. Why go through all that trouble?" her breath quickened. She was coming unraveled, completely unnerved that she was having this conversation."

"Loose ends. I needed to see if you recognized me, and I'm not going to lie, I really thought you did in the beginning. You acted all weird and wouldn't shake my hand. So I decided to put myself in front of you a few more times, just to make sure. Before I got rid of you, I needed to make sure there was zero possibility you remembered anything from that night or told anyone anything that could be linked back to me. This whole thing needs to be put to rest. With your case open again, I took care of the crooked cop, leaving you as my last loose end. I will say, I'm a little disappointed I don't have a reason to take out Kyle, too. He is annoying as hell."

Brad stepped in front of her and bent over, his face dangerously close to hers. She could feel his breath, but she never blinked.

"This was all supposed to play out way differently tonight, but you had to go and finally figure everything out. Now I'm going to have to revert to plan B."

Katie already had a plan B, and it didn't involve being a victim. Not again. Little did he know that their entire conversation was part of *her* plan. She had kept him talking long enough to free her hands behind her back. He reached down toward his ankle, and as soon as his eyes were off of hers, she swung her fist around with every ounce of energy she had. Nine years of anger went across his face, knocking him backward into the coffee table, his head hitting the mirrored vase on the way down. As soon as he was off his feet, she threw herself over forward, still strapped to the legs of the chair, and used her arms to pull her way toward the kitchen table as fast as she could.

She had one shot.

"You bitch!" he screamed.

He touched his head and pulled back fingers covered in blood. Pieces of broken glass lay scattered all around him. He wiped the blood on his pants and tried to stand, but stumbled forward, dizzy from the blow. On his hands and knees, he lunged toward Katie, grabbing hold of one of the chair legs. Only a few feet from the table, she stretched her arm to the top, reaching for her keys.

"You were always a feisty one."

He yanked the chair backward, causing Katie to fall face first into the floor. He pulled himself up next to her, shoved his hands under her stomach, and flipped her over. Her legs writhed in agony, still bound to the chair.

"Just for that, I'm going to make you watch."

He threw one foot forward and it slammed to the ground near her side. He made another attempt to go for his gun.

Katie flipped the lid on her pepper spray. "No, you watch," she growled.

Aiming at his face, she pressed the button and shot the blinding spray d d irectly into his eyes, holding the button until no more would expel. He grabbed his face, slinging his head and cursing, trying to escape the pain. Katie pulled herself up, her butt on the back of the chair, and ripped violently at the tape around her leg. Stuck directly to her skin, she felt each rip through to her bones. Brad heard the commotion and blindly swung, hoping to hit her, but he missed.

One leg free.

He kicked and thrashed, each move narrowly missing her as she worked on the other leg. Slits began to appear in his eyes and with his next swing, she had to duck to miss his fist. Now that he could make out her silhouette, his accuracy improved. She needed to get out of there, and fast.

Katie stood up and trudged toward the front door, dragging the chair behind her like an anchor. After only a few steps, it hung on the coffee table, impelling her forward, and she landed on her hands, jarring her wrists. Her body was exhausted. It took a few deep breaths to summon the fighter inside and she tried one final time to remove the tape. That final blow loosened it enough for her to run a finger between it and the leg of the chair and tear herself free. Finally shed of the chair, she ran for the door. Rounding the corner to the entryway, she came face-to-face with Brad.

"What's your master plan now?" he threatened.

Without a second thought, she reached out to the side and came back with the butcher knife she had left on the hutch, shoving it deep into his stomach. With all of the hate she could muster, she released a blood-curdling scream, and pushed one final time on the handle of the knife before turning it like a key. The force released the grip of his chemically stricken eyes and they opened wide, along with his mouth. He hunched forward and placed both hands on the knife. A gurgling sound erupted from his throat. With no strength to remove the blade, he fell to the ground, pushing it the rest of the way through.

Brad was dead.

Katie sat at the kitchen table, a blanket draped around her back, and watched as a policeman pulled a sheet over Brad's body. It was like watching the last page turn on that chapter of her life. It was over. After nine years, it was finally over.

It took a while for the police to arrive after she called 9-1-1, several roads impassable due to heavy rainfall, but the dispatcher stayed on the phone with her until they knocked on the door. Katie had called them from Brad's phone, pulled from his pants pocket while he lay dead on the floor. It was not something she wanted to do, but she had no other choice—her cell phone was at Amanda's and the landlines were still down. Before calling the police, she made another phone call. To Ty.

Katie's head turned at the sound of Ty's voice. "Let me in, I'm her husband," he demanded. He skirted under the yellow police tape and pushed his way inside. He saw Katie sitting at the table across the room and his heart leapt in his chest. On his way over to her, he paid no attention to the lump in the floor covered in a bloodstained sheet. He knew it was Brad, Katie told him on the phone, but Brad wasn't his concern. She was.

The rain finally a sprinkle, Ty was barely wet. He kneeled down beside Katie, ignoring his knee. He wanted to touch her, to wrap her up in his arms and shield her from the world, but he was afraid to. "I got here as fast as I could. I had to wait on Amanda to come get me. Please don't be mad, but I told her what happened. Once she could see how upset I was, it was the only way she would agree to bring me here."

Katie didn't say a word. She just stared at him.

"Hey, I'm sorry I said that to the cops, about being your husband. I knew it was the only way they were going to let me in."

You two just fit.

It was the second time they had been referred to as husband and wife. Katie thought back to Ty's nurse, Raye, and how she already knew they were meant to be together. She looked at Ty with a deeper respect than before.

"Katie, please say something to me," he begged.

"You're the one who found me that night … weren't you?"

Ty sucked in his lips and sighed.

And then he nodded his head yes.

Chapter 20

"When did you realize it was me?" Katie searched his eyes for answers.

"Not until last night, when we were talking on the couch and you told me where you were from. Actually, it was when you told me the name of the detective who worked your case when I finally knew for sure."

"Why didn't you tell me then?"

"I wanted to, I really did, but I couldn't find the right words to say. You were still processing your meeting with the detective's wife. It didn't seem fair to throw something else at you at the same time. I thought about it all night after I went to my bedroom, I hardly slept. Then this morning, when you told me about your dream, you were so excited. I didn't have the heart to ruin the moment; I could see how much it meant to you." Ty looked down. "I guess I was afraid that if I told you, it would make you uncomfortable to be around me, and you would leave. You needed a safe place to stay, and I was going to do whatever it took to protect you."

Katie reached out and took his hand, lacing his fingers with hers. "Tell me about what happened the night you found me. I need to know."

Ty pulled himself up from the floor and snagged a chair leg with his toe, dragging it over in front of Katie. He sat down, their knees touching, and leaned over to kiss the back of her hand, attached to his. He covered their union with his other hand and told her everything he knew.

"Shaun and I were driving from Fayetteville to Victoria, bikes loaded on the Jeep, and we were notorious for finding random places to ride. He had actually come across Black Bear Trail on a biking forum we followed, so we figured 'Why not?' It wasn't very far out of our way, and we could use the opportunity to stretch our legs. It was the one and only time I've ever been to Brownsboro."

"We unloaded our bikes, he went one way on the trail and I went the other. I came around the corner and skidded to a stop when I saw a pink jacket lying on a bench next to the trail. I had been riding carelessly, under the assumption we were out there alone because the parking lot was empty. I glanced around, looking for anyone that I might need to avoid, and saw you on the ground about forty yards from the trail. I threw my bike down and ran over to you," he swallowed hard. "Katie, your poor face." He reached up and brushed the side of her cheek. "You were unconscious and barely recognizable as a young woman." Ty stopped talking and looked away, his next words hung in his throat.

She grabbed his chin and turned his face back to hers. "It's okay, Ty. You can tell me," she assured him.

His chin quivered. "I took off my shirt and draped it over the lower half of your body. I couldn't leave you lying there exposed. Then I called for an ambulance. Shaun came around the corner and I screamed for him to stay back—to load his bike and get the hell out of there—and that I would call him when I was ready for him to pick me up. He was home on leave from the Army, and I didn't want him to get tangled up in anything questionable that might jeopardize his career in the military. Not to mention, he didn't need to see you like that."

"You are always thinking of everyone else." The edge of her mouth tried to pull up in a smile, but fell flat.

"I'm no hero, trust me. I kept telling you everything was going to be okay, but it felt like a lie. I didn't believe it myself. When the ambulance came and wheeled you away, my heart broke. I wasn't allowed to go with you. I followed your case the best I could from Arkansas, but your name wasn't released to the public since you were a minor. Even when the detective called me about six months ago, he still didn't give me your name."

"You talked to Detective Burns recently?" Her tired eyes offered a glimmer of hope.

"Yes. He said there was new evidence in your case and wanted to ask me more questions. His line of questioning had me feeling like I was being accused, which all makes sense now; the wrong man was in prison. Burns seemed frazzled, but determined. Sounds like he was trying to do right by you, up until the very end."

"I can't believe he's dead," she offered in a numb tone. "You know, perception is a funny thing. This whole time I thought I saw you two loading your bikes. I guess what I saw was you unloading them."

An officer approached and tipped his hat. "Ma'am, I know you've been through quite an ordeal, but I'm going to need you to come down to the station and make a formal statement."

"Is it okay if I change clothes first and put on something dry?"

"Of course. I will wait for you outside." The officer nodded and walked away.

Ty stood and pulled Katie to her feet, the blanket around her shoulders fell onto the chair. He wrapped her up in a hug and kissed the top of her damp head. "Don't worry, I will be with you every step of the way," he whispered.

"I should never have doubted you, Ty," she sighed. "It's just when I saw the picture next to your bed, and the locket, I jumped to conclusions."

Ty stepped back from Katie; his eyebrows pinched in confusion. "What does the locket have to do with anything?"

She reached into her pocket and then opened her palm, displaying the necklace. "This is mine. When you found it in the woods, why did you keep it all this time?"

"I didn't find that in the woods. The lady who stayed with me when I wrecked my Jeep gave it to me." He took the locket from her hand and opened the heart. He pointed to the picture of the couple on the left. "Her."

Epilogue

Ty waited in the truck at Katie's request. This was something she wanted to do alone.

She walked along the rows of headstones, pausing briefly in front of each one before moving on to the next. At the end of her second pass, she stopped in front of a flattened pile of dirt covered in short sprouts of weeds and green grass. A breeze shifted the wilted flowers that hung limply over the edge of a granite vase in front of the stone. The stone she was looking for. She leaned forward, removed the dead flowers, and replaced them with a bouquet Mrs. Greyson had put together. Blue irises, the symbol of hope. Next to the name on the stone was the picture of a dog. He had tall, perky ears, a pointy snout, and a long tongue that spilled out of his open mouth. Inscribed beneath the picture were the words: *Guarding you forever ~ Atlas.*

Victor Anthony Burns was buried in a cemetery outside of Athens, about a six-hour drive from Victoria. Katie calculated his age from the dates etched beneath his name. He was only forty-five when he died. She hadn't seen him since the day he stopped by her dad's house after the trial. That was more than ten years ago.

Katie squatted, placed a hand behind her to catch the ground on the way down, and landed softly in a seated position with her legs crossed. She brushed her hands together to remove the dirt from her palm and then reached into her pocket. "I wrote you a letter," her voice cracked as she pulled out two envelopes. She tucked one under her knee before she pulled a piece of paper from the other. "I know that may seem silly. It did to me at first, too, but my therapist thought it would be a good idea. She said it would help me sort through my feelings since I haven't been running much lately."

Sitting in front of his headstone, Katie unfolded the piece of paper and read the letter aloud.

> *Dear Detective Burns,*
>
> *I don't even know where to begin. So much has happened since the last time we saw each other. I know when you passed away that you were working on my case, so I wanted to let you know it's finally closed. It may have taken nine years, but the guy responsible is dead. I killed him. Don't worry, I'm not in any kind of trouble. The court ruled his death a justifiable homicide. The only regret I have in the entire situation is that it didn't happen sooner—maybe you would still be alive.*
>
> *I also know what you did with the evidence in my case, and I'm not mad—not even a little. I know it was wrong, but honestly, I think you did me a favor. Even though Damon wasn't the one who hurt me, what happened to me was because of something he did, and he was only out of prison for five months before he was arrested again. One of the first things he tried to do when he got out was find me. Thankfully, he didn't. I took a little time off work and hid out in a cabin in the woods. Dad said Damon was charged with aggravated robbery and injury to an elderly person for something that happened in Brownsboro. I didn't ask for any details . . . I would rather not know.*
>
> *I'm back in therapy again. I hate to admit it, but I actually enjoy going this time. I'm part of a group session for survivors of sexual assault. It's scary how many people have a past like mine. It's been helpful to be around people that understand me, but listening to their stories makes my heart break for you. Yes . . . you. I don't know how you did it. How you could see such horrible things every*

day and still want to try and help people. If I was ever rude to you when you interviewed me, I want to apologize. Yes, it was hard for me, but I never stopped to think about how hard that must have been for you, too.

I didn't get a chance to thank you for the letter you wrote me. It took a long time for me to read it, but it surfaced when I needed it most. In the letter, you told me that I was the reason you came to Brownsboro. At the time, I didn't understand what you meant, but I do now. Your wife told me about Roxie. Detective Burns, that young girl's death was not your fault. I know this because I, too, stood in my bathroom, staring into a bottle of pills, destined for a fate just like hers. Many of the women in my therapy group have experienced the same thing. It comes from voices inside that try to convince you that you are damaged beyond repair. Voices that nitpick your every move until you are convinced you somehow deserve what happened. Those voices are hard to silence and can be suffocating. So suffocating that you feel like the only way to shut them up is for your heart to quit beating. Roxie must not have been able to stop the noise, but that was not your fault. The only person to blame was the man that hurt her.

I feel guilty sometimes because I find myself being thankful you felt responsible. Otherwise, you may not have moved to Brownsboro, and it turns out I needed you as much as you needed me. You saved my life and you don't even know it. Not because you administered CPR or caught the man who attacked me. You saved my life by simply writing me a letter. My mother always told me I was the miracle that healed her broken heart. Your direction led me to the person who healed mine. Because of you, I finally found my happiness, something I never thought was possible. I have someone in my life who looks at me without judgement, who is patient and kind, and between you, me, and this headstone—is an incredible kisser. Sorry to drop that one on you, I can't really tell anyone else.

My best friend is his sister! Believe it or not, you actually know who he is. He was the one you interviewed the night of my attack, the man who found me in the woods. Talk about a strange twist of fate.

There are so many things about life I don't understand, like why my mom got cancer or why bad things happen to good people. Because of that, I still struggle a little with my faith, but I'm slowly coming around. Whatever happens after this life, I hope you can hear me, and that you are with Atlas. Oh, and I finally found my locket. You will never believe who had it!

Love,

Katie

The diamond on Katie's left hand glistened in the sun when she folded the letter and put it back in the envelope, then placed both envelopes next to the headstone. A twig snapped behind her and she turned around.

"How long have you been standing there?" Katie wiped her cheeks.

"Not very long," Ty smiled. He heard more than he wanted to admit. "I know I said I would stay in the truck, I just wanted to see if you needed anything."

"I'm good." She looked at her watch. "We need to get on the road anyway, if we are going to meet Dad for lunch at noon."

Katie held out both hands and Ty carefully pulled her up off the ground. She dusted her backside off and turned to look at the headstone one final time. Ty slid his arms around her waist and placed his hands on her belly. It was round and firm, two months away from her due date. Katie put one hand on top of his and the other on the heart-shaped locket that hung around her neck. She grinned, thinking about the letter that was in the other envelope.

Dear Mom,

It's a boy! During the sonogram, I got to see his arms, and his legs, and his other little leg. I know I wrote in your last letter that we were going to wait to find out, but we couldn't take it anymore. Ty cried when the doctor told us, but don't tell him I told you.

Mom, he's going to be such a good daddy. He talks to my stomach every night before bed, it's the cutest thing. I watched him put together the crib and he triple-checked every screw to make sure they were all super tight. We decorated the nursery, too. Ty wouldn't let me paint, of course, but I helped with everything else. We put a wooden rocking chair in front of the window that looks out into the trees. I'm going to read to our son, just like you used to read to me.

I left your letter here with Detective Burns this time, I hope that's okay. I'm sure he could use a friend. If you see him, tell him we decided on a name: Carl Anthony Duncan. We are going to tell Dad today at lunch. I bet he cries, too.

I love you, Mom. I will see you in my dreams.

Love,

Easter Egg

Letter from the Author

The premise for *The Locket* began after a dear friend of mine suffered a sexual assault at the hands of a stranger, or should I say monster. Katie's character, although fictional, manifested from what my friend endured during and after her attack. She allowed me to use details from what happened in hopes that others experiencing the same demons may find their way. It was not an easy path for her, but after years of fighting her way out of the trenches, she finally found her peace.

Less than a mile from her home, a man approached my friend from behind, put a utility knife to her neck, and drug her into the woods. Initially, she thought someone was playing a joke on her, but it was not a joke. What happened next was very real. She walked the same path numerous times each week training for an event in Dallas, Texas, and this man had apparently been watching her. He knew where she would be, and when, and he used that to his advantage. With earbuds blaring music in her ears, she never heard him approach. He left her alone in the woods … clothes torn, body beaten, and sexually assaulted. Again, she was less than one mile from her home.

Her experience at the hospital was less than ideal. Rape kits, STD prophylactics by the handfuls—which made her very sick—and nine million questions thrown at her by people who were doing nothing more than going through the motions. Once released to go home, fear and anxiety took control, and the life she knew before going for her walk that dreadful day changed forever. Sleep was elusive and, when she was able to sleep, her dreams were replaced with nightmares. The touch of her husband's hand on her shoulder rocked her to her core, and she was no longer able to do her job, which required her to be alone with people she did not know.

Next was her interview with a sketch artist at the Texas Ranger Station in Waco. Unlike Katie's character in the book, my friend had seen her attacker's face and described him in detail to the artist. When the artist flipped the piece of paper around, the image staring back at my friend was so realistic that she threw up. The blows just kept coming. His face matched that of a drawing from another victim and my friend's attacker was labeled a serial rapist. Although he had done it before, he was never found. Her case remains unsolved.

It took me longer to write this book than I would like to admit—nine years, to be exact—and yes, it is merely a coincidence that the past and present chapters of my book spanned nine years. At least I think it is a coincidence, it's hard to tell these days. More and more it feels like there are no coincidences in life. I've always enjoyed being a storyteller, but the thought of writing an actual novel overwhelmed me, especially on such a sensitive topic. I questioned my ability to do justice to the survivor's story, and after I was halfway through the manuscript, I pushed it to the side and walked away. Life happened, and time passed quickly. Over the next few years, I kept feeling nudges to finish the story. Some of those nudges were not so subtle, and felt more like being shoved forcefully into oncoming traffic. I soon realized that finishing the book wasn't about me at all, and I decided to give it another go. Imagine my surprise, when I went back and read what I had already written, to see a chapter of my life in print—before it ever happened—and in detail. In *The Locket*, Katie's mother died from cancer, something I experienced personally during my time away from writing. The pain and sadness that came from that loss, the agony of seeing your mother pass away, and the loneliness of not having her around, were all words I had written before I ever knew the harshness of their reality.

Coincidence? You tell me.

My mother told me one day this book would make its way out into the world. Now that it has, I regret not doing it sooner so that she would have the opportunity to see the finished product. Hopefully, in some way, she knows. Although the story covers a sea of emotions—grief, loss, love, tragedy, anger, hope—in the end, it all circles back around to faith. Something we could all use more of.

Thank you for having faith in me, Mom. I did it. I never gave up.

Every sixty-eight seconds, an American is sexually assaulted. Every nine minutes, that victim is a child. If you have been sexually assaulted or know someone who is a victim of sexual assault, visit www.rainn.org or call 1-800-656-4673 for access to trained support specialists who are waiting to help. You are not alone.

Acknowledgements

Since this is my first novel, I had no idea exactly how many people it took to complete a project like this. I thought I would write the story, click a few buttons, and it would be released to the world. Boy, was I wrong.

I have to start by thanking my husband, David, for putting up with me over the last nine years while I tried to get this story out of my head. For being my ultimate motivator when I was riddled with insecurities and self-doubt about my ability to finish. You've always been my biggest cheerleader and I couldn't imagine doing life without you. Like Ty and Katie, our paths crossed two different times, and I'm thankful that the second time we paid attention. You truly are the other half of me.

To my son, Corey, the Christmas you gifted me a hundred dollars to put towards the cost of editing helped push me to finish. You will never know what that gesture meant to me. It wasn't about the money, it was knowing that you were watching me and wanted to see me succeed. That money stayed in my sock drawer for way too long, Bubba, but I did it!

My dearest friend, K. You are the ultimate badass. Thank you for answering any question I had, and for sharing your horrific experience with me. I know it was difficult to relive such a tragic event, and you did so without hesitation. I admire your strength, your grit, and your ability to overcome.

To my sister in law enforcement, Leslie Lehman, your knowledge and direction helped tremendously. Thank you for sticking with me, even when I wrote a character that shed a negative light on your profession and for reining me in when I got a little carried away with his actions. Most importantly, thank you for your selfless service to your community for so many years.

Ralph Carroll, thank you for helping me find my wings. Your mentorship and guidance helped me realize I could do hard things. Not only do them, but to follow them through to completion. Thank you for holding me accountable, you will always have a special place in my heart.

A special thanks to my beta readers: Kim Pettiet, Wendy Milam, Brittany Ball, and Heather Carini. I trusted you with my baby, and you didn't disappoint. I appreciate the time each of you took to tear apart my unedited manuscript and offer suggestions. I never knew how important this step was in the process. Fresh eyes are priceless.

This may have been the hardest task I've ever tackled, but it is by far the most rewarding. I'm already dreaming of my next story and I can't wait to get started. I promise ... this one won't take me nine years to finish.